DC SUMNER

Echoes of The Fallen World

Contents

Acknowledgement

To my family, thank you for being there and supporting me through all the hours I've put into writing.

To my friends who are consistently letting me bounce different ideas for my stories off of you.

To the reader, without you none of this would be possible. Thank you for reading my books and allowing me to continue doing what I love.

Prologue

The Supreme Leader had never felt betrayal in such a way, not in all of his years on Earth. He was old, very old, and in all his time he had never met a man like Kenji. The man had learned the ways of sword fighting better than anyone the leader had ever met. He was incredibly gifted with a blade and Lucian could see that he would be a force to be reckoned with.

That's why he trained him to be the commander of his sentries, giving him the knowledge to command the Citadel's greatest defense force. Lucian's elder brother had gone undercover some time ago; so much time had fluttered by that the man couldn't remember how long he'd been running things alone. Sometimes he thought that his brother only did this so that he didn't have to make tough decisions anymore.

Lucian needed someone he could rely on now that his brother was on his covert mission to weed out traitors. *My brother and his antics,* he thought sourly. Not many of the nobles knew that Lucian was second in command to an elder brother. His brother was more into theatrics than Lucian and was his superior, so he didn't make much of a fuss over it. His elder brother craved to have all of their enemies brought down in an extravagant display of their power.

His finest warrior Kenji, leader of the sentries, had run away from the Citadel to start a rebel group. He attempted to recruit many of the sentries to join him before he left. Lucian knew of the traitor's plans and yet his elder brother allowed him to leave. He vowed to bring him in and destroy the rebels in the most ostentatious way possible. Lucian would let him have his fun.

Lucian pulled the revolver out of its case; the last known weapon of its kind. The leaders who made the Earth what it is—his predecessors—were sure to keep one of these around. He still remembered the day his father showed it to him and his brother. Their father explained that the device would kill a man in the blink of an eye. Lucian hadn't used it yet. He was saving it for a rainy day.

His brother used to make such an issue over being born a little before Lucian, claiming that he was in charge because he was the oldest. Once there was no one left in the world to oppose the Order, he would take control for himself and leave his brother to rot in a pit somewhere. It had been too long since the two of them were born and Lucian had grown tired of him.

The Order was his everything and the only way to protect it was to ensure he was its one and only member. The One World Order was known to have twelve leaders at all times, however, they'd successfully created the other ten members to be pawns. The others served only to make Lucian and his brother happy. Lucian wanted nothing less than to be the Supreme Leader and damned be the fate of humanity.

Captured

Disease, crime, war. Just a few of the things that plagued the human race. Mankind had always been inclined to fight for the things they wanted, despite whether or not their mission required them to hurt another person. With wickedness running rampant throughout the Earth's societies, the leaders of the world held a conference to brainstorm ways to rid mankind of its problems. Destroying firearms was the first item on the agenda; it was nearly successful.

Droplets of sweat rolled down Ryu's face as he trekked through the desolate land, the unrelenting sun beating down on him. Crumbled buildings cast shadows around them, giving a bit of relief from the heat. His companion, Storm, sat perched atop his shoulder, keeping her eyes peeled for any danger that may be lurking. Rocks crunched beneath his feet, the sound bouncing off the walls of decayed structures. Ryu's father had gone missing long ago, and the painstaking task of finding him continued to be tedious.

It's remarkable how bad the Order has let things get in the past thousand years, he thought to himself. The government lived for nothing other than themselves, and Ryu resented them for letting humanity delve into chaos. That's what his father told him anyway.

"Think we'll see any action today?" Ryu asked.

Storm cocked her head, listening. "So far I hear nothing, but I've been wrong before."

"I read something in father's journal recently," he recalled. "Talked about something called a firearm. Sounded like some sort of crazy weapon that the old world leaders decided would be better off destroyed."

"What was it capable of?"

"I don't know. It didn't say much else about it."

Storm was a Raven, wise beyond her years. She came to Ryu one day after his father vanished; startling him, and waking him from a nap, he thought it was a scavenger rifling through his pack, but was relieved to find the large black bird. Since then, they've traveled together, keeping each other alive, and sharing knowledge of their life before meeting. Storm was able to perfectly mimic a human voice—as if she had human vocal cords—and understood the common language better than some people.

There weren't as many humans on the planet as there once were, and the ones who still lived either belonged to the One World Order or were merely trying to survive. Ryu was sure to keep his sword on him at all times, as his dad taught him. The curved, single-edged blade had protected him many times, as he was attacked by animals, scavengers, and other human-like creatures. Some people were so doped up on Shade that they were unrecognizable as humans, foaming at the mouth and trying to tear others apart with their hands and teeth.

Storm snapped her beak twice in succession, making a faint clicking sound, alerting Ryu to stop as she sensed danger. Ryu grasped his sheath with one hand, his other on the handle of the weapon. He used his thumb to pop the blade out an inch from its casing. He crouched down slightly, ready to attack when necessary. Taking a life was no longer foreign to him.

"There, in the shadows to the right," she whispered in his ear.

He turned as a beast sprang from the darkness, its claws reaching for him desperately. His blade erupted from its wooden scabbard, slicing through the neck of the feline, killing it instantly. The starved cat had little chance against Ryu's blade, Sokushi—which his father had told him meant "instant death"—as it had dropped many foes and never dulled.

The sun was beginning to fade, so Ryu decided to stop for the night, making camp up against one of the decrepit buildings to at least protect his back from attacks. The duo feasted on what little meat was left on the predatory cat, roasting it on an open flame, taking delight in its gamy flavor.

Ryu cleaned his weapon, wiping it free of any blood or organic material. It was fitted with a steel blade, circular handle, and a handle wrapped in white and black fabric. He had yet to encounter another with as much skill with a sword as he, excluding his father who had taught him how to use it.

"The katana," he remembered his dad telling him, "is one of the most noble of weapons. You must treat your blade as if it were a part of you. It is an extension of your arm and you shall wield it nobly, just as the Samurai used to."

Another day of searching came to an end, and Ryu asked, "Will we ever find him?"

"As intelligent as I may be even I do not know that, little one." She spoke to him as if he was still a child, even though he was several years into adulthood. Ryu laid his head down on his pack, moving the contents around inside to make it more comfortable, and slowly drifted off to sleep.

Images flashed inside his mind; memories of his father training him in the way of the sword, and how to survive this broken world. The scene shifted to the day he disappeared; he went out from their dilapidated home, far away from where any civilization was supposed to be, on a journey to find resources to make their life easier. He was only meant to be gone for two days, but a week passed, and his dad hadn't returned.

Ryu awoke to Storm nuzzling him gently, the sun sending early morning streaks of light across the horizon. They began the usual routine, with Storm flying high up, searching for anyone that may be near. Ryu waited patiently for her to return, flipping through his father's journal, looking for a clue as to where he could be; he'd skimmed through most of the leather-bound booklet but hadn't memorized its entirety, although he was hopeful that clues remained in its pages somewhere.

A lot of its contents dealt with the Order and the fall of mankind. Ryu enjoyed reading about the history that his father put in the journal. One of his favorite excerpts read: *Upon returning to the surface, humanity's survivors learned that not all was well. Due to the nuclear radiation in the air, they'd all become infertile, leaving them forced to dodge extinction once again. Many years later, a scientist named Victor Yorkshire found the solution; he'd created a device that could grow organic matter. Using an array of chemicals, human DNA, and solar energy, human birthing pods were invented. In these, human babies could be born within 12 months, and thus humanity was saved again. Eventually, they would use this same contraption to grow plants and animals, although after tinkering with other variables, these began to mutate, causing different effects on a case-by-case instance. Some animals were born with extra limbs, some with claws where there would ordinarily be none. Some plants grew to be 10 times the usual size and others that would turn carnivorous.*

Storm returned, circling just above Ryu's head, sounding the all clear, a gurgling sort of croak emanating from her throat and rising in pitch. The sound was soothing to Ryu, and not just because it meant there was no danger near, but it reminded him he wasn't alone. He tied the red headband belonging to his father around his head, remembering the day he found it. After setting out to look for his dad, this and the journal were the only traces of his father he could find. He picked up his pack, tied the string for his sword around his waist, and marched on, ready to tackle the day of travel.

The city they were in was much larger than he first thought it would be; most of the places they crossed through weren't very big, but this one stretched on for miles. Crumbling buildings lay on their sides, and greenery had overtaken many of them, though most of it was inedible weeds. Only the most durable vegetation could survive since water no longer fell from the sky. The only critters around would scurry off at the sound of Ryu's boots on the hard ground. Storm caught a particular rodent with two heads, swooping down and grabbing it with her talons, and striking it with her beak. He was surprised there were no people around; towns with any sort of structures within were ordinarily found to have humans residing there.

The two of them approached the end of the city, an open desert before them where plants and animals were scarce. Before entering the barren landscape, they took a break; Ryu pulled the water interceptor from his pack, letting the small rectangular solar panel sit in the sun, and switched it on. The device whirred to life, gathering water molecules from the air, creating droplets that would pool in the bottom of the metal canteen. He didn't mind how monotonous it was.

Ryu peered into his bag, the white and blue fabric in the bottom triggering a memory from his childhood. Another gift his father had bestowed to him.

"This is a kimono," his father had said. "Mighty warriors once wore them. If you ever find yourself in a perilous battle, this will bring you good luck." Ryu was adamant about keeping the things his father had given him over the years.

He sat back and watched as Storm scratched her scar—which arced across her left eye—against the rock she sat on. She didn't say anything, but appeared to notice something; she floated down off the boulder and began hopping towards the back of the adjacent building. As she rounded the corner, Ryu heard her squawk, followed by what sounded like several sets of feet shuffling around the rocks.

Ryu shot up from the ground, but just before he could round the corner, something landed on top of him. He rolled onto his back, and a man, with wild eyes and a grotesque smile stood over him. Ryu kicked the man's feet out from under him and tried to recover. Before he could make it back to a standing position he was bludgeoned in the back of his head, and as his consciousness receded into his mind, he heard a voice say, "Alright, bag 'em up, you blokes."

Sokushi's Revenge

After ridding the Earth of most firearms, humans devolved to an almost barbaric state, using any sort of object as a weapon. Nothing could stymie the violence. Swords, knives, and pretty much any item that could be used to slice, stab, or bludgeon another being found its way back into the hands of nearly every person.

"Hold her still," Ryu could hear one of them grumble. Based on their voices and foot steps he figured there were around five of them; scavengers is what they are known to be called. Human vultures, attacking travelers and taking anything they had, usually killing them in the process, and then selling the possessions or trading them for Shade. They were known to eat their victims, with other sources of food being scarce, and Ryu was determined to not become another victim. Partaking in eating another human corrupted the soul, if they even had one.

He was listening intently after coming to, reaching up with bound hands to feel his head. There was a large painful bump but he found no blood. The scavengers were arguing over Storm who was putting up one heck of a fight, but unsurprisingly to Ryu, she hadn't let on that she could mimic human language. Animals with mutations such as hers would fetch a decent price in most markets. After noticing him stir awake, one of the men ripped the black sack off his head, revealing an inner room of a building. Trash and an assortment of makeshift weapons littered the floor, along with piles of clothes and other materials that this ragtag group of heathens most likely looted from other unlucky travelers.

"I'll give you one opportunity to let me go," Ryu spat menacingly, "give me my bird back, let me go, and I'll let you live."

The five men laughed defiantly, one of them picking up a black sack that contained Storm. The biggest of them smiled at Ryu through a mouthful of broken teeth, his muscles rippling through his ragged clothes, and seethed, "You're not one to be makin' demands of anyone, seein' as yer tied up and all."

The way he spoke was off putting to Ryu. He detested the man's intellect but knew the lack of a brain would make him dangerous in other ways.

"Let's go fry this bird up."

The group exited the building, leaving Ryu tied up without someone to watch him. With his hands tied in front of him, he was able to reach down and undo a bootlace, he pulled it up, weaving it through the rope around his wrists and biting down on it. He moved his arms up and down fervently, the friction burning through his binds, and then set to work untying the rope around his ankles.

Ryu did a scan of the room, but didn't see his sword which had been removed from his waist. Now freed, he crept to the exit quickly, being sure to step lightly over the debris lying around. He peered outside through the opening, the sun was still high in the sky and he saw a fire being constructed a few yards away. Strapped to one of the scavenger's backs was Sokushi. Ryu wasn't inherently set on killing people as were many others, but he didn't shy away from it. However, at this moment, seeing his second-most important possession strapped to this monster's back, he wanted nothing more than to end his life.

As he watched from the doorway, one of the men opened the bag containing Storm and yanked her out by the feet, she squawked and writhed in his grasp. Ryu bent down, picked up a large rock, and hurled it at the chump, smacking him in the temple with a loud crunch. He dropped immediately, releasing Storm who flapped away from the terrorizing men. The others spun around, grabbing their spiked clubs, and the one drawing the katana from his back.

A man with a dirty, patchy beard charged, spiked club raised high, but was not as agile as Ryu. As the man swung on him, Ryu dropped under the blow and swept his legs out from under him. He picked up the dropped club as another rushed him; they clashed weapons, the spikes getting tangled up on each other which allowed Ryu to pull him into an elbow. The blow struck him square on the nose, blood bursting from his face and flowing plentifully. The bandit clutched his face, screaming, and dropped down to his knees.

Storm swooped back down, clawing at one of the others' faces, while the last scavenger with the sword tentatively approached Ryu. They walked in a tight circle, facing each other, finally, the man became impatient and attacked. He lifted Sokushi over his head and yelled with fearful rage, but before he was able to bring the blade down Ryu lunged forward, grabbing the handle. He headbutted the man in the face, causing him to let go of the sword.

Ryu, now holding the weapon with a reverse grip, leaped forward while lowering his stature, slicing cleanly through the man's waist. With a look of disbelief on his face, his top half toppled to the dirt, and his lower half fell in the opposite direction. Two of the scavengers recovered while the other ran from Storm, who chased him unrelentingly. They both charged at Ryu, having regained their clubs, and the one who reached him first reared back his arm to strike. As he brought his weapon down, Ryu parried him easily and thrust the point of his blade through his opponent's chest. The other man saw that all was lost and got on his knees, begging for his life. However, this was the one who had pulled Storm out of the sack by her feet, and Ryu was not in a forgiving mood. He gently laid the blade on the man's shoulder, brought it back, and then swung. The enemy's head rolled into the dirt, leaving just one opponent left.

Storm clawed at the man's face, aiming for his eyes, one of which was already bloodied and useless. She herded him back towards Ryu, who waited patiently. As the man got within striking distance, Storm stopped her pursuit, and Ryu finished him with a thrust of his blade to the sternum. As the adrenaline wore off, Ryu's chest heaved, and Storm returned to his shoulder. Bile threatened to be released from his stomach; he had claimed many lives since the journey began, and yet at times, it still made him feel sick. It wasn't necessarily the killing that made him feel ill, but rather the elated feeling he sometimes felt while doing so. Ryu never looked forward to a fight, but once it starts, he seems to enjoy it.

"I'm glad you're okay. I wouldn't last long without you," he told her.

"And clearly I would certainly not last long without you.

That was dumb of me. I could have gotten the both of us killed."

"I had it sorted," he said stoically.

She snapped her beak at him as he gathered his things and began searching the scavenger's belongings for anything useful. He found some more weapons, but they were too barbaric for his taste. He also happened upon a few more water interceptors but decided to just take the solar panels that came with them. There were a few small knives that may be of use, so he stowed those in his pack.

After resting for a few minutes, and getting a drink, they got back out on their exodus. The sun was past midday, as they continued walking through the wasteland. *At least we don't need to fear scavengers or beasts out here*, Ryu thought. Not much had been erected since humanity began to rebuild, and what was salvaged soon fell again. Now, the world was full of crumbling ghost towns and cracked roads.

They had no idea if they were going in the right direction, or if they would ever find Ryu's father, but searched continually anyway. The sun dropped much faster than anticipated, and there was no protection from the cold of the night out in the open. The two of them stopped for the night, Storm circling overhead as Ryu pulled the small tent from his bag and put it together. Before the sun retreated entirely, he sat on the edge of the tent and opened his dad's journal again.

He read aloud for Storm to hear, "They continue to search for me; I've kept us hidden for now, but I fear that I may soon need to relocate. Ryu grows stronger and more intelligent every day and will be a fine young man soon. Before long I will have to tell him of all the things our government has done. Shade is being pedaled out to the people living in outposts. It gets you high at first, but after becoming addicted, the person loses all sense of humanity, trying to rip anything that moves to shreds."

This wasn't the first time he'd looked over this journal entry and it still caused him to have goose flesh. His dad never told him about any of this before he disappeared, but Ryu could assume that whoever was looking for him had been successful. The more he read about the Order the more he wished they could be stopped.

He pulled out his blade and began cleaning it, wiping it with a dampened cloth, removing the day's grime. His mind was light years away, playing a memory of his father training him. He was using a different sword back then, much smaller to fit his tiny body. His dad was throwing dried-up dirt balls at him, while Ryu sliced them in the air. This taught him how to react quickly and hit a moving target. When celebrating Ryu's twelfth year, his father gifted him Sokushi. He'd never seen the sword before; it was dug out of a wooden box, buried in the soil surrounding their home. His dad presented it to him, wrapped in a white cloth. It was beautiful, and to this day it remains his most valuable asset, excluded Storm.

Horrors of The Citadel

The nations leaders made the collective decision to open their borders, allowing anyone to stray into their lands. They claimed to have wanted a world where every country had open arms, inviting anyone and everyone into their home. They wanted to show that people of any origin was welcome. It didn't work out as planned and chaos ran rampant even further.

Bridger was born a noble but had quickly grown tired of the everyday life of a young boy in the Citadel. During his thirteenth year, he ventured closer to the Capitol; the outer lands within the Citadel walls weren't that far away from his home, but it wasn't often that Bridger got to visit the city. His mother and father were farmers so it only made sense for them to live on the outskirts closer to the fields.

The boy didn't tell anyone where he was going. He didn't see the need. Bridger knew which direction to walk, so he did just that as the scorching sun beat down on him. He hummed to himself and excitement rushed through him as the tall buildings grew closer.

Finally, on the streets of the city, Bridger made his way into a shop where goods were traded. He looked around, not seeing much that caught his eye. A glint from his peripheral halted him. It was a small knife that wasn't much longer than his hand. There were thin lines etched into the blade and its handle was made from the bone of some animal. It dazzled him.

The knife was so tantalizing that Bridger couldn't help himself. The clerk who worked the shop looked occupied with another customer. The boy reached out and snatched the knife from the shelf and hid it in his shirt sleeve. He put on his most innocent-looking face that he'd used on his mother countless times and walked out of the shop. Feeling confident that he'd gotten away with his crime, he pulled the knife from his sleeve to admire it.

He smiled as he rubbed his thumb across the fine blade, nicking the skin which caused him to wince. Shouts issued from inside the shop and the clerk came out, looking around frantically.

"You!" he shouted, pointing at Bridger. "You stole my merchandise, didn't ya, little brat?" Panic now hit the boy in the stomach and he willed his legs to move, but they wouldn't.

The man was stomping his way towards him. He looked at the knife that was still in Bridger's hands. "Give me that," he said, yanking the knife away. "You're gonna pay for this, boy." He grabbed Bridger by the collar of his shirt and began pulling him along.

"Please, don't" Bridger begged. "I'm sorry. I won't do it again!"

"Oh, but you did it once, didn't ya? I don't care for apologies. I'll let the sentry office deal with you."

Bridger knew of the sentries and how cold-hearted they could be. He had heard stories from other kids his age who also worked in the fields.

"I heard the sentries are giants with arms the size of tree

trunks," one kid told him.

"Well, I heard the sentries have powers that can take over your mind," another one had said.

There were many more rumors told of the sentries, but Bridger didn't believe any of them back when he first heard them. Now, however, it was all he could think about. He tried pulling out of the man's grip, but he was too strong.

Into a small building he was taken; several men in black attire stood behind a counter. The clerk flung Bridger to the ground. The hard floor hurt his hands and knees upon impact. "What is this?" one of the sentries asked. Bridger was thankful that they weren't giants, although the mind control couldn't be ruled out yet.

"This *miscreant* stole this knife from my shop. I want him punished."

The sentry speaking with the shopkeeper peered over the counter at Bridger. "Want him punished, huh? I don't know what led you to believe that you could just come in here and make demands, but whatever it is, is wrong. Now, get out of here before I break your legs just because of the interruption."

Bridger thought the man might argue. He huffed a couple of times, his face becoming red, and then he turned and stomped out of the building. The sentry came around and helped the boy up. "You okay, kid?" he asked.

Bridger nodded. "Yeah, thanks for helping me."

The sentry smiled as he looked at his colleagues before turning back to the boy and said, "If you *really* want to thank me, I have a little proposition for you."

Bridger smiled. Maybe this was his way out of the fields and into the sentry corps! "Sure! You name it."

He patted Bridger on the back. "Excellent. Follow me." To

one of the others, he said, "Hold down the fort. I'll be back."

Bridger followed the man through the back of the building. They walked down the street a bit before the sentry led him into another building. They went up a couple of flights of stairs and then entered a room where he had to scan his I.D. badge to enter. The metal doors slid open to reveal a bunch of nobles hunched over tables and milling about the area.

"What is this place?" Bridger asked but was ignored.

Instead, the sentry walked up to a woman with glasses and said, "I have that volunteer you've been needing."

She nodded to him and he departed without another word. The woman came up to the boy, asking, "What's your name?"

He told her, "Bridger. Yours?"

She smiled. "Bridger. I like that. You can call me Doctor."

"What will you guys have me do, Doctor?" he asked.

Doctor chuckled, "Oh, just test out a couple of new formulas we're working on. Nothing too crazy."

"Is it safe?"

"Don't worry. Everything will be okay." She smiled again, but Bridger was getting a feeling that things were not going to be okay.

Stripped down to his undergarments and strapped to a cold metal table, Bridger had tears streaking down his face. His chest was rising and falling rapidly, but he couldn't get a sound out. He was too scared. Nobles ran around the room in a loud commotion. Bridger could barely hear his thoughts.

"It's time, young man. Are you ready?" Doctor asked him.

"Get away from me!" he was able to muster, dragging in deep breaths when the final word left his mouth.

The woman frowned at him. "That's no way to treat your

new friends. What we're doing here—what you have the privilege to be part of—is going to further humanity's progress! You should be thankful you get to partake in something so grand." When Bridger didn't say anything she shook her head.

Doctor turned to another noble who handed her a large vile that was connected to a long needle. The vial had a liquid that shimmered with a verdant hue. Bridger struggled against his bindings but they would not budge in the slightest. "Hold still," she told him. "This may sting a little." The smile on her face was diabolical.

The needle plunged into his neck; the pain came instantaneously. The vial was emptied into Bridger's body and that's when the agony truly began. His body locked up, his muscles tensed so tightly that he thought they would explode. Bridger's entire body was freezing and yet he felt as if he were on fire. The searing pain waned after a few minutes and he felt his mind begin to drift.

"I'm sorry, Mr. Bridger," Doctor said. "I'd hoped your body would have tolerated the serum, but already you begin to mutate." She turned to a colleague and said, "Trial number 7,053 for human fertility serum: fail." She looked back down at the boy. "I'm afraid when you wake, you will no longer remember any of this." Bridger was thankful for the sleep that engulfed him.

There was a city marked on the small map that his father had left in the journal. Ryu and Storm traipsed their way through the desolate landscape, deteriorated edifices scattered about. Dark clouds rolled in, giving them solace from the overbearing sun, however, clouds never brought rain.

"I've been thinking," Ryu began.

"Something I seem to always warn against," Storm poked at him.

He moved to flick her with his finger but she easily dodged him. He laughed, "I was just thinking about what life would be like if we lived before the wars. How great do you think that would be?"

"I'd like to think the world would be covered in trees and water. These decrepit structures around us would probably be standing strong still. I certainly wouldn't be here in the same capacity. Neither would you."

"What makes you think we wouldn't be friends?" he asked.

Storm flew around his head in circles as she said, "If the wars had never taken place, the course of history would have been altered forever. Nothing would be the same. The birthing pods we came from most likely would have never been invented, as the need for them wouldn't exist."

Ryu chuckled, "Have I ever told you that you're too smart for your own good?"

She laughed, "Actually, you— look out!" A strange beast came lumbering out of the shadows of a building.

Ryu backed up and pulled his blade free. Storm hovered in the safety of the air above them. "It's a mutant," he said. The thing was once human, probably a boy younger than Ryu based on its height. It was slightly slouched to the right. The creature's face had shifted into something that was from a nightmare. The eyes were empty sockets, the ears and nose missing. Its mouth was a gaping hole with jagged teeth that could tear anyone to shreds.

Ryu was thankful the creature was still wearing a bit of garment over its bottom half. He'd dealt with similar beasts in the past and wasn't always lucky enough to not have to see their dangling participles.

Apart from that, the beast had arms that were far too long. The mutant's fingertips ended in nails that were more like talons. Ryu couldn't see how the thing was still alive, but that was one of the many secrets of the One World Order. Their unknown atrocities could outweigh the known and he wouldn't be surprised.

With a screech, the mutant lunged at him. Ryu gave it a merciful death; with clawed hands outstretched towards Ryu, the swordsman was able to duck and slash through its body horizontally. As the top half toppled forward, Ryu slashed again. The head rolled across the hard ground. He cleaned Sokushi hastily and put it back in its sheath.

Storm landed back on his shoulder. "Remind me not to get so lost in conversation from now on," he told her.

"I shall do just that, little one."

Old Relics

Deadly violence became the norm and the world leaders were at a loss as to how they would curb the rise in anarchy. The leaders turned to the world's elites—those who were exponentially wealthy—and devised a plan to redeem humanity. They concluded that the human race was a disease and they needed to create a cure. That cure came in the most devastating form.

Small wads of hardened dirt clanged off Ryu's blade as Storm hurled them at him. There wasn't much to do as one journeyed across the Earth's scorched surface. Ryu would destroy the targets with precision just as he used to with his father. Each time he practiced like this, a pang of longing and sadness would come over him, but Ryu knew his father would be proud that he was keeping up with his training.

"Father once told me of a class of warriors called the Samurai," he told the raven.

"Oh?"

"They were once revered as the most skilled fighters in history. Samurai were bound by a code of honor to their clans. The loyalty and pride with which they fought was a staple of their group."

"Do you think they trained with their friends like this?"

Storm asked, whipping another dirt wad at him with her talons.

He laughed. "No, I don't believe so. Father read a book to me about them. It had depictions of their training regiments. It would seem they cared about the mind even more than the body. They found it important to have a hardened mind so that one could withstand life's trials.

"The book showed many of the fighting tactics they learned. The Samurai were experts with bows and arrows, as well as spears and swords. There were probably more weapons than just that, but my memory fails me."

"I'm surprised that rock in your head remembers as much as you've told me already," she joked. Ryu gave chase to the raven and she easily evaded his grasp. The swordsman gave up the chase, covering one of his eyes with the red headband, and went back to a ready stance. Storm resumed throwing clods of dirt at him.

"Swords similar to mine were used by the Samurai and were somewhat popular throughout time," Ryu continued. "Even people who did not intend to use them would acquire them as a treasure of sorts. I remember reading that some of the Samurai would practice with their swords every day. Some would do up to 1,000 swings a day on top of dueling with their training partners."

"Wow," she said. "That's dedication if I've ever heard of it."

"Yes," Ryu agreed. "I think that if I had lived in that time, I would have enjoyed being a Samurai."

"I think you would make a fine Samurai," she told him.

Ryu switched the headband over the opposite eye. The sound of dirt on metal echoed around the open air. There were no buildings near them, but could be seen in the distance.

Weeds reached up from the cracked dirt, beckoning for a drop of water to quench their thirst. Ryu often wondered how anything at all could grow with no water, but thought that maybe these plants just happened to adapt and overcome their adversity.

It was a beautiful predicament they were in, in its own way. These living organsims had no way to combat the world. They simply had to survive with what they were given. Being resilient wasn't a virtue that came easy, or maybe that was the humanity in him talking. Maybe for a thing such as a plant, being resilient was as easy as breathing was for him. It was admirable.

"I think Father wanted to instill these virtues of the Samurai in me," Ryu said. "I think that's why he told me of them. Read me books about them. Trained me in the ways of the sword."

"I'd say he did a fine job in doing so. I've never known someone to be so loyal to their clan. So prideful of their swordsmanship."

Ryu felt himself blush. "What do you mean?"

"Just take a look at yourself," she said. "I mean, you've become a fine warrior and are using those skills to locate your father. You care so much about your craft that even as we trek across the world, you're training. You're constantly in search of ways to improve your skills as a swordsman. I may not be a human, but I can guarantee that no one else in the world is out here half blinding themselves whilst striking down targets being thrown at them."

"I just want to make sure we can survive anything that comes our way," he replied.

Storm swooped down and grabbed another chunk of dirt to toss. "Exactly. Whether you know it or not, I'm part of your clan. I always will be. Your loyalty to me—and saving your father—is what drives you to be the best fighter in any given predicament."

"I guess you have a point."

She chuckled, "Of course I do. For what it's worth, I believe you'll surpass even the best Samurai from history. Of course, that's something we'll never know. You shall be the last of them."

"I like the sound of that," he said. "The last Samurai."

Of the many skills that Ryu's father had taught him, scavenging for goods was one of the most important. Finding food or items with which to trade could often be the difference between life and death. Some buildings—such as the one he and Storm were approaching—still stood erect. However, this one had been covered in thousands of years of dirt, dust, and rocks so that only the top poked above ground.

The windows that were once part of the structure had long been shattered. Ryu peered down into the darkness; the closest floor was within jumping distance, but he wasn't sure he'd be able to get back out. It was extremely likely that this building had already been ransacked anyway.

"Want to check it out?" Ryu asked.

"I'll be back," Storm affirmed, falling off his shoulder into the abyss. Ryu found her black feathers, tinged with shimmers of blue, to be beautiful. However, they caused her to disappear in the dark almost instantly.

Ryu never enjoyed when Storm went off on her own, especially when he lost sight of her. He'd grown attached to her that way. He wasn't sure how he'd gotten along by himself before meeting her, and he didn't want to go back to that. Ryu had just pulled his father's journal from his pack and was about to crack it open when squawks alerted him to trouble below.

Disregarding not having a way out of the structure, Ryu tossed his bag and journal down onto the closest floor. He followed after it, rolling to the side as his feet touched down to avoid injuring his knees. He scooped up his belongings, tucking the journal away fervently. The squawks were coming from a corridor directly in front of him. His legs exploded with adrenaline as he burst down the hallway.

Rounding a corner Ryu could see that Storm was caught in a simple trap. It wasn't deadly, but she was panicking all the same. He knew that she didn't enjoy feeling trapped and always reverted back to a raven, rather than calling for help in the common language.

Ryu pulled Sokushi free and cut the net away that held her. She fell into his arms, causing him to drop the blade. She calmed as he cradled her in his arms. "Are you alright?" he asked.

"I'll be fine in a moment," she replied through heavy breaths. "I just need to catch my breath. I'm sorry."

He chuckled, "Why would you be sorry?"

"It was a silly trap that I got caught in. I saw something shiny and thought it could be of value. I tripped the net when I landed next to it. I've been getting myself caught too much as of late."

"Still. You shouldn't be sorry for an accident," he told her. "Although, it is odd that there would be a trap set in here. I wonder how recently it was created." As if on queue, a slinking sound next to Ryu made him jump. When he looked, there was a small child lifting his sword.

"Whoa!" Ryu shouted with surprise. "Um, hello there. I'm a friend. What's your name?" The kid stepped forward and now Ryu's eyes had adjusted to the dim light. It was a small boy, no more than nine years old. Storm hopped up to Ryu's shoulder and the boy eyed her.

Ryu knelt down to eye level. "Hey, buddy. Are you here all alone?"

The kid cocked his head to the side slightly. "Mother said not to talk to strangers."

Ryu was getting freaked out. He wanted his sword back. "Well, I'm Ryu. I promise I'm a friend to you. Just give me back the sword, please."

The kid looked down at the sword and smiled as he looked back to Ryu. Ryu returned the smile and held his hand out. Luckily, the blade was far too heavy for the boy to swing quickly. Although he tried. Ryu was able to narrowly dodge the blade. He held his hands up, "Come on, kid. Don't do that. Just give me back the sword and I'll leave."

It was as if something had possessed the boy. His face contorted as he swung the sword left and right. Ryu grew tired of it. As the boy swung, Ryu stepped in close and grabbed the handle and the boy's hands as they gripped the sword tightly. The kid tried to bite Ryu, but he shoved the kid away, causing him to trip. The boy began to sniffle. The sniffle grew into a sob and then wails echoed around the building.

"Ryu, you have to shut him up," Storm said. "What if there are more down here?"

He hated it, but she was right. Before Ryu could do anything, someone else emerged from a dark room next to the kid. It was a short, stocky man and behind him a woman. They crept out with wide eyes. The man snarled and charged Ryu. Ryu easily side stepped and bonked the man on the head with the bottom of his sword, knocking him out. He pointed the tip of the sword at the woman whose ribs were poking through her shirt.

She held her hands up in surrender, saying, "Go on. Take the boy. I don't want any trouble."

Ryu scoffed, "Not that I have any use for a little boy, but, he's your son. Why would you get rid of him so easily?"

She giggled maniacally, "He's not our son. Don't you know the Order only allows the nobles to have children these days? Unless you're lucky enough to find someone with a pod. No, we just found him. He's yours. Take him and leave."

Ryu looked at the boy. He'd stopped his wailing and now just stared at him. Ryu pondered the notion of having another in their party. It was ridiculous. As horrible as it was, he would have to leave the kid here with these people. They all would probably be dead within a couple of months, but it wasn't his problem to worry about. He had other priorities that were simply more important.

"The boy stays with you," he said. "Now, tell me how to get out of here and no one else gets hurt."

She smiled to reveal yellow teeth. "So kind of you, sir. Here," she held out a small rectangular device. He took it tentatively. "This should be worth something for trade. It's from the old days, before the wars." Something in her eyes led Ryu to think she was insane but he pocketed the small relic anyway.

"Thank you," he said. "Any chance you can also tell me how to get out of here now?"

She pointed down the hall. Ryu didn't want to follow where she was pointing, but gave her the benefit of the doubt. He and Storm found a set of stairs that led up to a small hatch. The hatch was the same color as the surrounding ground, nearly perfectly camouflaged.

"If only we had spotted this from the outside," Storm pointed out.

"I did not enjoy that. Those people freaked me out."

"Everything worked out in the end," she retorted.

He shook his head, exasperated. "Whatever. Anyway, let's hope this thing is actually worth something, otherwise that was all for naught." He pulled the gadget from his pocket and flipped it over in his hands. There was a black rectangle with a glassy feel to it on one side, and the other was white with an image of a silver fruit with a bite taken from it.

"Odd," Ryu noted. "I can't even imagine what this could have been used for."

"Perhaps, it's a weapon of some sort," Storm said. "I feel like you could throw that fairly hard."

Ryu laughed, "That I could, but I doubt it was a gadget that one hurled at their opponent's heads. Maybe somehow it has the ability to start a fire?"

She seemed to ponder it. "Could be. Although, I don't really see it. Let's get to a market. Maybe someone else can make sense of it."

"Agreed."

Ryu pulled out his father's journal and flipped to one of the maps that had been crudely drawn out. "I don't think my father documented any of this area." He drew it out himself the best he could.

"I'm going to fly up to get a better vantage point," Storm said, taking to the air. She returned a minute later. "I see another city toward the North. Appears to be movement there. Hopefully they have a market."

They headed North with hopes of trading their new relic for something they could use to aid their survival.

28

Shade

The hope for a more prosperous world was stamped out of the nation's leaders. They couldn't figure out how it had gotten to that point, how things could have fallen apart so quickly. I blame the leaders. The One World Order has always been and will forever be a vile organization. The elites and the leaders of the world hid in the most fortified bunkers deep beneath the Earth's surface and declared war on all of mankind. Nearly all life on the planet was decimated as every nuclear bomb known to man was unleashed.

Ryu made sure to keep his hand on his sword as he and Storm wound their way through the market. It was a small outcropping of crumbling structures that had been reshaped to fit the needs of those who inhabited it. The center of the small city was a market used for trading goods or services. The people here were able to grow their own food, which was surprising to Ryu. The Order was usually fairly strict about allowing people the freedom to own their own property, especially growth pods.

Without the pods, it would be ten times as hard to grow food. People had tried planting vegetation in the past, but the edible ones required more water than was available and never lasted long. Water interceptors were great for collecting enough water particles for one person, however, they couldn't produce the amount needed for vegetation quickly enough.

Ryu kept his curious eyes on a swivel. He didn't trust anyone but Storm. Taking his friend wasn't something he could easily put past a person.

"Care for some potatoes, sir?" A man with one eye asked him. "I'll trade that lovely morsel on your shoulder for several potatoes." Ryu could see his mouth basically watering as he eyed Storm.

"Come near her and I'll take your other eye," he said, moving past the man who sank back behind his cart of potatoes.

Ryu pulled the rectangular artifact from his pocket and held it out to a female vendor. He was thankful she didn't appear to be loony. "Can you make anything of this?"

She eyed it curiously. "Hmm. Looks to be some sort of communication device from the old days. Lookin' to trade?"

He chuckled, "Communication, huh? Well, I was wrong about that. What do you have to bargain for?"

The woman pulled out a bit of cloth reminiscent of a sleeve. She handed it to him and he looked it over. It was a dark sandy-brown color. "What is this supposed to be?" he asked.

"Here, let me show you." She took it back and motioned for him to bend down and he did. She slipped it over his head and down his neck, bringing part of it back up to cover his nose and mouth. "See? It's a dust shield. It can be used for many different things, but this one's the most useful I'd say. Windy day out in the waste'll get your nose filled with dirt."

She had a point, but something told Ryu this brick of a device was worth a little more. He looked at her indignantly until she caught on. He wasn't a fool. "Alright, I'll also throw in this bag of onions." Ryu looked inside and counted ten onions in the bag.

He smiled behind the mask. "You got a deal." They shook hands and he and Storm parted ways with the vendor. He couldn't remember the last time he'd eaten an onion.

Ryu didn't see anything else of value that he would want to try getting his hands on. At the end of the street where the market came to its end stood a small building that represented one of the oldest professions known to man. A slender woman stood outside the doors of the establishment and took notice of the two. She wore a dress with a slit on the side; her skinny leg popped out, revealing the skin to the top of her thigh. Her hair was dirty, her face grimy, and displayed a crooked-toothed smile.

She curled her finger to Ryu in a 'come here' motion and said, "An hour with me for that shiny sword you've got there."

"No thanks," he told her and tried to keep moving but she jumped in front of him.

"I'll throw in a second hour for free," she said, close enough for him to smell the stench wafting from her.

He grabbed her by the arms and pushed her up against the building, a whimper parting her lips. He told her, "Not if you were the last woman on Earth." She folded her arms, grunting in dissatisfaction as he walked away. There were less people milling around in this area. Most likely a combination of homes and unlivable buildings.

"That was a bit harsh," Storm whispered to him.

"There's no room for kindness in a place like this," he retorted.

"I disagree. There's always room for kindness. That is one of the reasons I joined you in your travels in the first place."

He chuckled, "I was a foolish boy back then."

"You're still a foolish boy," she joked.

"Hello, my friend," a voice shot out from the dark alley to the right. Ryu spun toward the voice, already taking a defensive stance. A tall man with a scarred face stepped out into the light, squinting. Ryu felt something off with him. His pupils were so large they nearly blotted out his irises. "I want to give you something," the man told him.

"I'm not interested," Ryu began sidestepping away from the man, careful not to take his eyes off him.

"It's free though. You don't even have to do anything. Just breathe in the dust," the man held his hand out. A small object lay in it and Ryu found himself curious to find out what it was. He took a couple of tentative steps closer and leaned in to look at the hand. There was a small piece of plastic wrapped around a nearly black powder. "Yes, take the Shade. It will make you feel… powerful."

As the last word left his lips, the man sprang forward, quicker than Ryu would have expected. Storm left his shoulder to get out of the way. He didn't have time to draw his blade, but he was more than just a proficient sword fighter. He and his father spent hours every day training for moments like this.

It was as if everything was happening in slow motion; Ryu cycled through his options in the span of a second. The man's hands reached for him desperately, his fingernails turning gray and cracked. The veins in his forearms bulging. His eyes were wide and wild-looking. Ryu took a sidestep to avoid the hands and delivered a swift uppercut to the man's chin, his head snapped back from the force.

He spat bloodied spit at Ryu's feet and grinned, "I just wanted the sword, but now, I think I'll have you as a snack as well." He began swinging at Ryu, his gnarly fingers poised so that if he connected the cracked nails would break Ryu's skin.

Ryu dodged or blocked the blows, almost having fun with the fight. It wasn't very challenging, but it had been a while since he'd gone rough and tumble with anyone. *So this is what the early stages of Shade poisoning looks like,* he thought. After a couple of minutes, he reached his limit of patience. The man didn't seem to be backing off at all, and there was no way Ryu was going to run from him for his pride wouldn't allow it.

He caught one of the man's wrists and then the other. He pushed the left one down and lifted the right one as he turned his back on him. Ryu thrust his hips back and bent over at the waist, throwing the man over his shoulder. There was a sickening crunch as his head connected with the hard ground. He didn't move. Ryu wasn't sure if he was dead or not, but decided to move on without confirming. The guy wouldn't be able to find them if he were to wake anyway. Ryu searched the body and found more pouches of Shade. He couldn't understand why anyone would want to ingest something so vile. He collected the drugs and disposed of them.

Storm fluttered back down to his shoulder, "Let's get out of this city. Too many crazies."

"Agreed. However, I could trade you for a nice set of knives I saw back there," he joked.

She pecked the side of his head playfully. It wasn't hard enough to bring blood, but got her point across. Ryu often wondered where he would be had the two of them not found each other. Would he be alive or dead? He didn't want to imagine existing in this life without her as his companion.

The days after his father disappeared and before Storm found him were terrifying. He was consistently scared of everything that moved. His sword didn't do much to make him feel safer, and the feeling that everything and everyone out there was trying to kill him left him wrought with fear. With Storm, he not only had the company of an intelligent creature but also an extra set of eyes and ears to help keep him safe.

If he could go back to when he was a child, Ryu would have made sure to go out with his father the day he disappeared. He remembered it more vividly than almost any other memory. He had ruffled the boy's hair and said, "I'll be back, my little Samurai."

Ryu didn't realize how much he would miss the man until now.

He pulled out the map that his father had made of the different places he'd traveled. He found what appeared to be the correct city and marked it off. Ryu worried about what would happen when he ran out of cities on the map to explore. There were only a few left now. This meant he and Storm would soon be venturing off into wastelands that neither of them knew of. There was no way to tell what was safe and what wasn't. Of course, nothing is ever really *safe*.

"Where to next?" Storm asked.

"Can you fly up and see if there is anything near?"

"Be right back," she zoomed off into the air. It took several minutes before she returned, saying, "It's not going to be a quick trek, but there is something to the North East."

He sighed, "Then that's where we shall go."

"What bothers you?" she asked.

"I'm tired of searching," he admitted. "I just wish we would find him already. Or if he's dead a sign would be nice."

"I understand you're weary, but let's not give up on hope. Once your hope flees, there's nothing left." He knew she was right.

The buildings of this city were behind them and they were on to the next. Ryu figured they would reach it within the next couple of days. Every day was an adventure; a horrific, beast of an adventure with no end in sight. Fighting for your life, for your survival did have a way about passing the time though.

Ryu pulled out his father's journal and perused the pages once again. He'd already read its contents a couple of times, however, this time he found something new. There was a narrow slit in the spine of the booklet. It was previously stitched together, but at some point in his last couple of skirmishes, the stitching popped open. A piece of paper folded down to a tiny thing was tucked inside.

"Look at this," he said as he unfolded it.

The Resistance grows strong. We have recruited around forty rebels now. The sane people of the world are sick of the Order and how they've corrupted mankind. Living a lavish life while the rest of us suffer. We will amass enough warriors in our ranks to take back what is ours and overthrow the tyrants, I only fear that we will lose too many in the battle for it to matter.

"You have to hear this," he told Storm and then reread the excerpt for her.

When he finished she said, "It seems this was written before you were created. He was part of this Resistance, maybe even a high ranking member."

"You're right," he said. "I wonder what made him leave the Resistance and why he never mentioned it to me."

"Perhaps there were certain things he wanted to protect you from."

"Maybe," he said.

"You'll just have to ask him for yourself."

Hope. Ryu forced himself to cling to the hope that one day they would all be together again.

Wrestling With Perturbation

Hundreds of years after the Earth's devastation, they returned to the surface as their rations began to rapidly disappear. It appeared that all was clear above ground. The descendants of the elites were able to take to the surface in hopes of reclaiming the Earth and starting anew. Unfortunately, the radiation lingered. The human race slowly became barren as the newer generations were being born and mankind, once again, faced extinction.

Ryu was once again walking across the broken ground—something that was once known as a highway—as Storm floated nearby, just a few feet above his head. She told him that she wanted to do a quick perimeter check, and flapped away. She was far away from Ryu, but he could still see her when she dive-bombed something. He didn't see what it was, nor did he notice anything on the ground until she tackled it. Ryu presumed she was taking out a rodent or some other small prey, until their bodies thrashed around wildly, locked in a grappling match. Storm's calls hackled through the air as she struggled to gain the upper hand.

Immediately, he knew something was wrong; after traveling together for so long they knew each other very well, and he knew what her different sounds meant. She almost always reverted to raven calls when in trouble. Ryu flung his bag from his back, and sprinted across the acidic dirt, the morning sunbeams shining brightly in his eyes. As he got closer to the battle, he noticed it was a fairly large lizard.

Ryu reached the two of them, grabbing Sokushi, and pulling it from the scabbard. He ran to her aid, getting a closer look at the lizard. It was bright green, with large spines running down the length of its back, and orange spots encircled by blue all over its body. The reptile had one of Storm's wings locked in its jaws, ignoring her rapid pecking of its bony head. Ryu raised the sword high above his head, his blood boiled as he readied himself to slice the beast in two.

"Don't! Its blood is like acid!" She alerted him.

Heeding her warning, Ryu dropped the blade and jumped on the beast. It was more than half his size, its massive body bulged with muscle. Under the weight of Ryu, the animal gave up its fight for a meal, turned, and bared its fangs. He rolled off the beast's back, but before he could get to his feet it struck at him. It missed his face narrowly as he rolled to the side. He popped up to one knee as the lizard struck again, but he was ready; Ryu caught it around the neck, putting the bend of his arm snugly into its throat. He squeezed for an eternity, finally bringing the monster to draw its last breath.

His body stung from the scratches left by the lizard's sharp claws. The lacerations weren't too deep, he wasn't in danger of bleeding out. He would need to clean them to ward against infection though.

Ryu, breathing hard as if he'd just run a mile, shuffled over to Storm who was lying still on the ground, her chest rising and falling rapidly. He inspected her wing, noticing bite marks, and some blood gathered on her feathers.

Concern furrowed his brows, "Are you okay?"

She looked down at her wounds, "I'm more concerned with my talons growing back. That thing's blood burned me when I clawed it."

"What were you doing? You're usually not so reckless. That thing was almost as big as me."

"I was going after a rodent, apparently the lizard had the same idea, but I got in the way."

He picked her up, and walked back toward his fallen gear, "I'm just glad you're okay."

Once they reached the rucksack, Ryu cleaned his friend up the best he could, showing a gentleness unbecoming of a swordsman. He pulled out his water canteen, a small mixing bowl, and an assortment of herbs. Combining the materials into the bowl, he blended them together until a thick salve was formed. He applied it to Storm's wounds and wrapped them with some extra cloth he found.

"You have to keep moving," she told him, "you can't wait on me to heal, I'll just slow you down. Leave me, Ryu."

"You've known me long enough to know I'd never do that."

He picked her up to his shoulder where she clutched his shirt with her good talons and preened his dirty hair affectionately. He packed up and set out in the direction of the lights they observed the previous night. Storm's keen sense of direction kept them on the right path, never straying from where they were headed.

Ryu's newly acquired face mask was already ruined. The massive reptile had ripped several holes in it with its claws. Luckily, his face was unharmed. "Well, this thing is done for," he told Storm, discarding it into the dirt.

"I'm sure you could have found another use for it," she said.

"It's okay," he reassured her. "I'll probably come across another of those devices eventually."

Finally, structures began to take shape in the distance; Ryu felt that he'd been walking for an eternity. He could see tiny shapes of movement just before the buildings. They were like ants from this distance.

"See that?" he asked.

"Yes. Definitely people up ahead."

Storm was unable to fly, but still had better eyesight than Ryu; she relayed there were around 10 people up ahead. The group seemed to be watching them, waiting. Beads of sweat dotted his brow, the heat's intensity ever-raging. He wiped the perspiration from his face, uneasy at the amount of people, and their appearance. They looked pretty well put together, staggered around with their weapons, varying from different-sized blades to blunt objects. To their backs was an eroding city with short buildings casting shadows. To anyone else, the formation may have seemed random, but Ryu could see its complexity. Once they entered their area of defense, if they decided to attack, there would be no escape. Ryu would be forced to fight all of them at once.

His experience with people was sparse; his father kept him away from others most of his life, and since his travels began, most of the people he'd run into were not looking to be friendly. He decided to try being amiable, holding his hand up and waving it at the closest member. They all studied each other in silence, Ryu and Storm examined each of them carefully.

A few of them looked harmless enough if their weapons were disregarded, some of which Ryu didn't have a clue as to what they were. Apart from that, they all had some sort of assortment of blades, and one had a giant hammer. He appeared to be a threat, with his robust stature, but the others looked relatively normal. One of them was a female, with dark brown hair tied into a tight bun on the top of her head. She had a slim figure, and Ryu found himself lingering too long on her appearance. The guy closest to him was definitely the ugliest. His face looked like it had been bashed in more than once.

"What brings you here?" The man in front of him said with an awful voice, he was burly and had an assortment of blades strapped to his belt.

Unsure how much to tell them, Ryu asked a question of his own, "Who wants to know?"

"We'll be asking the questions here, boy. I won't ask again. What brings you here?"

"I don't owe an explanation to you, or anyone else. You have a problem with that? Then just try me." Ryu made it evident that he wasn't to be trifled with. His hand rested upon the hilt of his blade.

Storm subtly whispered, "What happened to being nice?" He ignored her question. The guy had pissed him off already and the niceties were tossed out of the proverbial window.

This was the wrong answer, the man pulled two knives out from his belt, one in each hand, and flung them in succession at Ryu. In one fluid motion, Ryu dove to his left, reached up to his shoulder, and grabbed Storm, placing her gently on the ground as he flipped sideways. He landed with his right foot in the dirt, his thigh facing the sky, his left knee planted in the soil. His face turned to the ground while black bangs dangled in his face as he clasped the hilt of his sword as the other members of the group began to surround him. The two blades had soared past him, landing in the dirt.

Storm cowered behind him as they stood back to back, in an attempt to make sure they could see everyone. The motley group of people menacingly stalked forward, closing in on their targets. Ryu pulled his blade free, mulling over his options in his head. None of what he could think of would keep both him and Storm alive. Before he could finish his thoughts or any of the others could attack, a voice rang out, "Stop!"

Everyone turned, and the gang spread back out as a new member approached them. Ryu noticed the man looked battle-ridden. He had long brown hair that parted down the middle, a scar deformed his bottom lip, and one of his hands was missing. He was still tall and muscular despite looking so mutilated.

"Kenji?" he asked, looking at Ryu with wide eyes. Did Ryu hear him right?

Murmurs flitted throughout the crowd. Too stunned to answer, Ryu found himself wrought with confusion, his head tilted quizzically as he pondered why this man would call him by his father's name.

"Ah, I see I've made a mistake," he said, his voice deep and rough, with an accent Ryu had yet to hear, he continued to get closer, "You look remarkably like a man I once knew, albeit quite younger. You can call me Abe."

He reached his hand out, now a couple of feet away; Ryu sheathed his sword and declined to take the man's hand, just holding his apprehensive gaze. Ryu was suspicious of Abe, but curious as to how he knew his father's name. He bent down and picked up Storm, perching her back onto his shoulder.

"My name is Ryu. Kenji is my father. How do you know

him?"

"That, my friend, is a very long story. Come," he motioned with his hand for Ryu to follow, "I'll tell you everything."

"Why would I trust you after this bunch just tried to kill me?" Ryu pointed as he posed the question. "I mean, I'm assuming they're with you, right?"

"I'm sorry, we thought you were with the One World Order," The man who'd thrown the knives hissed his lame apology.

"Why would you think that?"

"Look at your face, boy. It looks almost too perfect, unscathed, free of blemishes."

"I can't help that I have this face, just like you can't change the fact you look like a wild dog's rear end."

Ryu expected him to retaliate in some way, however, the man threw his ugly head back, laughing heartily. The others joined in, including Abe, and Ryu let a grin slip through his steely demeanor.

"Yep, that's Kenji's boy alright," Abe mentioned as he turned back to walk away, "come, we'll get you all cleaned up once we get back to the bunker."

Something about him lured Ryu in. What was it? He couldn't think of what it could be, however, Abe seemed so trustworthy. Ryu felt safe with the group. For the first time in his life, Ryu found himself blindly trusting the word of strangers.

Ryu raised a brow, "Bunker? What bunker?"

Abe turned, holding eye contact with Ryu, "Welcome to The Resistance."

The Resistance

Victor Yorkshire, one of the first children born on the new surface became a studious man of science. He invented water interceptors in his youth as a way to gather water without drilling deep beneath the Earth. Many scientific practices had been passed down from the ancestors, but people cared less about innovation as time moved forward. The most notable of Victor's work is undeniably the birthing pods.

The Resistance, this must be what Father meant in his journal.

Ryu walked behind the group of people, bemusement rifting through his brain. He couldn't believe that the rebel group was *actually* real. The sun was beginning to fade as the aggregate walked through the city, dirt and rocks crunching beneath their feet. Ryu continued to eye them from behind, trying to discern any trickery that they may be holding onto, but didn't detect anything in their mannerisms.

One thing he did notice was how they wore better clothes than a lot of the other people he'd run across. They looked fairly dirty, but the garments were more intact, less rips and tears. Their weapons looked to be made of finer quality; many of the armaments he saw were poorly put together. One of these rebels carried a double-edged sword with a cross guard.

It didn't have any chips or nicks in it and appeared to be sharp enough to cut through flesh and bone. A woman carried a bow and arrow; her bow looked rather rough, but the arrows were fine. Any other arrow that he had come across was crooked and warped, but these were straight and would fly true.

Storm napped on his shoulder, cooing softly as she exhaled. She awoke and looked around, and then nibbled Ryu's ear, making him chuckle. He held his hand up to her allowing for her to hop into his palm. With his other hand, he unwrapped her bandages, the wounds healing nicely. The poultice he made was a trick his dad showed him when he was a young boy after he sliced his leg open on one of the defensive spikes that surrounded their home.

The plants used in the concoction were difficult to find and scarce in most places. They only grew in areas with plentiful shade. It healed wounds quickly and mended damaged tissue, often regrowing that which was missing. Already, Storm's talons had mostly healed, and her wing appeared to be fine.

She hopped off his hand and flew around the sky, a bit shaky, but her wing would be perfect within another hour. The sun dipped beneath the horizon, and Ryu began wondering how close they were to their destination. The group mumbled small talk, none of it aimed at Ryu. As the dark began to surround them each of the people reached into their pockets and pulled out a minuscule device, a small light erupting to life, as they flicked a switch. Ryu was baffled, he had never seen a device like this in all his years of traveling. A light that you could hold in your hand, without it being fire, was like magic to him.

"What is that?" He asked the person nearest him, the woman with the bow.

She scoffed, "It's a flashlight. Never heard of one?"

"No, never." His admission made her shake her head.

Abe finally halted their movement. There was nothing visible to Ryu that signified they'd arrived, but Abe reached down behind a short scraggly bush. He pushed a small button that blended in with the sand, the ground began to shake, causing Storm to squawk in surprise as Ryu was forced to shift his weight to avoid falling over.

The ground split in front of the group, revealing a circular entrance into the ground, roughly six feet in diameter. Ryu was bewildered at what he was seeing and wondered if they were secretly with the Order. The young man was naturally skeptical and they were showing him things he never thought possible. However, he didn't see the point of lying to him; he wasn't important enough for the Order to take notice. One by one, they entered the Earth, descending the metallic spiral staircase, with Ryu being the caboose. After his head cleared the entrance, the ground shifted back into place, closing the hole. The stairs were lit with bright, white lights attached to the walls. Ryu looked down, attempting to see the bottom, but couldn't make any of the details out.

After going down what felt like a million stairs, they finally reached the bottom; the staircase opened up into a hallway, where they entered through a windowless metal door. Going through the door, they were led into a large, well-lit cavern with high ceilings. More lights dangled from the rocky overhang, illuminating a large group of people bustling about. The ones with Ryu and Storm dispersed, the only one hanging back being Abe.

He spread his arms wide and said, "This is our main hub of activity. From here we plan raids and house some of our people. Come this way."

Abe motioned with his good hand, and Ryu followed, awestruck by the scenery around him. He'd never seen so many humans in one place, much less some of the weaponry and technology around him. There were rectangular machines, with images of words and letters floating on them. The technology was a tad overwhelming. Abe walked him down a long hallway and they passed a wall full of an assortment of blades and other weapons. Ryu thought himself to be fairly knowledgeable on various weapons, however, some of these he had never seen in his life.

Rounding a bend in the hallway, Ryu noticed a door at the end; Abe led him through the door, and inside was a single table, a chair, and a small device atop the table. Abe motioned to the chair and said, "Have a seat."

Ryu pulled the chair out and sat down, a wary feeling blanketed his mind, something felt off. Abe began tinkering with the boxy contraption on the table, it hummed to life after he pressed the red on switch. He punched a series of buttons on the top, and lights flashed around it.

"Now, if you are to join us, the first step is to remove that," he pointed at Ryu's wrist where the black tattoo lines sat; each person gets one while being formed in their pod. The black stripes are a symbol that the Order uses to show their ownership over the people. Each pod is designed to automatically apply the ink in the early stages of child formation. Ryu hadn't decided if he would formally join this organization or not, however, he didn't think he'd miss this reminder of the control the Order has over him.

"I'm not saying that I'll join you, but go ahead and take it. I have no use for it."

Abe grabbed his wrist and laid it in a slot in the box, pressing one of the buttons. The device buzzed, and light flashed through the hole his hand was inside of. Ryu grimaced slightly as something burned the markings off his wrist, and when it was over he pulled it free to reveal a puffy, red blister. Abe gave him some ointment-soaked cloth to wrap around the wound which he took gratefully.

Abe asked, "So, what's with the bird?"

"Her *name* is Storm, and she has been a better friend to me than any person I've come across," Ryu told him.

Storm snapped her beak at him, to which he raised his hand, surrendering. "Hey I meant no disrespect, Lady Storm, it's awfully nice to meet you. I once had a very nice cat named Garfunkle."

Storm made a low-pitched hissing noise out of disdain for one of her natural predators. Ryu looked at her, contemplating when he'd reveal that she could speak, and after thinking it over for a minute decided it should be up to her. She wasn't his pet after all. He often felt like she could read his mind.

Looking into her red eyes and nodding, he said, "When you're ready."

"It's nice to meet you as well," she told the man.

Abe jumped back in astonishment, shock displayed on his face. "Wha- ho- uh." He stumbled through words, unsure of what to make out of what he just witnessed. Gathering himself, he croaked, "I uh, have never met such an animal that could speak."

"Most haven't," she said, "and I'd assume a man of your intelligence can see why it's better kept secret."

"Yes, of course. You have my word not to out you. I do wonder, why would you tell me?"

She tilted her head slightly, "You seem... trustworthy."

Abe smiled, "That is most joyous to hear. Thank you."

She bowed her head to him as a sign of respect. Abe turned the machine off and turned back to the door, motioning for them to follow. They snaked back down the path to the area from which they entered, and Abe led them to another room, but this one was more like a lounge. Furniture was spread around, a table here and there, and some other devices Ryu didn't recognize.

Abe sat at a table and invited Ryu to have a seat; once they were both seated, a woman with short, blonde hair brought them both a glass of water. Abe looked at Ryu and said, "We have many things to discuss, and I know you'll have some questions for me, so let's hear it."

"Right," he said. "Well, first off, what is this place? Who are you guys? And most importantly, why did you call me by my father's name when you first saw me?"

He took a deep breath, "I'll answer them in order then. To your first question, this is the main refuge for our rebel group, the Resistance. Many of us live here, while others live in different locations where they're able to carry out missions. Our goal is to overthrow the One World Order; the way they've treated humanity is abhorrent and has gone on for far too long.

"The nobility sits in the Citadel, surrounded by their sentries, feasting on fat hogs, and sipping wine, while the world's people suffer in what's left. Creating and dealing out Shade—the psychoactive drug—to any who will take it. Their goal is to keep people away from the Citadel. We're unsure of how it came to be this way, but they've been very selective about who they allow to be part of the Order. They only permit the nobles within the walls to make children for themselves. I shudder to think what they'd do if anyone outside was caught with a birthing pod."

Abe paused, looking at Ryu, deep in thought. He continued, "Anyway, after outlawing the creation of children by those not in the Citadel, we are left with a vicious cycle of continued oppression as new nobles are created. I'm sure your dad has told you all of this already."

Ryu was bewildered, most of that information he'd never heard before. "Um, not exactly. He did tell me a bit of their corruption but never mentioned the Resistance or anything. Although, there was a hidden log in his journal that he left behind that you may be able to make sense of." He pulled the journal from his pack and read the entry about being scared of someone finding him.

Abe got lost in the page, clearly thinking about it hard, but when he didn't answer, Ryu continued. "Maybe he was waiting for me to be older, but then he disappeared when I was fifteen, and that was ten years ago. I haven't seen him since."

After a brief silence, Abe said, "Ah well, I was hoping you'd be able to shed light on where he's been, but I see that is not the case. As for your last question, Kenji and I were great friends many years ago. We both worked for the Order back then as sentries. He worked his way up, earning the rank of Commander, in charge of all sentries, and now I'm assuming he stole a pod to grow you in during that time."

Ryu interjected, "How was he able to join the Sentries? I didn't think he was a noble."

"Oh, he's not a noble," Abe continued. "The Order will occasionally let outsiders join the Sentry Corps, but only if they see something of value in them."

Abe waited for a response but continued after Ryu nodded

his understanding. "He and I lost touch for a while until he came to me one day, begging me to leave with him. He spoke of the great evil he'd witnessed from the nobles and wanted out. He talked about having a plan to rid the world of their vileness and creating a new government that treated all people fairly. He started the Resistance with me, but he was our leader, our Commander. Then one day he vanished without a word. I now assume he left to raise you away from all of this."

Answers

I've already picked out your name; you will be called Ryu. It's been only six months that I left to grow you in the pod. You look like a small blob still. I hope that you come out healthy when it is time. I only wish Sari could be here to share in this occasion with me. I'll have to tell you all about her one day. I've learned that writing every experience I've had down is therapeutic. I hope that this helps you when you need it.

Ryu was processing everything that was said, trying to formulate a response, but failing to do so. He sat silently, his intertwined fingers pressed against his lips, his thumbs tucked under his chin.

How could he never tell me any of this?

Abe interrupted his thoughts, breaking the silence, "I know this is probably a lot to think about. If you're up for it I'd like to hear your story. Perhaps if we share our knowledge we will be able to locate him. I'd like to find my missing friend as well."

Ryu let out a deep sigh, "Okay, let's talk. Storm, if I misspeak, correct me," she bobbed her head up and down and he continued, "I'll start as far back as I can remember. Dad had us living in this tiny, old house. It had nothing but a bed for each of us, and we spent most days with him teaching me things about survival. He told me the One World Order was evil, and how they weren't to be trusted if I were to ever come in contact with them. He said he moved us far away from where anyone else lived and built our house from any spare materials he could find.

"He never mentioned how I came to be, and I never questioned it. My training started when I was very young. He taught me how to fight," he pulled Sokushi from its sheath, handing it to Abe, "we trained and sparred almost every day, starting when I was around six. He taught me how to hunt animals, even though there weren't many. We had to spend several days searching each time to find anything edible. He said that one day I may have to fight without him by my side. I didn't know what he meant, but I'm guessing this was when he became paranoid, although I've no idea who might have taken him."

Abe chimed in, "I can only assume that it would be the Order. To work for them you have to pledge your undying loyalty, promising to do whatever is asked of you by the nobility. Any faltering in this vow is punishable by death, but at the time we joined, it was so difficult to survive without their resources, we thought it to be the best option."

Ryu began to worry, sweat beading his brow at the thought of his father being put to death by the government. His hope was waning faster than ever before, until Abe said, "Now I understand why you'd be fearful of the worst. Let me reassure you that I believe him to still be alive. He was very valuable to them, and the nobility favored him over many others. He helped increase their efficiency as he was a fearsome warrior, which I'm sure you are well aware of.

"Kenji completely revamped the system put in place for the sentry program. He trained them to his specifications in all kinds of weaponry. Then he developed traps that would ensnare those who attempted to break into the Citadel. The Order is made of ten members of the nobility and the Supreme Leader; it's something one can only be born into, the leadership positions that is. None cared for Kenji besides Lucian, the Supreme Leader, who favored him above all others.

"As I said earlier though, the leaders do not take kindly to betrayal, so it would make sense that they'd hunt him down until they found him. Even Lucian would be unforgiving of Kenji's treason. I'm sure they brought him back to the Citadel to force him into working again, probably keeping a pair of eyes on him at all times and I highly doubt they'd give him anything he could use to defend himself with."

Ryu thought about all of this deeply, emotions rattling his body, his eyes beginning to fill with tears, but he refused to let them fall. He fortified the dam in his mind, and with a steely resolve, he pushed the knot that had developed in his throat back down. Storm noticed his struggle and nuzzled into his neck, attempting to comfort him.

He asked, "If he was just a sentry, why was he trusted more so than others?"

Abe said, "Your father isn't just a warrior, he has one of the brightest minds I've seen. His time spent reading books alone would be more than the years you have in life. Not only that, but he had a way with words that he could bend almost anyone to his will. He was determined to fix what was broken and they trusted him and gave him the resources to do so even. One of his greatest ambitions was to solve the non-reproductive disease that plagues us. The Order even gave him the resources he required. Until they discovered his plan, that is."

He looked down, shaking his head slightly. "They took everything from him, burned all of his research. I've no idea if he was close to an answer or not, but to not allow him to even try is despicable."

After a deep breath, Ryu said, "Okay, so let's say he's still alive. If he is being held captive at the Citadel, how do we rescue him?"

Abe smiled at the question and said, "I believe what we need to do is infiltrate the Citadel. The outposts have become increasingly more dangerous, and most of the people there are either strung out on Shade or fear the nobility too much to be of any help. We need to sneak past the sentries located there and make our way to the Citadel, get past their gate, and find Kenji."

Storm said, "Somehow I don't think it will be that easy."

He chuckled, "Right you are, yes. This will require much planning and training to pull off, so I say we get some rest, and then first thing in the morning we begin our preparations."

Abe stood and left the room with the other two in tow, walking quietly through the halls. He walked them through the central room with computers and across the other side to another door. They passed the girl that Ryu saw above ground with the bow and arrow, they made eye contact and she smiled, but he didn't return the gesture. He found himself attracted to her; he'd never met a woman who looked good enough to draw that kind of attention from him. It wasn't just her appearance though; she had this air about her that gave him the feeling that she was incredibly kind.

The feeling left him unsettled. Controlling one's emotions

was a valuable asset to the Samurai that he longed to portray. If he lost his faculties in a battle, he would most definitely lose. But when she smiled at him, he had a feeling in his gut that was foreign to him. He shook it off.

The air got colder as they traveled further underground until they finally made it to a blue metal door with the number 987 written across it. Abe pushed it open and flicked on a light switch, illuminating the inside of the room. There was a small bed laid out on the floor, a metal cabinet of sorts pressed up against the wall to his right, and a large wooden tub in the back. It wasn't a large room, but it was adequate.

"You'll find fresh clothes in the metal lockers, along with some soap to wash yourself, trust me on this, you need it." He gave Ryu a grin and a wink, "If you need to relieve yourself just go back down this hall, you'll find the waste chamber down there. I'll come get you for food in the morning."

Ryu thanked him for his hospitality and bid him goodnight. He unloaded the contents of his pack into the locker, pulling a set of fresh clothes out, along with the soap. He hadn't taken a formal bath since he was a kid, only able to rinse off here and there since leaving the house. It took a while for his small water interceptor to collect water, and using it for bathing seemed like a waste. Storm didn't seem to mind his smell either, or at the very least kept quiet about it.

He unrolled the tent from his bag and propped it up, carefully placing one of his blankets inside for Storm to sleep in. She was cleaning herself in the pot of water while he did these other tasks.

He asked her, "Feel refreshed?"

"Like a new bird."

He paused, gathering his thoughts, "So, what do you think

of all this? I need your opinion."

She took a moment to prepare her response, "I think we were lucky to find the Resistance. It's good to get a few answers, even if we don't have all the pieces of the puzzle yet. I feel that we will find your father sooner than you think."

He smiled, "I sure hope so. I'm excited for the two of you to meet. I know he'll love you as much as I do."

She gurgled at him, showing affection, and hopped away into the tent. Ryu stripped out of his dirty clothes, hoping they'd be salvageable; they were important to him as they helped him fight with more agility than others he'd worn. He stepped into the bath, which sent shivers throughout his body, making his teeth chatter. The water turned a murky brown as the dirt left his skin. After a minute he relaxed some, his body getting used to the cold water. He untied the red headband from his head, causing his hair to hang more loosely. Gathering some soap around the cloth, he scrubbed the dirt from it.

Satisfied with the cleanliness of the headband he submerged completely, eyes closed, and just sat there. He broke the surface with a gasp and wiped the water from his face. He cleaned his entire body and then cleaned it again. He hopped out and dried off, changing into the olive green shirt and black pants, his skin immediately itching.

Ugh, there's no way I'm wearing this longer than I have to.

"I'll be right back," he said to Storm, "I need to relieve myself."

Normally, he'd just go outside, so he was curious as to what this waste room would look like. He swung open a wooden door, an acrid smell hitting his nostrils causing him to recoil from the doorway. After a few seconds he regained his wits and entered; looking around he noticed the room had four rocky walls, and on the far wall there were three metal doors attached. He walked over and grabbed the handle of the middle door, wrenching it open, the scrape of the metal on the floor echoed around the chamber. Inside was a large hole in the ground, roughly two feet in diameter. He couldn't see the bottom, which made him glad it wasn't big enough to fall into.

Ryu finished up in the waste quarters and headed back to his room, but collided with someone as he rounded a corner. Just after contact was made, he felt his feet get swept out from under him, someone clasping his wrist and bicep with their hands. He looked up to see dark green eyes peering at him through dangling brown hair.

The girl said, "I'm so sorry. You scared me."

It was the archer he met above ground. She grabbed his hand and helped him to his feet as he said, "No, it was my fault. I should have been paying better attention."

There was an awkward silence, Ryu looked around the hall, words eluding him as that weird feeling buzzed in his stomach again. She broke the silence saying, "Your name is Ryu right? I'm Amelia." She reached her hand out towards Ryu.

He took her hand in his and shook it, only now realizing his palm felt clammy. He stared at her, feeling like his breath had been truly taken as she smiled at him. This was an emotion Ryu had not processed before.

She giggled, "Okay, well it was nice meeting you. I'll see you around, yeah?"

"Oh, uh, yeah. See ya."

They went their separate ways, and upon making it back to his room, Ryu shut the door hard behind him. He leaned against the door, his back on the cold steel, his chest heaving. Storm, startled, jumped out from her makeshift bed with a squawk.

"What happened? Are you okay?"

Ryu nodded his head, caught his breath, and said, "I have a problem."

He explained the experience he just had and how unnerving it was to be put in such an emotional state by a female. Once he finished, Storm chortled. A concoction of raven sounds escaped her, but when she recovered, Ryu just looked at her incredulously.

She said, "I'm sorry, but have you considered the possibility that you are infatuated with her?"

Puzzled, he said, "I don't know what that means."

"When someone feels attracted to another it's called infatuation. You think she's pretty don't you?"

"Yes, I can't deny that."

"Good, then I will help you win her heart."

He laughed heartily, "I just realized I'm getting lady advice from a bird."

"Well, I'm a female too you know."

"Yes, I'm vaguely aware of that.

They went to bed, unsure of the hour, and both fell asleep promptly. Ryu snored lightly, dreaming of this new girl, Amelia. The feelings he had in the dream were nothing compared to reality. He slept peacefully that night, without having to think or care about anything else.

The Bunker

Many forms of technology from the old world have been replicated. They are few and far between, usually. I've only seen some of them whilst working for the Order. I'm a smart fellow but I'm no inventor. I hope someone is able to replicate some of the wonders I've only read of one day.

Ryu walked around the main corridor of the bunker, looking around at all its accessories. Square-shaped devices glowed as rebels peered at them, pouring through data of sorts. When Ryu asked a particularly short man about it, he just gave him a dirty look and went back to studying the screen. Storm sat atop his shoulder, fluttering around the steel support beams covering the ceiling every so often. The ugly man who attacked Ryu sat in a metal chair, glaring at the two of them, and they returned his gaze. He gave Ryu an unsettling feeling. He tore his eyes away from him and continued walking.

Ryu heard a slight rumbling and a few minutes later, Abe came sauntering down the stairs that they'd descended initially. He walked up as Abe was speaking to a couple of other people; they were in a serious conversation, and Ryu caught the words, "four-armed beast," from one of the people he had yet to meet. The two skittered away as Ryu approached.

"Ah, Ryu, good to see you, my boy. How did you sleep?"

"Fairly well. What was all that about?" He asked, too curious to let it slip by.

"You will be filled in all in good time. Storm, how are you?" Ryu didn't like being left out of the loop.

She responded, "I am well. And you sir?"

"Good, good. Listen, I need to meet with the scouts and raiders to discuss recent and future missions. Would you like to listen in?"

Scouts? Raiders? Ryu thought about it for a moment before saying, "Yes, but just so you know, I've still not decided if I'm going to join your group or not."

Abe's eyebrows furled and the corner of his mouth twitched as he said, "What is there to think about? The One World Order must be overthrown, I thought we agreed on this."

"I agree that they should be stopped; I just don't see how it's my job to stop them."

Abe took a few breaths before responding, "A wise man once told me that if good men didn't dare to stand up to tyranny, then the world would be better off without them. You know who told me that?"

Before Ryu could form a response, Abe said, "Your father told me that. That's the sentence he used to get me to leave my post as a sentry and join his crusade for justice. The elites, with all their power and resources, have ruled for far too long. It's time for a new leadership to rise and restore some equality to mankind. If you want to have a hand in saving humanity from evil, you can follow me through that door."

He pointed at a large metal door, then turned away, shaking his head as he walked through the door. Ryu was leaning further toward joining the rebels.

He asked his companion, "What do you think we should do?"

Storm thought a moment and said, "I think this group is our best chance at finding your father. Don't think about it too much. The brain can be a faulty thing, but the heart will lead you to do what is right."

He did know what was right; he turned to the door and proceeded through it. On the other side was a small room with chairs and tables; there were already around 30 people in attendance, and upon looking at the faces turned toward him he saw the ones he'd met outside the night before. Amelia was there, she had a slight smile on her face as she patted the empty seat next to her. Ryu sauntered over, feeling silly as he tried to appear cool. He sat down, the cold of the chair seeping through the itchy clothes he wore.

Sitting so close to Amelia, his face was warm; he searched his brain for words to say to her but none would come. Luckily, she spoke first, saving him from saying anything embarrassing, "So, how are you liking the bunker so far?"

He found his words, "Oh, it's great. Unlike anything I've seen before."

The awkward silence returned, the two of them weren't used to making small talk it would seem, but then again, most people weren't. It was completely natural to not trust people. One's survival depended a lot on whether or not trust was placed in certain people. Abe took to the front and center of the room, addressing the faces that peered up at him. He gave a nod to Ryu before he began his speech. By entering this room, Ryu was showing that he had decided to join the Resistance. When Abe spoke, his voice sounded different, more commanding than before.

"I'd like to thank you all for gathering with me this morning. Your continued dedication to the cause does not go unnoticed. Before I drone on about upcoming operations, I'd like to ask Trish to come up and give us all a debrief of the scout's most recent findings."

Ryu watched a small girl make her way to the front; her short spiky hair went well with the metal rings dangling off her ears. She cleared her throat, "As you all know, we recently scouted the most nearby outpost, roughly 100 kilometers to the East. Once arriving, we observed from a distance as the drug pushers traveled to and from the Citadel to the outpost. It seems they weren't going outside the gates into the wasteland, so we can only assume that those living in the outposts are venturing out after receiving the Shade. We waited for the gate sentries to change out personnel and then sneaked past them. They were well equipped with an assortment of weapons, including explosives."

Ryu didn't know what explosives were and dared not ask with so many ears around.

"Next, we found something truly disturbing. The connector bridge that goes from the outpost to the Citadel is roughly 5 kilometers long. Along the path, we encountered something that wasn't entirely human. It appeared to be male, was over seven feet tall, and had the fattest belly I'd ever seen. He had four arms, two where they'd normally be and the others around six inches below. Its jaws appeared to expand, and the worst part was that it seemed to smell us.

"The thing sniffed the air as we got closer, hunkering behind rubble, we could see it turn toward us, looking in our direction. It was then that I gave the order to turn back. I believe this creature will be the biggest obstacle in reaching the Citadel."

Several people around the room shuddered, collectively repulsed by the story they just heard. As Trish was making her way back to her seat, Abe said, "Thank you, Trish. Now, I'd like you all to assist me in welcoming our newest rebels, Ryu and Storm." He lifted his good hand out, gesturing to Ryu. He stood with Storm on his shoulder, the gathered crowd applauding them.

Ryu said, "I thank you all for welcoming us, I wasn't sure at first if I would be joining your ranks, but after thinking it over, I believe it's the right thing to do. I'd like to help in any way I can. I'm rather handy with my sword, so if I can join as a scout or raider, I fell that would benefit you all. I don't know where I would fit elsewhere."

Storm squawked in agreement. The bulldog of a man stood up, crossing his arms, chuckling, "Who do you think you are to demand that we allow you to fight alongside us? We've worked together for years, since before you could even tie your boots. What makes you think you and your silly bird are needed around here?"

Ryu's fists clenched, his jaw muscles flexed as his teeth ground together. He wanted to shove his fist into this jerk's face, but before he could make a move Storm said, "Who are you calling silly?"

The crowd recoiled, some of them jumping from their seats and putting distance between themselves and the bird. The man's face went slack, he said, "Tal—a talking bird?"

Ryu said, "Yes, she speaks. Her name is Storm and she's far smarter than you, I can promise that."

The man sat back down, defeat apparent on his face. Abe just laughed as the people in the room took their seats, awe on their faces. Ryu noticed that Amelia's bottom jaw was open, and he hoped she wasn't too freaked out.

Storm spoke again, "Yes, I too agree to help in any way I can."

Ryu went back to his seat, Amelia just staring at the two of them as he sat down. Abe went back to the front, "Yes, well. Now that you've all met Ryu and Storm I'll continue. In two days the raiders will venture out to a neighboring city to the North. Many people were observed residing there, they did not appear hostile, but as always we can't be sure until we get there. Remember, the priority is recruitment, we need to gain as many as possible for when attacking the Citadel. If a conflict occurs protect each other at all costs and salvage what you can from the area. Dismissed."

Abe walked around with Ryu and Storm, showing them the rest of the bunker's facilities. The place was massive; it held many rooms with weapons, stockpiled food and water, and other supplies. There were corridors leading to an infirmary where he witnessed a man lying on a mattress with a blood-soaked bandage wrapped around his head. Abe told him the man was bludgeoned by a wooded club in a recent mission, luckily there were no spikes or metal attached to it. There were training areas where members could practice whatever they wanted; Ryu stood in the doorway of a large chamber, watching several people practice fighting with short daggers.

They came to a bold expanse, entering through a set of steel double doors. Rows upon rows of books lined the underground walls, stretching from the floor to the ceiling. Rolling ladders rested up against the massive shelves; Ryu couldn't wait to crack some of them open, a virtue he inherited from his father. He walked in eyeing them greedily for he enjoyed reading almost as much as fighting with his sword.

"Feel free to peruse whatever catches your eye. Don't hesitate to ask if you need anything," Abe told him.

"One thing," Ryu said. "I want to be on the raid you mentioned before."

"Of course. I'll let Jax know, he leads the raids."

Abe turned, leaving Ryu to find a book that sounded interesting. Storm fluttered up in the air, taking advantage of the open space of the library. He saw her land on a shelf, grabbing a thick book with her beak, and pushed it off. She swooped down and caught the book with her talons, floated down closer to Ryu, dropping it into his hands. He noticed it wasn't made like any normal book; its cover was made from leather, and the pages appeared to be poorly crafted. Leather was extremely rare. This book seemed old, and the title was messily scrawled across the spine reading *The Rise of Man.*

"This one stuck out to me, I thought you may want to look at it," Storm said to him.

He opened it, flipped to the first chapter, and began reading silently to himself. *The goal of the One World Order is to restore balance to the world; making the rich richer and the poor poorer. We do this by creating a way for us to be separated. Forming a central location for our government to flourish, and leaving the others to fend for themselves. Give them something to distract from their poverty, something that will make them happy, but ultimately destroy them. In the end, all that will be left is us, after the remaining people eliminate each other through division and feral madness, then we will populate the rest of the Earth with just our noble DNA.*

Ryu had to put the book down, he closed his eyes, choking back bile at the words written in this book. At first, he thought of the Order as an organization that was just corrupt because that's how governments tended to be in the past. After reading this, however, he was utterly disgusted at what these people were capable of and yearned for the day he would take over the Citadel with the Resistance. After calming down he asked Storm to return this book to its place on the shelf, unable to read further for now.

"How does all this work?" Ryu asked one of the rebels sitting at what they called a 'computer'.

She pointed up, replying, "Back before the wars, there were these devices called satellites sent into outer space. Many of them are still intact up there and we can connect to them. We can't do much with the computers besides track rebel inventory and movements, log data, stuff like that."

"Interesting," he responded.

"Yeah, I like the techy stuff. Keeps me occupied."

"Well, thanks for explaining it to me. I'm not sure I understand it fully, but that's alright."

She giggled as he walked away, stalking back to his sleeping chamber.

Raiders

For Ryu, when you're old enough:

My boy, there are many things you have yet to learn about me. I have not always been the kind man that you've come to know. I've done wicked things—just as anyone who works for the Order—in my life that I do not boast about. Perhaps I shouldn't have trained you in the ways of the Samurai as intensely. I hope that you'd forgive me for any transgression I've dealt to you.

The time had come for the raiders to head out on their operation, Ryu's first mission with the group. He planned to learn the ins and outs of how they operate, as well as build some camaraderie with them. There were eleven of them in total with Jax as the leader of the motley crew. He was the dog-faced man who had much distaste for him, but Ryu was determined to change his opinion of him during this mission. Apart from him, there was Amelia, Rob, Chester, Greta, Lincoln, Gabriel, Gregor, Toby, and the youngest in the group whom they called Chubbs. Ryu discovered that he'd been given the nickname because he was on the chunky side, which was rare to see.

Before departing the bunker, Ryu placed his journal under his pillow. He'd recently begun writing things down to his father's behest. He hadn't felt the effects that his father spoke of yet, but it didn't hurt. He left it behind, lest he lose it on this trip.

The device in Ryu's ear felt weird, foreign to him. He was told it was a communication device. It was no bigger than the tip of his finger, but he wasn't accustomed to it yet. They did a sound check before leaving the bunker. The earpiece was only to be used if they got separated and needed to speak over a longer distance.

Ryu was excited to go out on his first raid and to have more time to get to know Amelia better. Storm had chosen to hang back, resting for the first time in a while. He asked her what she would do while they were all away, and she responded, "Oh, I'll just hang around and eat my weight in whatever I can find scurrying about."

Ryu had to remind himself that she would be safe in the bunker, despite his angst of leaving her behind.

He felt weird in a new set of clothes; he'd only worn the same raggedy outfit for a long time. It didn't make sense to carry a bunch of clothing around which would only make his pack heavier. The Resistance outfitted him with a new long-sleeve shirt which was very soft and comfortable, and a new pair of pants that weren't too thin or too thick. The new clothes would do well at protecting him from the elements and keeping him cool. He wore the same boots, too accustomed to them to let them go as they hadn't yet fallen apart on him.

The raiders departed the bunker early in the morning, pink streaks split the sky open, and Ryu was happy to see it once again after exiting the ground. They left from the same way they'd entered, and he learned that this was the only way in and out. As they exited, he saw Abe coming back to the opening and bid them a safe raid.

In the two days before leaving, Ryu learned more about the bunker. It used to belong to the Order before it was abandoned. Abe and Kenji found it after leaving the Citadel and got it up and running. They got their power from large solar panels located roughly a mile away; surrounding the panels were enough booby traps to capture a decent-sized army.

There were several small bases spread around the bunker, most of them miles away from anything else so as not to attract too much attention. Each one had a different duty, from growing edible plants to growing animals, and from these bases, the Resistance got its supplies. The stations were instrumental in keeping the rebel group afloat. One of them was responsible for creating and raising humans, and once they were old enough to make their own choices they'd be given the choice to either leave on their own or join the Resistance. It wasn't much of a choice, but it was necessary if they were to win this war. Some of the rebels had the sole job of traveling around and trading goods between the stations and also delivering them to the main bunker. Each base had one duty in particular that was the same; lookout for enemies and sound the alarm if things go awry.

They walked in a straight line in pairs, side by side, leaving only Jax to be alone in the front of the group as they headed toward their destination. Amelia took place next to Ryu, her bow and quiver strapped across her back, the hood of her olive green cloak on top of her head. The group kept a steady pace, walking as fast as possible without overdoing it. Ryu peered at the colors of the sky as the sun peeked over the horizon; his hand rested on the handle of Sokushi, his boots crunching in the dirt. The pairs talked amongst themselves, but Ryu wasn't close enough to make out any conversations. Amelia and himself hadn't said anything to each other, and the more time that passed, the more awkward he felt.

"You don't talk much do you?" Amelia asked without looking at him.

He wondered if his silence bothered her, but said, "I haven't had much interaction with people. Well, not good interaction anyway. I've met a few friendly people before running into you all, but my blade has claimed more lives than friends I've made along the way."

"What were you doing out there anyway? It seemed so random at the time."

Ryu pondered how much detail he should go into, not wanting to reveal too much about himself, but finally came to the conclusion that he could trust her. He said, "Let me know if I start to bore you. About 10 years ago my dad suddenly vanished while on a supply run. He always made me stay home when he went out for extended periods. When I realized he wasn't coming back, I grabbed my sword and a bag and set out to search for him. I knew the direction he left in so that's where I started. All I could find was this headband and his journal, so I figured something bad happened to him. I couldn't imagine anyone being able to abduct my father, I mean, he was strong. I had to believe he was still alive.

"I continued searching, and then one day Storm found me. Freaked me out when she spoke to me for the first time, but I'd heard of weirder things happening. I questioned why she decided to stay with me, and she told me she sensed that I had a kind soul. Said that she felt that we needed one another. I didn't argue with that. I was lonely and scared, with no idea of how I was going to survive out there. She and I work well together and she's been the best friend I could have asked for. I've asked people along the way—those who didn't try to kill me—if they'd seen my dad, but none recognized the description I gave."

He stopped his explanation, missing his father more than ever, his eyes welling up. He hadn't talked about his dad this much in a while and was becoming overwhelmed with emotion, but dared not let a tear slide down his cheek. Amelia pulled her hood off and stopped walking. Ryu followed suit, turning to her, confused as to why she was stopping. When he looked at her, pain was written across her face.

"I'm sorry that all of this happened to you. It sounds horrible, and I just want you to know that I think you're so strong for dealing with it like you have. I mean, it's incredible that you've survived on your own for so long. I've been surrounded by warriors my whole life."

He chuckled, "Thanks, but I'd be dead if not for Storm. She may not be a fierce warrior, but her brains make up for her slight form."

She didn't respond so he said, "Alright, you've heard my part, now what about you? How'd you become part of the Resistance?"

"Well, it was an easy choice for me. I used to be part of a scavenger pack. My earliest memories involve being the bait so that my pack could trap and steal from travelers. I always hated it. When I became old enough, I ran away while the others were asleep. Jax found me on the brink of death and brought me back to the bunker. I've been with the Resistance ever since."

Ryu noticed her expression darken as she was telling him her story. "Look on the bright side. All the things that happened in your past have made you into the strong person you are now."

"You may be right about that," she said.

He chuckled, "I try to remain positive about things."

It took a full day before the decrepit city came into their view; the sun was dipping below the skyline, resulting in Jax stopping them for the time being. They erected their tents and started a fire. The supply shop had given them each some dried meat to keep them fed while they traveled. It wasn't much, but was better than what Ryu was used to.

Ryu had a restless night of sleep due to a nagging feeling in his gut, but he couldn't figure out what it was. He silently crept out of his tent before the sun had fully risen; with the city so close, Jax told them to sleep in, but Ryu wasn't able to sit still any longer. He stretched his arms wide, yawning, and breathed in the cool air. Movement caught in the corner of his eye and he turned his attention to it and saw that Jax was hunched over outside his tent, his hands tinkering with something.

Upon completing what he was doing he stood up and tossed the thing in the air. It was a bird. It flapped away, disappearing quickly. Ryu found it curious but didn't want to anger the man by bringing it up. He was still trying to get on Jax's good side. Perhaps the man had caught the bird and decided not to eat it, or maybe there had been something unsavory about it. He let it go and went to packing his stuff up.

The raiders took off in the direction of the city, all excited to reach their destination. Finally, the features of the city came into view. It was rather small but was fortified better than anything Ryu had yet seen. He could see two guard towers with archers standing tall above the ground. There was a wall made of piled-up rubble that surrounded the town. The front gate had spears jutting through it, removing the possibility for people to ram it.

Archers stood with their arrows aimed at the group, bowstrings taut, but they approached the big gates anyway. They were made of wooden slats so tight that no one could see what was on the other side, but in the center of one door was a small rectangular slot. Jax pounded on the door with his fists, after a second the slot slid open to reveal a pair of eyes looking at the group.

A gravelly voice said, "Yeah? What do ya want?"

Jax spoke for the group, "We were sent by the leader of the Resistance. You've no doubt heard of us, yes?"

A grunt was the only response Jax was given.

"We have a proposition for you. Is there someone in charge we could speak with?"

Without answering, the man slid the slot shut and the doors began to creak as they slowly swung open. The rebels had to scatter to avoid being impaled by the sharp tines. Once there was enough space they entered; Ryu noticed there was a stool with a tiny man standing on it. He was pointing down the street towards a building not far from their location.

The buildings didn't look too bad as far as Ryu was concerned; they looked nicer than most others he encountered. People milled about, taking notice of the raiders and staring. Ryu noticed that they were all fairly old, there were no kids around. He wasn't sure they would make a good addition to the Resistance and would end up being fodder. It took a few minutes for them to reach the building.

It was the nicest one in the town, and even now people were cleaning its front steps. There was a man outside the front door with a large knife strapped to his belt. He had a long thick beard and had a blank expression on his face. Jax led the crew up the stairs and tried to enter, but before he could reach the handle the bearded guard stepped in front of it and said, "What's your business here?"

Jax said, "We wish to speak with whoever is in charge."

He huffed, "Suit yourself. He'll be upstairs in the first room to the right."

He slid to the side and let them enter; Ryu noticed there were several elderly people in there dusting the various shelves with books and intricately designed vases on them. They stomped up the stairs and entered the room, its door wide open already. Ryu was in the back of the formation, checking over his shoulder just before stepping across the threshold. The cleaners had stopped what they were doing and watched them enter the office.

Behind a large wooden desk sat the town's leader. Ryu's heart skipped a beat as he stared into the man's scarred face. His features were gaunt, his eyes sunken inside of his skull. His hair grew in strange patterns on his head, as if part of it had been burnt off a long time ago. His fingers were long and bony, a golden ring on each of them. He had stubble on his chin patched with silver hairs. The man looked mad, like someone who had spent much of their life being tortured and beaten.

He pulled a burning stalk from his lips and laid it down in a glass bowl, finally looking up to acknowledge the audience before him. His eyes met Ryu's gaze and he tilted his head slightly, as if he recognized him from somewhere. The look passed and he cringed at the sight of their dirty boots on his clean, polished floor. After a moment he smiled, his teeth were crooked and jagged, as if filed down to purposely mimic a wild beast.

"Well, well, what brings this filth into my town?"

76

An Unforgiving Host

"Sir, I apologize for the interruption. We didn't realize you all were so sophisticated out here," Jax said, seeming to feign sincerity. Ryu looked around the office; the walls were blank, completely devoid of any decoration. The only items in the room were the desk with papers strewn about with other accessories.

"What do you want? Why do you disturb me? Do you not know who I am?"

Ryu thought about it, trying to figure out if he should know the man. *Is he supposed to be famous?* he thought. Then Jax said, "Forgive me. I don't know who you are. We were sent by Abe, leader of the Resistance. We've come with a proposition for you and your town."

The man seethed, tossed his head back, and laughed heartily before saying, "Perhaps you should have heard who I am before telling me the organization you come from." He let his words hang in the air for a moment, relishing in their naivety. Then he continued, saying, "I am Darius the Deadly, former Vice Commander of the One World Order's elite sentries." He smiled a disturbing grin as Ryu waited for the man to spring into action, but he didn't. Several moments passed by and he just held the grin, passing his eyes over the entire group, but lingering only on Ryu slightly longer than the others.

Darius coughed, breaking his gaze away from the raiders, and wiped a white rag across his mouth which was then stained red with blood. "You're sick," Amelia observed, concern crossing her face.

He eyed her and said, "Right you are, my dear. You can see that I've been brutally deformed by the government. They do not take lightly to failure, whether you are responsible or not." His expression darkened, and Ryu felt a bit of sympathy for the poor man.

"Well then," he said, "best not to dwell on the past. What is this proposition you have for me?"

Jax said, "Our current goal is to spread our forces and recruit more able-bodied men to our cause. We'd like to extend the hand of partnership. We can offer you many supplies from any of our stations, in return for you lending us help in times of need. In time we will overthrow the nobles and rebuild society. You can have your revenge on the Order."

As Jax spoke, Darius' expression grew more intense, and once the speech was over he sat for a long time with his fingers crossed in front of his face. Ryu was becoming impatient with the man, wishing he'd either accept or turn them away. Finally, the man stood up; he was tall and narrow, a thin layer of muscle wrapped tightly around his skeleton.

He thrust a bony hand toward Jax and said, "I'd love to assist you all in this endeavor. Please, accompany me to my home to make this alliance complete."

Ryu felt a bit of apprehension about the man's sudden change in demeanor but attributed it to his chronic distrust of people. Still, he followed as Darius led them all back out of the office, and clamored down the stairs, where at the bottom gathered those who were cleaning before. They all cowered as Darius passed. Ryu noticed a woman who held a dirty rag to a mirror, her hands trembled. A look was exchanged between Darius and the man guarding the entrance to the building, but he wasn't sure what it meant.

Down the steps and taking a street to the right, they trekked down the cleanest road Ryu had ever seen. This town became more and more peculiar the more of it he observed; doors slammed shut and people peered through windows as they walked by. Soon enough a building loomed before them, it was two stories tall and looked pristine as far as structures go. The wood was scratched up but looked solid. There was a large porch wrapping around the entire house. It was filled with windows, none of them broken which was unusual to see.

Out of earshot of anyone else, Ryu leaned over and whispered in Amelia's ear, "Is it just me, or does this place give you a creepy feeling?" Amelia shrugged in response.

"Please, follow me into the lounge. I will have some tea made," Darius said as he opened the massive door for them to enter. Just as before at the last building, there were several people scattered around cleaning every surface of his house. Ryu gripped the hilt of his blade, hoping he wouldn't need it, but his nerves were ever-increasing.

The group followed Darius into a large room with sky-blue walls, the sun shining brightly through the ten-foot-tall windows. A large black device sat in one corner, a man with brown hair, and wearing a solemn expression sat behind it on a small bench. He sat up straight as he noticed the group. Darius motioned his hand towards him and said, "Allen, play something light if you would."

The man began pressing white rectangles on the device with his fingers, a delightful sound began dancing around Ryu's ears. He stood, fixated on the sounds emitting from it, and couldn't help himself. He asked, "What is this?"

Seeming annoyed by his question, Darius stepped toward him, clenched his jaws together, and answered through gritted teeth, "That's a piano. Never heard of one, eh?"

Ryu merely shook his head, and Darius turned back, striding across the rug on the floor. There were long couches spread all over the room, and as Ryu—being the last one standing—took a seat, Darius called to another.

"Bridgette, would you be so kind as to bring us some tea? You know, the kind reserved for special guests?"

A young girl stood in the doorway to the right of Darius. She hesitated at his question for only a moment before offering a short bow and slinking away. Clanking could be heard in the adjacent room as the girl made tea, which Ryu wasn't exactly sure of. Luckily one of the other raiders asked Darius what it was, saving Ryu more scolding from their host. He explained that it was a drink made from boiled water and ground-up leaves from various plants.

Ryu was sure to keep aware of their surroundings, taking notice of each time someone floated past the entrance to the lounge, each one looking ghostly as they sauntered by. Darius gave them a history lesson of his time working for the One World Order, not sparing any detail despite their consistent yawning.

"I was Vice Commander of the sentries for many years, defending our way of life from scavengers and the Shade-doped devils. I'm not entirely proud of the things I've done, but it seemed better to be on the side that had wealth and resources versus the demons trying to take us down. And now look at me, ha!"

A wild look entered his eyes, making him appear as if he was a crazed lunatic, laughing madly as he droned on, "Getting into the metaphorical bed with what was once my enemy. Surely, with my knowledge, the nobles will fall easily."

Bridgette returned with a tray full of tiny glass cups. She passed them out, one to each of the raiders and then one to Darius. There was a large porcelain container that held the tea; she poured a small amount of translucent brown liquid into their cups. Ryu looked into his cup as colors swirled; the bottom showed a tree, and as the steaming tea hit it pink flowers blossomed from its branches. He was mesmerized and the suspicions he previously held had since left his brain.

He sipped the hot liquid, scalding his tongue and wincing. Darius said, "Best to blow it a bit so you don't burn yourself."

He was very attentive as Ryu blew his brew and took a drink, followed by the rest of the group. Darius continued telling them about how he had been wronged by one of his closest allies, and his betrayal is what led to the nobles punishing him. Their cruelty left him disfigured, and they gave him this small city as a gift, calling themselves merciful in doing so. He would have rather died than live like this but was too much of a coward to take his own life.

"Since that day, I vowed to get my revenge if I ever got the chance. And it seems, my chance has finally come." The man chuckled maniacally.

Ryu's eyelids became heavy, and he thought it was the fatigue of the trip that was causing this. He couldn't get the fog to leave no matter how many times he tried to shake it off. His eyes tried to close but then snapped open as he heard a loud crash on the floor. Frantically looking around, he saw that several of his fellow rebels had passed out and fell onto the hard floor. He looked into his cup, realizing what was happening, and Darius stood up, pouring the contents of his cup back into its original container.

He strolled over to Ryu and squatted down, his head lolling to one side. Darius had a devilish grin on his face as he said, "Your father, Kenji, was the friend who betrayed me. He ran off, with that fool Abe, dead set on overthrowing the nobles. I knew you were his boy the moment I laid eyes on you. You look just like he did when we first met."

Tears filled Darius' eyes, and rage contorted his face as he said, "I loved him like a brother. And look, "He pointed at his disfigured face, "look at what he's done to me! This is all his fault!"

Ryu felt his consciousness fading in and out, only half understanding what was going on at this point. Darius was barking orders, but his voice was too far away for Ryu to make out what was being said. Darius came back, turning his attention back on Ryu, his hot breath pouring only inches away from his nose as he breathed heavily.

He grabbed Ryu by his hair, wrenched his head back, exposing his throat, and said, "I will get all the information I need out of you lot. You will lead me to Kenji or I'll slaughter every last one of your friends while you watch. And then, I'll find your little hideout and smite whoever remains there as well."

Darius released Ryu's head, letting it fall forward. Ryu mustered the tiniest bit of strength; he tried to draw Sokushi as he stood. His feet faltered and slipped out from under him, causing him to crash to the floor. Darius paused, looking over his shoulder with a smirk on his face.

The light faded from his vision, and Ryu passed into oblivion, his consciousness slipping from his grasp. The last image that crossed his line of sight as he lay motionless, was the burly man with the thick, twisted beard grabbing him by the ankles and dragging him away.

He was drowning, no, that was just a bucket of cold water being thrown into Ryu's face. He sputtered and spat water from his mouth as his eyes opened, he tried to regain his composure as the liquid dripped down his face. He blinked rapidly and tried to wipe the water away with his hands but they wouldn't cooperate. He shook his head, clearing the liquid off his eyes, and looked around frantically. Ryu was in a cage with his group of raiders; they had already woken from the forced slumber, and all looked around with desperation in their eyes. To Ryu, they all looked scared, except for Jax. He looked composed.

Ryu slowed his breathing, forcing himself to calm down. His hands were tied to the thick bars of the steel cage, as were his comrades. They all sat on the floor with their legs splayed out in front of them. The chamber they were in was dark, but he couldn't tell if it was a building or underground. He noticed Amelia's hair was slickly stuck to the side of her face, and she still looked beautiful.

The only other person he could see was the bearded man from that first building. He stood in the middle of the cage, holding a metal bucket with water slowly dripping off its lip. Along with the beard he had thick brows, large ears, and a fat nose. His hair was long on top and short on the sides. He was a giant, towering over the raiders; his shirt had no sleeves, allowing his large muscles to show. It was rare to see tattoos—

apart from the ones that people are born with—but the man's arms had thick black lines all over.

"Welcome to our quaint little prison, lads. I've been tasked with getting specific information out of you. If you give me what I need then we can all be on our merry way. If not, Darius will come to take over for me and believe me when I say this, you would much rather have me here than him."

He took his shirt off, revealing large abs and pecs, turned his back to Ryu, and pointed at three long, jagged scars running diagonally down his back. "He gave me these when I first arrived here. Believed I was a spy working for his enemies. Only after killing my mates and giving me these did he let me go, with the agreement that I'd work for him. At first, I didn't want to work for someone so vile, but over the years I've come to enjoy my job. These," he gestured to the tattoo markings, "represent how dedicated I am at getting the truth from people. Each line is either a lying soul I've taken from this world or a confession of candor."

Ryu, feeling brazen said, "So, what, you just torture innocent travelers for information that they don't have? How pathetic."

The titan dropped his shirt and the metal bucket to the floor, the clang echoing around the chamber. He slowly turned, eyes locking on Ryu, and smiled with broken teeth. "I usually start these things off nice and slow, but you've just made my job much more fun, mate."

A Scathing Escape

The Order is no doubt angry with me. I left abruptly and they don't take well to deserters. There were few who joined me when I abandoned my post. I'll live the remainder of my days looking over my shoulder. I just couldn't take their wickedness any longer. Many of my brothers and sisters at arms fail to see the corruption. They weren't born on the outside as I was.

The gnarly man sauntered over to Ryu, dropped down into a deep squat, breathing in his face. He asked, "Where is Kenji? Tell me and I may forget about your insult."

After several seconds of silence, the giant became impatient with waiting for a response. With his large meaty hand he slapped Ryu across the face, the sound of the strike reverberating off the walls. His head snapped to the right and heat welled up in his cheek where the man's palm had landed. Again, the man smacked him in the face, this time on his other cheek with the back of his hand. Ryu's anger contorted his face, his cheeks stinging from the slaps. He could feel a small lump forming just below his left eye.

"Hey," Amelia yelled from across the cage, "How about you just let us go already? We don't deserve this; I'm sure there is some decency still left in you"

The giant turned around slowly, a smile danced across his face as he purposefully looked the girl up and down. She shifted on the floor as he stalked closer to her. Squatting back down, he said, "What's your name, darling?"

Ryu expected her to ignore him but instead, she answered, "Amelia. What's yours, pig?"

Ryu chuckled, the smile faded from the man's face as he said, "Don't you worry about that. Just call me pig all you want. I like it when they talk dirty."

He looked around at the group of people, taking his time in eyeing each of them separately. While distracted, Amelia reached out with her foot and kicked at the man. She was too slow; he caught her foot in mid-air, turned back to her, and pushed her legs into the floor with his hands. He jumped on her, straddling her legs and effectively pinning them to the floor with his body.

"No, get off me!" She struggled under his immense weight which was easily double hers. Ryu felt more enraged than ever before. He looked around frantically for anything that may help him get loose of his bindings but was unsuccessful. The others just watched, horrified by the scene that was unfolding before them. The large man ran a single finger down her face, caressing her cheek gently.

"You know," he said, "you remind me of my first lover. She was petite, just like you."

"Oh yeah? And what happened to her? You kill her?"

He looked up, a shadow of regret crossing his face as he said, "I did what was necessary." He leaned in close to Amelia, looking as if he was going to whisper in her ear, but she didn't give him the opportunity.

With a grunt she threw her head forward, connecting

squarely with the man's nose. He flew backward and landed on his back right in front of Ryu. Not wasting this chance, Ryu wrapped the man up in his legs. He struggled to recover as his life was being choked out of him. Ryu continued to squeeze with all his might, straining heavily from the intense effort. Finally, after what seemed like an eternity, the man's retaliation slowed and then came to a halt. He fell back completely, motionless. Ryu held on for another minute, his breath ragged, until he was sure the guy wasn't going to get back up.

He let go, his chest rising and falling rapidly, he looked around at the wide-eyed, slack-jawed faces of his companions. Amelia looked terrified, like at any moment she would burst into tears, but she didn't cry.

Jax said, "Well, now what?"

Ryu racked his brain, searching for any possibility of escape, but nothing would come to him. He looked around and his eyes had adjusted better to the room they were in. It was fairly dark but there were cracks in the walls and he could clearly see daylight through them. In the dim light, he was able to see ropes bound their hands to the cage bars, but he couldn't detect any debris lying around that would be able to cut them free.

He pulled down on the ropes, they were solid. He stood up, sliding his arms up the bars as he went; looking up toward the ceiling, he was now able to see a notch in the bars. It was high above his head, but he could see a gap. This would be his way out, and after he got loose he would be able to save his friends. He turned his body so that it faced the bars but was unable to change the position of his hands. His wrists remained crossed over one another at an awkward angle.

He leaned back as far as he could, placing a foot on the bar in front of him. He applied pressure until he was able to kick his other foot up onto the adjacent bar, and pushed until he was able to hold himself upright. The pressure on his wrists caused him to wince as the rope dug into his skin. His legs wobbled, clearly still spent from the effort of choking the giant. He inched his way up the bars, sliding his rope along the metal shafts. The raiders watched him, cheering him on, and encouraging him to reach his target.

Once he reached the break in the bars he looked at the ground between his legs. He was fairly high up, roughly 12 feet by his estimate. With a great deal of effort, he yanked his hands upward, the rope slipped through the chink in the metal and he plummeted to the floor. He landed on his feet but heard a sickening crunch as his right ankle exploded with pain. He screamed out and clutched his ankle, already feeling it swell inside his boot.

Ryu looked around at his comrade's faces peering down at him, reading the pitying looks on their faces. After a few deep breaths, he began dragging himself toward Gabriel. He hauled himself up clumsily, grasping the bars of the cage and pulling up. He untied the binds around Gabriel's wrists, taking most of his energy to hold himself up on the one foot. After they were loosened enough he slumped back down onto the floor as Gabriel began releasing the other raiders.

Gabriel worked quickly to untie Chubbs who was next to him, and they continued to release the others. Once everyone was liberated from their binds, they found the door of the cage which was locked. Jax was able to find a set of keys on the supine man and promptly unlocked the barred door. They all filed out, in search of an exit. Gabriel and Chester—the biggest men besides Jax—helped carry Ryu out of the building once the exit was found.

Once outside, Ryu was nearly blinded by the sun, which was nearing the bottom of the sky with only a few hours left of daylight. His eyes adjusted and he noticed other people slinking back into the safety of whatever structure they were next to. Anxious eyes watched the raiders as they shuffled their way back down the street.

"Keep your head on a swivel," Jax told them. "Let's get in that house, retrieve our gear, and get the hell out of this place."

Ryu felt like a piece of him was missing without Sokushi strapped to his waist. That blade was an extension of his arms and had never failed him in battle. And now he was even more useless with this busted ankle. He hobbled down the road, arms straddled over his comrades. Within a couple of minutes, the lavish house came into view and the group sneaked across the street, taking cover behind the corner of a nearby building. Ryu was lowered to the ground and the rest of the raiders scurried into Darius' house.

He watched them all enter through the front and, through the windows, was able to observe them splitting up, going in different directions to search more efficiently. Ryu looked back and forth, up and down the street, on the lookout for anyone who may approach. Luckily he was being vigilant because a small group of men appeared, jogging down the street carrying an array of weapons, some sharp and some blunt. From his position he was able to keep out of sight; finding a group of small rocks on the ground, he began picking them up and hurling them at one of the upstairs windows in the house.

The sound of the shattering glass was inaudible to the men,

the scuffle of their feet was too loud. Ryu flung another rock, smacking the window again. A few seconds later, Amelia's face popped up in the window and Ryu pointed at the enemies. She gave a thumbs-up and disappeared seconds before the group reached the porch of the house. Ryu suddenly had an overwhelming sense of unease wash over him as chill bumps sprouted all over his body.

"Hello there," a familiar voice whispered from behind him, hot breath touching his neck. Slowly Ryu turned, the ghostly face of Darius smiling at him. He looked delirious. His eyes were thick with madness, his smile cruel. Normally Ryu was able to stay calm and keep his reserves about him, but in this moment he felt true fear. His body shook slightly as he tried to drag himself away, wincing at the pain in his foot. Darius straightened up, holding the smile, and laced his fingers into each other.

"Ryu," he said, taking the overcoat off and letting it fall into the dirt, "don't be unreasonable. Just tell me what I want to know. Where is your father?"

"I don't know."

Darius laughed, "You expect me to believe that? I know what happened. He took a pod the day he left, created you, and then started the Resistance with that moron, Abe."

"Listen," Ryu told him, "I haven't seen him in years. I've been searching for him for a long time now. If I knew where he was, I probably wouldn't tell you, but I don't know where he is. That's the truth."

Ryu heard a boisterous commotion coming from behind him; he looked over his shoulder to see bodies flying around in front of the windows of the house. It was all too fast to see who was being flung around, and he began to panic, dragging himself faster toward it. Darius then reached down and wrapped his bony fingers around Ryu's ankle, gripping it tightly to keep him from moving further away.

Ryu grimaced, pain shooting all the way up to his knee. "I swear I don't know where he is! Let go of me. Please!"

Smiling again, Darius said, "I'd be a fool to believe you. Right now, my men are ripping your friends apart. Once they come out, I'm going to put you through unimaginable pain. You *will* tell me what I want to know."

As if on command, they all emerged from the house; the raiders came first carrying gear bags, but no weapons. Darius' men came next, holding more weapons than before they entered, clearly they had won the fight.

Something is off, he thought, wait, *where's Chubbs?*

Ryu thought back to when he first met the kid. He was so full of life and energy. It was impossibly to be in a poor mood with him around.

He'd grown rather fond of the young boy over the little time he had gotten to know him. The worst thought began running through his head, and he was about to ask, but the only word he got out was, "Where-" before Amelia sternly shook her head at him.

Darius spread his arms wide and said, "You may have taken down Andre, but you're no match for my elite group of defenders. I recruited them straight from the Citadel's failed sentry corps. Now then, who shall we kill first?"

He walked around the circle of raiders, looking at each of them from head to toe. He stopped at Amelia and said, "Hmm, I doubt this one will be missed." He grabbed her by the back of her head, and she struggled to break his grip but he was far too strong despite his bony frame. Darius dragged her to the middle of the circle, and Ryu hobbled up to his feet, putting all his weight on his good leg.

"Let her go, you bastard!"

"Oh name calling, are we? I'll make sure to wash my hands in this one's blood."

His shark tooth grin sent tremors of rage through Ryu, but he didn't know what to do. Not only were his options not good, he couldn't even think of any plausible options. Darius reached behind his back and withdrew a six-inch blade. The handle was made from some sort of bone and had a skull etched into it. He poked it into Amelia's back, just enough to make her wince but not do any real damage. He smiled at the look of indignation on Ryu's face.

Before anyone else could do anything an arrow came flying out of nowhere; the dart struck one of Darius' men in the back and protruded through his chest. This gave Amelia enough time to twist out of the man's grip and duck under his arm. She shoved him from behind and jumped to Ryu's side, giving him a little bit of support. The rest of the raiders turned on their captors, grip fighting for possession for the weapons. Ryu saw a bald man with a shortly-trimmed beard raise Sokushi over his head and swing it down toward Gregor.

Gregor was not quick enough in blocking, though he tried, and it was a fatal blow. The blade's edge buried itself deep into the muscle fibers of his neck. It sliced into his arteries and blood spurted through the air. As Ryu watched the man fall to his knees, he screamed, "No!" and with the help of Amelia began hopping to the action. More arrows were flying through the air and Darius ducked out of the battle just as Ryu made it to the bald man.

He lunged off one leg and tackled the man; they tumbled

into the dirt and pain shot through his ruined ankle once again, a groan of pain escaped his lips. He wrestled the man for his sword and would stop at nothing to have it back. Amelia jumped in to help, placing her knee into the man's esophagus. She crushed his windpipe and he sputtered, struggling to breathe. He let go of the sword and Ryu stood back up, hopping on one foot, and held the sword just above the man's head.

He was about to put him out of his misery, but something dark took over him, he wanted this man to suffer. Ryu wanted him to agonize in his last moments for what he did to Gregor. He bent over at the waist and yanked the sheath from the man, tying it around himself. Looking around, he noticed that all their enemies had been defeated, but he didn't see Darius anywhere. Chubbs came running in from where he'd been firing arrows, a smile on his face.

The two of them slapped hands, a grin crossing Ryu's face as well, "Good job, Chubbs. I'm pretty sure we'd all be dead if not for you."

The young boy beamed, and then they all turned to Gregor, any sense of elation now gone from their bodies. They stood for a moment in silence as Gregor lay in a pool of his own blood. Greta had tears slipping down her face as she mourned in silence.

"Alright," Jax said, "We can grieve more later. We have all our gear, now let's get out of here. Rob, Chester, you two grab Gregor. We aren't leaving him hear. Someone else help the gimp hobble his way out. We're gonna be moving fast."

People began moving to action, when suddenly a sickening thump rang out, and a gargling noise filled everyone's ears. Turning to the sound, Ryu saw Chubbs with a knife sticking out through his throat. Blood streamed from around the wound and leaked from his mouth. Amelia screamed in horror at the sight; the knife was ripped out and Chubbs fell face-first into the dirt, lifeless.

No one could move, only stare at Darius, holding the bloody knife with a crazed look in his bloodshot eyes. He raised the knife up to his face and licked some of the crimson liquid off, laughing maniacally. Ryu had seen enough of this madman.

Springing forward, Ryu launched himself off one foot with all the power he had. He sailed through the air, at a speed too fast for Darius to react. With a rageful scream, he thrust his blade forward. Its tip plunged into the monster's gut as Ryu landed back on his good leg. They were face to face now, Darius' mouth hung open in surprise. Ryu didn't want to wait for him to respond to the attack, he then gripped the hilt of his sword with both hands and turned it so the edge faced the sky.

With all the power left in his arms, Ryu yanked upward, the blade gliding through flesh, muscle, and bone as if he were cutting into water. Sokushi angled outward, leaving Darius split clean through from his navel up and through his collarbone and shoulder. Ryu breathed heavily at the effort he'd just expound. Amelia walked over and pulled him into an embrace; even though he was taller than her, he still rested his head on her shoulder. He breathed into her neck, wanting to stay there forever.

Jax ordered them to do as before, except this time it was two bodies they'd be hauling out. Ryu refused any help, determined to keep pace with the group and make it back on his own. He was putting a little pressure on his ruined foot as they hastily made their exit from the city. People were now coming out of their hideouts, watching them move down the street. They were moving at a jogging pace; Ryu was struggling along with those carrying the bodies of their fallen raiders.

There was an hour of light left in the day, and then they'd have to deal with the cold of the night. Before approaching the towers that stood sentry at the gate, Jax sent two of the raiders up onto the roof of a neighboring building to see if they were still there. If the guards were in attendance they were to be shot down with arrows immediately. The two returned and gave the all-clear.

The tiny man still sat on the stool, however, he was napping as they approached. Jax kicked the stool out from under him, causing the man to panic as his eyes snapped open. Jax ordered him to open the gate immediately which he complied with and then slammed it shut as they crossed the town's threshold.

After making it a small distance away, the sun was creeping beneath the horizon. Jax ordered the raiders to stop and make camp, and after doing so wrap the bodies of their fallen friends in whatever spare cloth they had. Ryyu hadn't spoken to Gregor much but was still pained by his demise. Chubbs had a way about him that forced everyone to adore him. He was kind, silly, and kept everyone around smiling. His death hurt Ryu more than he wanted to admit. He sat beside his body after helping wrap him up, silently hoping that the boy was at peace wherever he may be now.

Abounding Anger

Ryu, it's your tenth birthday. You've got a fire in you that I can tell will lead you to do bold things one day. I can feel it. Call it a father's intuition. Having great emotion is not a bad virtue, as long as you're able to control it. I write this as a reminder to you in case I am not there to say the words in person.

Upon their arrival back at the bunker, Jax gave a full debrief to Abe as to what transpired while the others tended to their wounds and fallen friends. It took Ryu forever to get down the stairs with his busted ankle, still refusing help from anyone and was the last to touch down at the bottom. He saw Jax and Abe enter a room with windowed doors. They appeared to be having a heated argument, but Ryu wasn't sure why. Perhaps Abe was reprimanding him for allowing two raiders to die, however, Ryu couldn't imagine it being Jax's fault.

They exited the room and Abe's visage shifted back into that of a humble leader, rather than a reprimanding boss. Ryu hobbled away from everyone as the other raiders shared what happened, and slunk back to his quarters. Storm was waiting for him when he got there and was very concerned when she saw him limping to his bed. "You're hurt," she said, fluttering down from her perch, "what happened? You should be in the infirmary."

Ryu explained everything that had happened since the raiding party left, and that he didn't want to be around anyone at the moment. He told her about Chubbs' death, and how it made him feel, sharing his innermost thoughts with her. Storm listened intently, bobbing her head up and down every so often. He stripped down and plopped into the bath, soaking in the cool water. He closed his eyes, listening to Storm's retelling of her time in the bunker.

She spent a lot of time with Abe, learning about the ins and outs of the bunker and the intricacies of the Resistance as a whole. Ever the intelligence gatherer. It was a fairly large force, but still smaller than the manning of soldiers and mutants in the noble's possession. Every day they grew closer to laying siege to the Citadel, but not yet. There was still much work to be done.

"Your father seems very important to him," Storm told Ryu, "but storming the Citadel is more so. He seemed almost giddy at the thought of taking down the Order."

"I don't blame him there," Ryu admitted.

Abe told her how innovative he was even before leaving their sentry duties; Kenji would often come up with clever ways of keeping unwanted beings out of the Citadel. He was a master swordsman—which was no secret to Ryu—and was also great at setting traps. He told her that Kenji once dug a hole in a popular creeper area, which was the name they'd given to people drugged up on Shade. These were the ones who had lost all sense of humanity; after digging the hole, Kenji put spikes in its bottom. He covered the hole with a sand-colored cloth, weighed down on the edges with rocks, and then covered the whole thing in dirt. When a creeper would walk over it, they'd fall straight onto the prongs, being impaled and trapped in the deadly crater.

Ryu lost track of how long he listened to Storm speak; eventually, she stopped and he drifted off to sleep. He later awoke to a knock at his door, "One second," he said as he rolled out of the tub. Storm was asleep in her little bed, breathing softly as he pulled on some clean clothes. He noticed his fingers were soft and wrinkled from being in the water for such an extended period of time.

Opening the door, Ryu stepped out, face to face with Amelia. She smiled softly at him, but he felt that she was looking at him in pity, which didn't sit well with him. "What are you doing here?" he asked. A hurt look crossed her face but fled quickly.

She said, "I just wanted to come check on you."

"What makes you think I need to be checked on?"

"I'm sorry I just—"

"Just what? Just wanted to let me know that you feel sorry for me? Well, no thanks, I don't need pity from you or anyone else."

Amelia stared at him, shock displayed with her mouth open slightly, and after a few seconds she responded, "Okay," she whirled around swinging her arms hard as she walked away, turning over her shoulder she said, "When you want to stop acting like a jerk, come find me."

Ryu shook his head, annoyed that she was right, he was acting childish and wasn't sure why. He walked back in, slamming the door, and waking Storm in the process. Startled, she jumped up alert for danger, and upon noticing it was Ryu, laid back down. She looked at him for a minute as he sat on the edge of his bed, staring at the floor. He was both hoping she'd ask him if he was okay and also afraid that he'd break down if she did ask.

She didn't press him, instead laid her head back down and drifted back to sleep. Ryu wasn't exactly sleepy now but didn't want to move from his spot. A dull pain throbbed up and down his leg, keeping rhythm with his heartbeat. He laid back on his bed, staring at the ceiling for a long time, until slowly falling back asleep.

Several weeks after their return to the bunker, Ryu's ankle was mostly healed. A twinge of pain would hit him if he twisted it a certain way, but other than that it was okay. He was relieved to not have to use walking sticks anymore. The infirmary staff told him they were called crutches, but he still called them walking sticks. His mood hadn't improved much as far as talking with others, no matter the topic.

Many of the Resistance members had tried starting conversations with him, but he usually shrugged them off and aborted back to his room. Storm was the only one who could get anything of substance out of him. He'd passed Amelia in the halls a few times, but she paid no attention to him, which was fine with him. He didn't feel like dealing with anyone, not even her. His mind was in a conundrum, torn between wanting to talk to Amelia and avoiding her at the same time.

"You realize she's probably going through the same thing right? You weren't the only person who lost something on that mission," Storm lectured him.

The words hung in the air, guilt eating away at Ryu's gut until—with a grumble—he heaved himself off his bed. "As much as I hate to admit it, you're right. I'll be back."

Ryu wound his way slowly through the halls, looking for

Amelia. His ankle was much better now but still wasn't back to its original state. He found her sitting in the dining hall alone, poking at some food with her fingers, a look in her eyes told him that her mind was miles away right now. He walked over and plopped down in the chair across from her; she blinked rapidly as he disturbed her from her trance. Her eyebrows furrowed as she realized Ryu was the one sitting in front of her.

"I'm sorry, okay? It wasn't fair of me to take my frustration out on you. It's just..." his voice trailed off as he second-guessed whether to share this much of him with her.

She pursed her lips, "It's just what?"

"The only time I've ever lost something that I cared for was when my father disappeared, and even then, it was more of a realization that I had to find him. I didn't have time to process what was happening inside of me, and even if I did, there was no one for me to share it with."

Amelia listened to him, taking his words seriously, and said, "But what about Storm?"

"I didn't meet her until a couple of years later. Of course, I shared my story with her, as she also shared her life with me. But it's not the same. I don't feel for her the way I do you."

A smile expanded across Amelia's face, "Oh? Is that so? And how exactly do you feel about me?"

Realizing what he'd just implicated, his eyes got big, his cheeks flushed and his palms perspired. He rubbed them frantically on his pants, looking down and shaking his head, "Umm, ya know. Uh.."

She burst out laughing, "You're *such* a boy."

He kicked himself for not trusting in Amelia's ability to be so understanding sooner. She came around to his side of the table and hugged his neck. Resting her chin atop his head, her hair dangling into his face. He couldn't help but laugh along with her, the embarrassment receding from his body. She let go as he got up and they walked hand-in-hand back to his room where they discussed more of their past together.

"I have a task for you if you're feeling up to it that is." Abe had found Ryu in the waste chamber. Ryu hadn't seen much of the man in a while. He was grateful for the rest; Ryu wasn't eager to go out on any missions after the last, not yet at least. *Not the best place to be asking favors*, he thought as they exited the room.

"I guess that depends on what you have in mind. My ankle is still pretty sore." It wasn't a total lie, sometimes if he twisted hard enough it would ache, although Ryu knew that he was well enough to fight again. Now though, he was a bit scared to go back out on a mission. Not fearful of losing his own life, but seeing a comrade fall again without having the power to save them. He didn't want to experience that again but suspected it was inevitable.

"Don't worry, my boy, nothing crazy. The Resistance has solid numbers, although we are still lesser than the Citadel. The time to march on them approaches as we get stronger, and we are going to need as many capable members as possible. I would like for you to train as many of the Resistance in sword fighting as possible. Even if someone's weapon of choice is a spiked club or metal bat, they can learn something from your skill. No one in all our ranks handles a blade better than you."

Ryu felt honored that Abe spoke so highly of him; he pondered the acquisition for a moment and then decided, yes, he would train them. He was ready to do something useful again. Had he not busted his ankle up, the mission may have gone very differently for them, but now was the time to get back out there and be productive. If he could mold more skillful warriors, then perhaps he wouldn't have to lose any more friends. He'd grown very close with many of the rebels since arriving and didn't want to lose any of them in battle.

"I'd be glad to help where I can. Let's have groups of ten meet me in the training bay, that way I don't get too overwhelmed. I've never taught before, so it should be interesting."

"Works for me. I'll gather the trial participants and send them there first thing tomorrow."

The two of them parted ways, and Ryu was happy to be helpful again. Back in his room, he told Storm about the proposition Abe gave him and asked if she would relay a message. He wanted her to tell Abe of the things he would need to properly train their forces. She flew out of the room as Ryu began formulating a training curriculum.

"He said your supplies would be waiting on you in the training bay tomorrow," Storm told Ryu after flying back to their chambers. Ryu cleaned and sharpened Sokushi with great attention to detail, leaving not a single blemish behind on its surface.

The next morning when Ryu entered the training bay, he found all the things needed to begin. There were swords carved from wood—old wood that wouldn't last—but wood just the same. They'd do well for drilling different techniques. There were plentiful swords of different shapes and sizes, along with dummies made from pieces of cloth shaped to appear as human, and bound with strips of twine. They were stuffed with bits of whatever was available.

I'll probably need more of these, he thought as he looked at the training dummies.

After looking over everything twice, the students began to arrive, and to his pleasant surprise, it was his group of fellow raiders. There were two new guys that he recognized from around the bunker but hadn't learned their names yet. They all gave their greetings, the students seemed happy to be there, except for Jax. He looked grim as if he'd rather be anywhere else right now.

"How's it going, Jax?" Ryu asked, but the man just turned his back to him.

"What's up with him?" he whispered to Amelia, but she just shook her head, saying she wasn't sure. He's been getting grumpier as time went on it seemed.

"Alright, let's get started."

They all spread out in a straight line, as Ryu passed out the wooden swords. He paired them up with partners of similar weight and height, teaching them some basic sword fighting techniques. They were all quick learners and caught on to what he showed them, and he moved through the lessons swiftly. He instructed them to begin sparring, one pair at a time, watching them closely to see how they moved and if they were using the techniques correctly or reverting back to their method of hack and slash.

Overall the trainees were doing well, evolving as fighters, although Amelia was probably the least of them. Ryu spent more time instructing her privately, but even with more attention she was still losing her sparring matches. "I'm seriously just no good at this," she said, as he began correcting her form for the millionth time.

Ryu reassured her, "Don't worry, you'll get it down. Even if I have to spend a little extra time with you to perfect your form." He winked at her; he'd grown more comfortable in her presence, but he forgot there were other eyes watching. This comment and wink gathered some hoots, hollers, and groans from the other students.

When it was time for Jax to spar with his partner—Rob—the expression on his face showed boredom. They started off striking at each other with a decent pace; not going too fast, but with a battle-worthy tempo. All was going well until Rob's wooden tip struck Jax on the knuckle. After wincing, Jax's face contorted with what could only be rage; he lashed out with a flurry of blows that had Rob scrambling to defend himself.

"Stop! That's enough!" Ryu yelled for them to halt, but Jax wouldn't listen. His ears had gone deaf to any sort of instruction and he wouldn't be stopped. Ryu grabbed a wooden blade of his own, about to step in and break up the duel, but before he could take control, the fight ended in an unsavory way. Jax's teeth gritted in anger, he raised his sword and brought it down with a mighty force, knocking Rob's sword from his hands. Immediately after disarming him, Jax swung the blade upward, striking Rob directly in the face.

Rob flailed back, landing on his butt and clutching his face as a groan of pain escaped him. Ryu jumped between them, placing his hand on Jax's thick chest, and said, "You're done."

Jax, still with a look of madness in his eyes grabbed his wooden blade with both hands and broke it across his knee. Ryu didn't let his gaze drift, adrenaline pumped through him as the man stared at him. Finally, Jax turned and stomped out of the training bay, slamming the door on his way out. Ryu turned around and squatted down in front of Rob, who had blood running down his face. He gasped for air as a couple of others peeled his hands from his face to examine the damage.

Luckily, Rob only suffered a nose break; it would mend

within a couple of weeks. Had he lost a tooth or an eye, those wouldn't grow back. Ryu sent Rob to the infirmary and continued with the training session. Giving them real blades now, he lined a stuffed dummy in front of each of them. Grabbing one for himself, he demonstrated a series of strikes that would prove fatal to any opponent.

"Picture a blade in your opponent's hands. You want to be clear of their weapon, go to the right or left, and strike like this."

He simulated pummeling their blade to the side, hopped opposite of it, lifted his blade, and struck downward and diagonally where the enemy's neck would normally be. He then showed them how to deal multiple blows in one sequence; slicing with a similar pattern as before, but this time as soon as his blade made it through the fabric he changed direction. Angling the sword's edge, he cut it horizontally through the body of the dummy.

Two chunks of stuffed fabric flopped down to the floor, applause ensued from his students, and he charged them to try it on their own. Ryu felt like he had bubbles in his stomach as he watched them practice the art that he loved. It took time, each of them struggling in different ways to cut through the dummies. Some of them failed to cut at the correct angle, while others didn't put enough force behind their strikes to slash all the way through.

When Ryu was satisfied with their training for the day he dismissed them and set out to find Jax, determined to figure out what his problem was. He searched everywhere he could think of, but couldn't find him. Giving up the search, he went to Abe and asked if he'd seen him. He said he hadn't and asked if there was an issue, so Ryu explained everything that happened. Abe looked worried as the story progressed, and said he'd find Jax and get to the bottom of what was wrong with him. After that, he strolled down to the infirmary to visit Rob.

It took a whole month before Ryu was satisfied with the progress of his trainees; each day they would review some other movements that he'd shown until they looked solid enough to satisfy Ryu. Amelia still struggled in some areas, but she improved highly in Ryu's opinion. When Rob returned to training Ryu made sure to spend some extra time with him until he was at the same knowledge level as the others.

When the month ended, Ryu got another set of ten troops to mentor. This happened again and again. Before long, all the rebels at the bunker were trained up. They started swapping out people who were stationed at the other Resistance bases so they too could be trained. Six months had passed and Jax was still missing; Abe let on that this was a major blow to their ranks as Jax had been commanding the raiders for nearly two years and was one of their most skilled fighters.

After a while, Ryu increased the number of students he was willing to take on; he went from training ten at a time to twenty-five. He figured within the next year, or maybe a year and a half, all of the Resistance would be up to par with his standards of sword fighting.

Chains of Steel

The floor was dirty and his raggedy clothes dripped off his body as if they were melting. His grimy hair dangled in his face and the sun heated the box he was in. One of the luxuries of betraying the Order. Kenji sat in this metal box whenever Lucian felt like he needed the reminder of who was in control. Even the slightest disobedience would land him in the metal box. How long has his torment continued?

One of the nobles had ordered him to clean their boot with his tongue. He was many things, but deprived of his dignity, he would never be. Even if the punishment was death he would not stoop so low as to lose his dignity. Kenji knew they wouldn't kill him; the government enjoyed using him as a show of their strength, parading him around as they treated him like a dog. It was a reminder to the rest of the Citadel to never cross them for they were not quick to forgive, and would never forget.

The Order felt betrayed by his leave of absence and starting the Resistance. Luckily, the rebel group hadn't made a move on the Citadel yet and as long as that stayed true, the Order would not venture out in search of them.

Ryu, if you're alive, I swear I'll find you, he often thought this and similar things to himself. Believing that Ryu was still alive was the only thing that would keep him from taking his own life. If he were to somehow catch wind of his son's death, he would be sure to kill himself, thus taking the power that the Order held over him.

Lucian, or the Supreme Leader as he liked to be called, would be out to visit his box and release him from his punishment later today. One thing he was grateful for was the monster's issue with the unclean. He would allow Kenji to bathe once he laid his eyes upon him, but before that happened there was a commotion coming through the nearby gate. Someone Kenji didn't recognize was being shuffled along the street with his hands cuffed in front of him. He was a big guy who looked strong and fit, however, his face was horrible.

Hours later, Lucian showed up with the man, now unshackled. He walked behind Lucian as if he held some air of authority and Kenji was immediately wary of him, watching them stride toward the box through a crack in its wall. He didn't like the look in his eyes.

"Hello there, Kenji." The guy's eyes doubled in size, realization spreading across his face as Lucian spoke his name. "I trust you've learned your lesson, again?"

"Oh, yes sir. For sure. I will do better next time. Who's your new friend?"

Lucian opened the door of the box and gestured with his hand toward the newcomer and said, "This is Jax. It would seem this gentleman has turned from his wicked ways and decided to join us here at the Citadel."

Kenji was wrought with confusion. Jax clarified, "Your old friend, Abe, sends his regards."

Kenji's eyes widened. He said, "You come from the Resistance?"

"That I do," he replied.

"So, Abe is still kicking, is he?"

"It would seem so," Lucian said. "Now, you behave yourself, Kenji. Seracuse will keep an eye on you while Jax and I pay your old friends a visit." Lucian grinned wickedly, motioning toward a man dressed in black—the garb of the sentries—and departed from him.

Kenji watched at the front gate, not daring to attempt to set foot outside of the Citadel walls. As far as he knew, Lucian hadn't left the Citadel in many years. Now, however, he rode out of the gate with a crew of killers on large hoofed beasts. Kenji wasn't sure who was alive within the group of rebels, but he hoped they were prepared for the attack that was headed their way.

The horses they sat atop would put the Resistance at such a large disadvantage, Kenji just hoped they had adequate traps and archers at the ready. He highly doubted they were aware that a threat would be approaching.

Two of the horses pulled a large wooden wagon that was filled with supplies. Kenji could only assume the supplies within would be used for the destruction of the Resistance.

What kind of setup were they running now? How far had they come as a group since the day Kenji was left? The man still often wondered who had gotten the drop on him. He never saw his captor and Lucian never let him in on the secret.

Jax had grown tired of the Resistance; that's why he did what he did. He wanted to live a luxurious life behind the confines of the Citadel. When he approached the sentries along the way, he wasn't sure if they'd try to kill him or not. He was ready for them either way. Luckily, he managed to get to the Citadel with no issues.

When he brought up that he had vital information about the Resistance, the sentries jumped at the idea of being the person to bring him to their Supreme Leader. Lucian was a scary man. Jax learned that within several minutes of meeting him. When Jax told the man that he had locations of rebel hideouts, he nearly drooled with excitement, like a starved dog spotting its next meal.

The two of them developed a plan and agreement that if Jax helped him destroy the rebels entirely, then he'd be given free passage into the nobility. Jax would be welcomed with open arms as if he had been a member of the Order the whole time. His treason as being allied with the Resistance would be forgotten and he would have the life he only saw in dreams.

Lucian made it sound so tantalizing. Jax almost changed his mind a couple of times, but all that went away when Lucian lured him in with promises of grandeur and luxury.

Jax had never ridden a horse before and now sat in the wagon, giving directions. It took a while but they eventually made it to the bunker. Explosives were placed all over the ground which was the roof of the Resistance's main hub. The sound was nearly deafening.

Blasts rumbled the ground and Jax could feel it beneath his feet even from a safe distance. The horses made sounds of discomfort as the explosions continued. When it all stopped, Jax walked over to the massive crater that was now opened up on the surface of the Earth. He peered over the edge to see a gaping hole so deep and dark that he could not see the bottom.

Rumble in The Bunker

You never know when you've written your last sentence or spoken your last word. I am leaving on an expedition tomorrow to see if I can find more supplies for Ryu and I. I've felt the presence of someone watching me when I ventured out last and my paranoia rises. If the Order is to apprehend me, I shall do my best to leave clues for my boy.

Ten months into living in the bunker, Ryu was feeling at home; he and Amelia spent most of their free time together. His feelings of affection for her had grown rapidly with time, and he found himself missing her more and more the longer they were apart. One day Ryu, Storm, and Amelia sat at a table in the dining hall; the raven delighted in eating a small mouse she'd caught earlier, while the other two ate some meat from whichever animal farm it was bred in.

They were conversing lightly when, out of nowhere the walls began to shake as booms rattled above ground. Crumbles of rock and dust dropped from the ceiling as Ryu and Amelia ducked under the table for cover. Storm followed suit, squawking in fear.

"What in the world is going on?" he shouted over the chaos.

Feet scurried around their table, and bigger chunks of rock

fell around and began crushing wooden chairs. *I refuse to die here,* Ryu thought to himself, "Come on, let's go!"

He scooped up Storm and dove out into the falling debris. Grabbing Amelia by the hand, they ran, narrowly dodging the crumbling rock. He dragged her to his room, tossed Storm into Amelia's arms, and then strapped his sword around his waist.

Exiting the room, Storm took flight. She weaved this way and that, dodging falling rocks nimbly. They ran back up the hallway toward the control room but their path was blocked by a massive boulder. Screams of terror rang out over the loud explosions coming from above. They turned around and ran the other way until the training room came into view.

The door was being propped open by Abe as he waved rebels into the room, "Come on, run! Let's go! Keep moving!" he shouted commands over the rumbling bunker. Booms continued to echo around. They ran inside, the last of the Resistance to make it there; on the far end of the training bay, there was an open door. Ryu hadn't noticed a door before, but upon closer inspection realized that it was a secret passage. The wall was opened to reveal a staircase that led them deeper into the ground.

Ryu turned to see Abe hurrying behind them as the bunker continued to shake. They ran down the stairs as fast as possible, the rocks and dirt caving in behind them. If the rebels were any slower they would have been crushed beneath the rubble. The air around Ryu became colder the further they ran down the steps, and he began to shiver as the sweat that slicked his neck turned icy in the chill of the air. There were very dim lights strung together along the walls leading down the steps.

Finally, the ground stopped caving down on them but

blocked their path back to the bunker. Ryu was thankful for the lights, dim as they were. He asked, "What is this? Where are we going?"

Abe panted as their boots clanged on the metal stairs, "Don't.. worry.. just keep on.. going. We're almost.. there." he said. Many minutes later, Ryu touched back down on solid Earth. The other rebels grouped together in front of him, although their numbers had dwindled exponentially from this disaster. Looking around he noticed they were in a long, wide tunnel. Lights stretched for as far as he could see.

"Everyone listen up," Abe said. "This was a direct attack by the Order; there is no other logical explanation for what just occurred. The explosions we all heard were not natural, but man-made. This tunnel was crafted in secret, by myself and a few others that I trusted highly. We created this tunnel for circumstances just like this. Perhaps I should have informed you all, and maybe we would have more survivors. That is the guilt that will remain with me until I pass from this world. It was kept secret for the protection of us all, in case we were to be infiltrated by the One World Order. You can mourn your fallen comrades later, but for now, we must push forward."

The group turned around, beginning their journey away from the bunker. Amelia transferred Storm from her hands to Ryu's shoulder. She whispered to him that she would scout ahead and fluttered down the path, disappearing in the dim light. She returned several minutes later, stating that there was no danger ahead.

They all walked through the tunnel, shivering in unison; no one spoke, the only sounds that could be heard were chattering teeth, heavy breathing, and the echos of several pairs of footsteps bouncing off the rocky walls.

Refuge

Ryu's ankle throbbed dully as the group of rebels walked down through the dim tunnel, his old injury reminding him that it hadn't fully gone away. Their pace became slower the further they trudged. Ragged breathing haunted the cold air of the dark passageway. Storm shivered atop Ryu's shoulder so he pulled her down and cradled her in his arm, using his body heat to warm her. Many of The Resistance had fallen back, the numbing cold and exhaustion of trekking so far getting the better of them. Ryu knew they most likely weren't going to make it out and it would do no good to try helping them along. Their numbers had dwindled quite a bit so taking down the One World Order would be even more difficult than before.

Who did this? he thought, *I'll find the ones responsible and make them pay.*

"Hey," he said to Abe in a hushed voice, "what do you think happened? Like you said earlier, this was no accident. The bunker was destroyed by someone."

Abe took a moment before answering, "It seems clear to me that it was the Order with some massive explosives. What I don't know is how they found us."

"Is it possible we have a mole?" Ryu asked, dumbfounded. From what he'd learned, the Order didn't normally venture out very far from the Citadel. They wouldn't have shown up unless they'd known for certain where the bunker was hidden.

"That is the question, isn't it?"

They continued to walk in silence and Ryu noticed Amelia's pace was slowing down. He fell back and grabbed her hand, pulling her along to keep up. She looked up at him with weary eyes, too tired to form a smile. After what seemed like an eternity they finally made it to the end. The lights on the walls stopped and a ladder appeared before them.

"Okay everyone," Abe commanded his troops, "Up this ladder and we're done. I know you're tired, but now is not the time to give up. If you feel strong enough, hang back so the weaker ones can go first. Move!"

One by one they began climbing, moving as quickly as possible. Ryu pushed Amelia up to be one of the first to go and then fell back to Abe's side. He asked him, "How are you going to make it up there?" he gestured to Abe's nubby wrist.

Abe laughed and then pulled something from his pocket that resembled a cup with a hook attached. He fastened the cup portion over the nub and strapped it on tight. It was their turn to climb and Ryu motioned for Abe to go ahead of him; he started climbing using the hook as a hand to grasp the rungs. Ryu let him get a few steps ahead and then hopped on the ladder, the cold steel made his hands scream. Storm clutched onto his shoulder with her talons. It was so cold that his hands felt like they were hot, baking in the midday sun. After climbing for a couple of minutes the air started turning back to normal, the cold dissipated and his hands began to throb as they warmed up.

Finally, they were topside, the sun blinding Ryu even though it was low in the sky. He looked around, observing their surroundings as Abe was already barking orders to them. He saw a structure in the distance which Abe was pointing at, and the rebels began marching off towards it. He returned to the back of the group next to Ryu and Amelia.

"That's one of our smaller bases over there. They should be able to house us, seeing as our numbers have shrunk vastly." Abe's face became grim and he looked down at his feet.

Amelia placed a supportive hand on his shoulder, "We'll just have to take more time now. It's horrible that we lost so many, but we knew this war wouldn't be easy."

Abe smiled at her and nodded, but Ryu didn't think he looked very convinced.

Storm hopped off Ryu's shoulder and floated around, getting some blood back into her wings. Circling back, she landed on Amelia's shoulder and said so that they all could hear, "I'm going to fly back in the bunker's direction to see if anyone is there. I'll be quick."

Ryu told her, "Be careful."

"You too, little one."

With that, she took off and quickly disappeared as she flew farther and higher away. Ryu cursed himself for the anxious feelings that plagued his soul each time they separated. He had to keep reminding himself that everything would be okay. His eyes were counting the rocks as they walked toward their new destination.

"What's wrong?" Amelia snapped him from his trance.

"Oh, nothing."

"I think I know you a little better than that. Even Abe could see that something is bothering you. Can't you Abe?" They both looked at him waiting for a response.

"Hmm? What's that? I'll be right there." Abe trotted off and began making conversation with someone in the middle of the pack.

Amelia chuckled, "Come on, you know you can tell me."

Ryu thought about it. Being vulnerable isn't something he was well versed in. Especially to the likes of a girl that he'd grown quite fond of. "I haven't ever really been vulnerable to anyone before."

"Besides Storm?"

"Right, but that's just it. She's been here for me through a lot of my life. My dad was taken and I had no one. Then she showed up and filled that hole in me. Since we've met, she's often left my side, but never for very long, and yet ..." he sighed.

"Yet what?"

"No matter how many times she comes back, I can't help but fear she won't return."

Amelia put her arm around his waist, and he threw his around her shoulder, accepting the intimacy. His cheek fell over onto the top of her head and a few wild hairs tickled his face.

For such a long time he's been guarded, not allowing any of the people he has met along the way to break down his barriers. When he arrived at the bunker he was determined to not allow anyone in yet again. Then he met Amelia; he recalled how beautiful she was the night they bumped into each other. Since then she had been one of the greatest friends he could ask for, second only to Storm.

He stopped walking and grabbed Amelia's hand, pulling her back to him as she turned, wondering why he had stopped. He gazed into her green eyes as she peered up at him; he made note of the brown flecks that danced around in her irises. They were inches away from each other.

"I love you," he muttered, pulling her into a kiss without waiting for a response. An explosion of butterflies erupted in his gut as they held their passionate embrace. When they finally separated, the rest of the group had gained at least fifty feet on them. They looked at each other and Amelia giggled, her face was flushed. Ryu returned the laugh as she turned around, pulling along as they trotted to catch up with their convoy.

They walked with their fingers intertwined as they were coming up to the entrance of the base. Ryu could see that it looked like a small village surrounded by a fence. There was some sort of metal wire wrapped around the top of the fence with points that he assumed were to keep anything from climbing over. The front gate was already swung open and a man was jogging to meet with Abe, who was now at the front of the rebels.

When the two of them reached one another they clasped hands and gave each other a brief hug, patting each other on the back. Ryu could see two men standing just inside the gate, each equipped with a bow and arrow. Before making it to the gate, Ryu heard the squawk of his dear friend, Storm. He turned around as she swooped in for a landing, but she didn't land with him. Instead, she flew straight to Abe and he knew something was off. He ran to the front of the group, Amelia following close behind.

As he caught up with the raven he saw that her chest was heaving from the exhaustive flight. She had waited for him to catch up before briefing them on what was found. Allowing for her breathing to normalize, finally, she said, "You were right. We were attacked." The man standing next to Abe jumped back in surprise, astonishment was written across his face as he listened.

She explained that she found a camp filled with a group of men who must have been members of the Order, although one of them she recognized as the first man they met from the Resistance. Ryu was shocked that Jax could be involved in something like this, but Abe didn't appear to be surprised in the slightest.

She told them about the hoofed beasts they had, the carts full of weapons and other supplies. There weren't enough to outnumber what was left of the rebels, but if this base didn't have sufficient weapons then they would be doomed. Abe listened to the story intently and then ordered everyone inside so they could get a plan together.

The rebels got inside the front gate just as the sun dropped out of sight. Several flashlights clicked on, sending strobes of white around the area. The man whom Ryu saw with Abe was introduced as Kelvin, the man in charge of this base. Ryu felt lucky to be here as he learned what they were tasked with producing. They called this encampment M3 due to being the Resistance's sole proprietor of chicken, cow, and hog. Kelvin led them to a small building where a few yellow-colored lights were turned on. There was a table with chairs set up so that some of them were able to sit.

Kelvin had one of his men show the rest of the group back to a place where they could get some rest. The only people Ryu recognized were Abe, Amelia, and a couple of what was left of the raiders. They sat around the table and began discussing what was going on.

Abe told Kelvin about the blasts that shook the bunker and crumbled it into bits. He told him how they had lost many people in the attack, but luckily he'd formed a tunnel that no one knew about, just in case they were to ever find themselves under siege. Apparently, that idea was one of the best Abe ever had, given their current situation.

The planning for the next day began; according to Kelvin, the animals Storm described sounded like horses. None of them had ever seen one before, but Kelvin read about them in a very old book. He shared with the group that horses were capable of running very fast and pulling heavy loads, which explained how they were moving around so much equipment.

"According to my estimate, if they leave at sunrise, and assuming they know where to go, they should reach our gates within a couple of hours," Kelvin said confidently.

"Jax knows about this place. If they were to find the tunnel, it would be easy to put together where we're at. The passage is pointed in this direction so I'm certain this is where they'll be headed."

Ryu chimed in, "What are our options? What does the weaponry around here look like? With the fence and gate we may be able to hold them off, although if they have any more explosives, I'm not confident about that."

"We don't have many fighters here, mainly just myself and the guards. The majority of our troops tend to the animals. I have eight gate guards that rotate throughout the day and night, and they are all very good with the bow and arrow. As for me, I'm fairly skilled with a sword, but if they have any long-range weapons I'd be toast. Did you all bring anything useful?"

Ryu held up Sokushi for him to see and he said, "That looks like a fine blade. But how well can you use it?"

Ryu smirked, "Would you like to find out?"

After accepting the challenge, Kelvin went to go retrieve his sword, which made Ryu believe he'd already won the bout. No great swordsman would be caught without their weapon on them. Upon his return, Kelvin led the group to a different room in the building that had more space. He flipped on some dim lights and they crossed swords to begin the battle.

Kelvin attacked first, swinging clumsily at Ryu with a shout. Ryu easily sidestepped his attack and pointed his sword at Kelvin's chest. Kelvin knocked the blade away with an upward whirl of his own and then struck again and again. Ryu was blocking each of his strikes, and finally, as Kelvin's energy began to wane, Ryu launched a counterattack. He smacked the blade down, the tip of it scraping into the hard surface, and kicked Kelvin in the gut. He fell back onto his butt, and as he tried to stand, Ryu swung mightily with his sword. Kelvin's blade flew out of his hand and skidded across the room; Ryu held the tip of his blade just an inch from the man's neck.

"Okay, I yield. You win. You're much better than me." Kelvin laughed with his hands up in submission. Ryu reached down to help the man to his feet, feeling satisfied with his victory. He didn't want to humiliate the guy, but he enjoyed a little friendly competition.

"Ryu is the finest sword fighter I've met in all my years, next only to his father, Kenji."

Kelvin's eyes grew wide, "You're Kenji's son? How can that be?"

"As you know, Kenji and I left the sentry corps and started the Resistance. When Kenji disappeared he must have taken a pod with him and used his own DNA to create Ryu. And then according to Ryu's testimony, his father raised him away from any other humans and taught him the ways of the sword."

"So then, do you know where he is?" he asked Ryu.

"No. He was taken away from me years ago. I set out to look for him and that's how Storm and I found each other. We believe he was captured by the Order."

Kelvin slowly shook his head, "I can't believe it. This is crazy news. Well, it's great to have you here, Ryu. I'd be glad to fight by a skilled swordsman like yourself any day."

They went back to the previous room and resumed hashing out their plan for the next day. They agreed that it would be foolish to try venturing out and meeting their adversaries with an attack, especially since they would be on horses. The best thing they could do is be on defense at M3. They discussed any sort of traps that they could lay out and different ways to distract the enemy in order to flank them. There were no explosives at their location, and the only traps around were being used to secure the solar panels.

After much talk, it was agreed that they would hold down their position with as many bows and arrows as possible. Kelvin showed them to the small hut that he referred to as the weapon shack. Ryu wasn't accustomed to seeing people use slingshots and partially looked forward to seeing them in action.

They would be most effective if they were to launch small rocks at the opponent's from a medium distance. They gathered up all the weapons in the armory and took them to the front gate. With the small numbers of their attackers, it was unlikely that they would be spread out far enough to hit the base from multiple angles.

There was only a short period before the morning would arrive so they all adjourned to sleeping quarters. Ryu flopped down on a dusty bed, coughing as the dust particles floated around him. Storm nestled herself up against his side, and they both promptly fell asleep.

Ryu's eyes flew open as someone gently shook him awake, his mind was already in attack mode, but the soft lips of Amelia took that away as she kissed him. Ryu noticed Storm sat on the open windowsill, looking at them as they broke apart, which made him a tad uncomfortable. Amelia smiled and left the room so that he could gather himself. Storm continued staring at him as he laced his boots on.

Without looking at her he said, "What?"

"I didn't realize the two of you had become so... intimate. Were you going to tell me?"

"I didn't know I had to," he replied.

"You're right. It's none of my business."

Before he could protest, Storm hopped outside and vanished from his sight.

What is her problem? he asked himself. *No, that was all me. Why did I get so upset over that? I should have just told her in the first place I guess.*

He left the building, looking around for Storm so that he could apologize, but he didn't see her anywhere. The sun was peaking over the horizon, casting those morning colors that Ryu loved so much. It would be a beautiful sight had he not been worried about the incoming battle. Kelvin and Abe were already at the front gate when Ryu arrived; they were sorting weapons into categories. Blades, bows, slingshots, and blunt objects were separated from each other. As more people gathered around they were instructed to pick something they were comfortable with, and if that object didn't exist then they were to grab whatever was left over.

Altogether Ryu guessed there were about 20 people in the group. Kelvin had told them that most of their rebels were too old to be fighting battles anymore. They were adequate at growing meat and butchering it, but that was mostly it. He was getting up there in age too, but said he felt younger than a newborn hog. Ryu believed the guy was putting on a front, but thought it best to not point that out.

The warriors that were assembled grabbed what they could and spread out a little along the fence line. There were large piles of rubble lying around that would allow them to climb up and over the fence or take cover behind them if they needed. They wouldn't do much to protect them from explosives though. Ryu saw a black dot appear and then take the shape of a bird. As it got closer he recognized Storm, she was cawing with alertness.

When she was close enough for their leaders to hear she shouted, "Here they come!" and then flew along the soldiers and repeated the message.

Ryu peered out from the direction she'd flown from, trying to see anything, but at first there was nothing. After a few minutes, however, in the distance, he could see a dust storm billowing up into the air. Shadows began emerging in his vision, and then those shadows took shape. Massive beasts—the horses he'd heard about—were barreling toward their base. Ryu could see large carts being dragged along, and people sitting atop them and the horses. He tried to swallow, but his mouth had become dry suddenly. He desperately wanted Storm at his side, but she circled high above them, watching from the sky.

The group of enemies slowed down as they got closer and then stopped, just out of the range of their archers. The dust flowed around them like a brown fog, draping over their heads, and time seemed to stand still as Ryu waited for them to launch their attack. After the dust settled he could see a man with a gold and red tunic sitting on a horse at the front of their formation. Ryu thought to himself that the black horse was gorgeous, and it was horrible that it was being used to carry out such deeds. They were too far away for Ryu to make out any of their faces.

"I'll give you this one chance to surrender. If you refuse, I will have no other choice but to exterminate you." The man on the black horse yelled out to them. His voice sounded off to Ryu, almost like it was too nice, too inviting. There was no way this guy would let them go. He was probably faking it just so they'd lay down their weapons and then he'd attack them, defenseless.

Ryu heard Abe yell back, "Come and get it, Lucian!

The man squinted his eyes and said, "My gosh, is that you, Abe? You're looking rather dreadful. How's that arm?" Lucian chuckled.

Lucian made a motion with his hand and the group of men began charging toward the fence. Arrows started flying, a few of them finding their targets and many of them plunging into the ground. Ryu had been instructed to wait until the enemies breached the gate, and then unleash hell on them with his sword. However, as he watched the chaos break out, one man in particular charged the gate. He stood up on the horse's back, crouched slightly. The feat of dexterity surprised Ryu.

Ryu released his blade from its casing as the man turned parallel to the fence. He got closer and then dove over it, flipping in the air and landing on his feet. Ryu rushed toward him and stopped a few feet away, blade at the ready.

The man's face turned upward; Ryu would recognize the face anywhere.

The Real Swordsman

The devastation of the bunker left Jax filled with chagrin. His old home had been nearly obliterated along with those he used to call friends. What did he expect? The morose feeling that now plagued him was not what he thought would happen. The man had grown tired of living under the ground like a rat.

Jax tried to leave but it would seem that Lucian expected as much. He turned to flee from the scene and was immediately surrounded by sentries. Lucian waltzed up to him and asked, "Leaving in a hurry, are you?"

"I was just-"

"You are feeling guilty," Lucian stated matter-of-factly. "It is only natural. You've just given the Resistance, your old friends, into my hand. They now lie beneath us, utterly defeated."

Jax just stared at the ground, unable to speak.

Lucian continued, "Your job is not over yet, however."

Jax looked at him. "What else could you possibly ask of me?"

"Ask? You think I ask anything? No, this is an order that you will follow blindly, or I can have my best and brightest peel the skin from your bones." A cruel smile splayed across his face.

The descent into the pit that was once the bunker was tedious. Jax and a few others went down to check for survivors, possible prisoners that they could interrogate. Once at the bottom of the bunker, Jax and the others began climbing over the rubble.

Much to his horror, there were massive boulders with appendages poking out from underneath. Pools of scarlet leaked out from under much of the wreckage. They searched to the best of their ability and ended up blasting some of the large debris into smaller pieces so they could search the rest of the bunker.

What have I done? he thought to himself, regret evident on his face.

Then he smiled when they found the tunnel. It was clear that not all of the rebels had escaped, but Jax hoped it was enough to still have a good chance at defeating the Order.

Back on the surface, one of the sentries explained to Lucian what they found in what was now a grave. Jax couldn't help but laugh when Lucian's face screwed up into a scowl. "I wouldn't be laughing just yet if I were you," Lucian said.

"Why's that?" he asked.

The Supreme Leader pulled out a small brown box and withdrew a vile of creamy white liquid. Strong hands grabbed his arms and another pair held his head still as he struggled to break free. Lucian approached and plunged the needle of the vial into his neck, releasing the warm liquid into him.

It was painful at first, but once he stopped resisting the urge to fight whatever was happening inside him, the pain subsided. A fog took over his brain and it felt as if he were floating in a basin of water.

Lucian's voice sounded wonky when he ordered, "Punch him," pointing at one of the sentries. Jax wasn't sure why he obeyed, but the longer it took to reach his goal, the more the pain increased. When his fist finally connected with the man's chin, all the torment was released from his body and he was left with a euphoric feeling.

Jax stood before Ryu, crouched on the ground, a crazed look in his eyes. His hand was on the hilt of a sword, as he stared up at Ryu. It was clear that Jax was here as part of the Order now. Ryu lunged at the man but was too slow. Jax easily dodged the strike and slashed at Ryu with his own blade. It caught Ryu in the stomach, slicing through his shirt as if it were made of water. Luckily, the laceration was shallow, however, its searing sting reminded Ryu to be more careful.

There was no time to investigate the severity of the wound; Jax slashed again and again as Ryu dodged each attack. After bounding away he was able to pull his blade back from its scabbard and began defending the attacks. The metal of their swords clanged together sending sparks flying through the air with each clash of their blades. Ryu knew from the moment he met Jax that the man was dangerous, however, he never thought it would have come to this.

Ryu could hear explosions and screams but was unable to take his attention off his opponent because he knew that he would be slain if he didn't give this fight everything he had. As options coursed through his brain he wondered if there was any possibility of them both walking away from this alive. Any scenario he came up with resulted in one of them being killed by the other. Ryu didn't wish to end Jax's life, despite the former ally's betrayal.

Thoughts ran through his brain. If Jax has been to the Citadel, then they could use whatever intel he had to their advantage. He would need to do his best to not strike down the man before him.

Ryu was trained by his father to overcome any threat so there had to be a way for him to win without either of them dying. Jax rushed in, trying to stab with the point of his blade, but Ryu deflected it and dropped to the dirt. He swept his leg in a circle in an attempt to trip Jax, but he jumped over the sweep.

As he landed, Jax brought his sword down from a vertical position. It came down quickly but Ryu dodged, jumping out of the way, and dragging his blade's edge across Jax's forearm. Jax's eyes had a far away look about them. The deranged man didn't even flinch as blood began dripping from his arm.

What the heck is going on with him?

"Jax, whatever they've done to you, we can fix it!"

His pleas fell on deaf ears as Jax began another torrent of attacks. This time faster, chopping and slashing, their blades sending a spark show into the air until the man got the better of Ryu. He ducked under a slash from Ryu and then stabbed at his thigh. The blade would have most likely torn through muscle, tendon, and bone had Ryu not shifted slightly as he saw the blow coming in. Ryu twisted as the tip made contact sending it completely through roughly an inch of flesh and muscle on the outer side of his thigh.

Ryu released a howl from his lips. He hobbled away as crimson dribbled down his leg. He glanced down to quickly check the gash; the blade had narrowly missed any major arteries, but if he didn't get it wrapped up soon it could be fatal.

Ryu looked back to his opponent. The man had fallen to his knees. His face contorted, his muscles taut as he struggled with whatever spell he was under. Saliva dripped down his chin and with gritted teeth, he groaned, "Kill me! Do it now, Ryu."

Jax watched through his own eyes as he leaped from the back of the horse and over the fence. With the instructions to kill Ryu. He never cared much for the young man, but he didn't want to end him this way, unable to control himself. His movements were not of his own volition. It felt wrong.

He hurt Ryu but the wound wasn't very deep, he'd live. He begged his body to slow down or make a mistake so that Ryu could gain the upper hand. Jax regretted his decisions now. It was paramount that Ryu beat him.

Explosions rattled inside Jax's head as the attack plan ensued; explosives with short fuses were being tossed as the horse riders rode around in an attempt to dodge the arrows that they knew would be coming. Jax described the base almost perfectly as Lucian ordered, detailing the fence and the front gate with the razor wire spiraling the top. These were being destroyed by the blasts now, and soon they would lay siege to the entire operation.

As their battle continued, Jax was gaining the upper hand against Ryu. The serum in his blood made him a better fighter. He would have never been able to defeat Ryu without help. Through excruciating pain, Jax was able to force himself down to his knees and plead for Ryu to end his life.

Ryu couldn't hesitate any further; it seemed that—for the moment at least—Jax had control over whatever it was that had gotten into him. He leaped forward on his good leg and swapped his sword over to his weak hand. Rearing back with his strong hand, he threw his fist as hard as he could toward the man's face. His knuckles landed squarely across Jax's jaw, a thud and a crunch echoed in Ryu's ears as the older man's head whipped around and he landed face-down in the dirt.

Ryu shook his hand, the force of the punch vibrating through the bones in his arm. *I'll have to leave him here for now.* Ryu ripped a few pieces of cloth from the man's shirt and began bandaging his leg up. He tied a piece above, below, and across the hole in his thigh. It stung enough to make him grimace.

Limping, he went back around the corner, assessing the damage inflicted upon M3. The front side of the fence and the main gate were both obliterated. Explosives had riddled the base, sending shrapnel from the fences and other bits of material scattered around everywhere. Ryu hobbled as quickly as possible in search of Abe or any of his comrades.

He scanned the area and observed that what remained of the forces were still fighting. Amelia was shooting arrows, but their enemies had thick, full-body shields and were inching closer to the fence line. The other rebel archers were mostly incapacitated by the explosions. Ryu saw several of them lying on the ground, moaning and clutching their missing limbs.

One by one, Ryu dragged survivors back to safety, wrapping their wounds up as best he could. He put his trust in his allies to keep the Order from advancing all the way while he tended to the wounded. There was one man whom he didn't recognize who was missing both legs; Ryu knew the man wasn't going to make it and decided to put him out of his misery. He told the man to close his eyes and that everything was going to be okay. Then, he pulled a small knife from his pocket and plunged it into the man's neck, severing the carotid artery. He gurgled for a moment, the blood washing over Ryu's fingers, and then the life fled the man's body. Ryu pressed on, dragging other survivors to safety.

After the last survivor he could see had been taken to a safer area, Ryu charged back around the building, limping as he did so. The anger of having to take his comrade's lives swelled within him. It was unfair that his life had come to this. The adrenaline he gained was enough to take his mind off his injured leg, and it was as if his energy had been restored. He knew this wouldn't last forever so he took advantage of it.

Analyzing the battlefield, Ryu could see there were several shielded enemies almost to the fence line now. Amelia and the others who were still on their feet had run out of arrows and now flung rocks from the slingshots, and they bounced off the hard barriers. Behind the shielded members there were several others with clubs or knives, and then in the very back, doing nothing but sitting atop his steed was the one called Lucian.

Who does this guy think he is? No way I'm letting him leave here alive after all this.

Ryu rushed in from the side and the enemies saw him too late. He lowered his shoulder before any of them could let loose a warning cry and plundered into the nearest shield-bearer. The man he smashed into bumped into the one beside him, creating a chain reaction of chaos in their formation. The rock slingers were then able to smash them in the face with small rocks just big enough to cause some damage.

Several of them began clutching their face as they were pelted with debris and Ryu began taking them out, one-by-one. He slashed with a fury he'd never felt before and in his rage, he didn't see the man sneak up on him with the large metal club. Ryu saw the shadow too late, and as he turned around the blunt weapon was already swinging toward him. As he tried to duck he knew it would be futile.

Inches from his head, the club was smashed by something that fell from the sky and missed Ryu's head completely. It was Storm; she'd picked this moment to intervene and save Ryu. She hit the ground hard, flopping and rolling over several times before coming to a stop. Ryu swung his sword at the man who was too slow to stop the strike; his head rolled into the dirt and the rest of his body slumped to the ground. He glanced over to Storm to find her motionless.

His heart was about to explode, his comrades were falling and his closest companion was hurt. He slowly turned to face the man on the horse, who still sat there with a smug look on his face. His body was sleek and slender, but he looked strong.

Ryu seethed absolute hatred for this man and lusted to feel his blade go through the monster's chest. He craved to kill him as slowly as possible, and as these feelings coursed through him, it was as if the man could sense it. The man smirked, hopping off his steed, put his hands behind his back, and confidently strode in Ryu's direction. The rest of their enemies had fallen, picked off by Ryu's friends and himself. Out of the corner of his eye, he could see Jax dragging himself to his feet.

"Jax, come," the man ordered. Jax walked over and stood behind Lucian obediently.

Abe stood behind Ryu, breathing heavily. Lucian appeared to look past Ryu, smirking at Abe. "Be careful," Abe told him.

Lucian and Ryu walked toward each other, and upon closer inspection, Ryu noticed that he had an extraordinarily thin sword strapped to his waist. Lucian looked to be amused by the whole situation. Ryu wiped the crimson from his sword.

Ryu said, "Just want my blade to be nice and clean when I remove your head from your shoulders."

"Oh, please. No need for the false sense of confidence, boy." His voice sounded even worse to Ryu at such a close distance. It was like it belonged to a man much older than the one who stood before him.

"Careful, Ryu. He's dangerous," Abe warned.

Ryu looked between the two men. Something passed between them. A look of mutual hatred, perhaps?

Amelia's voice entered his ears as she said something in a hushed tone to Abe. Ryu had returned his gaze to his opponent, but he wanted her away from this fight, "Amelia, go check on Storm. She's hurt pretty bad. After that, I want you to tend to the wounded. I did what I could but it may not be enough."

"But I-"

"Go!"

He heard her footsteps scurry away and then Abe stepped up beside him. He still wore the hook where his hand should be, but now there were bits of human hanging from it. His breathing was steady, "How do you want to do this?"

"I want him for myself." Ryu had never felt more sure that he was going to win a fight. He didn't believe this would be easy, but he knew because of his motivation that there was no way he'd let this monster win.

Lucian smiled and said, "Abe, nice to see you again old friend. Say, are you ready to join my side once again?"

Abe responded calmly, "You should know better than that, Lucian. My enemies still thrive."

"Very well. After I'm done with this little pawn of yours, maybe I'll hang around and see what other fun I can have here. Maybe even have my way with that pretty one. What was her name again, Amelia, was it?"

Abe yelled, "You will do nothing of the sort!"

"Alright, that's it." Ryu heard enough; he charged Lucian.

Ryu began slashing furiously but to no avail. None of his attacks landed as Lucian twisted away from each one, his hands still behind his back. He had a wicked grin on his face as Ryu continued the unsuccessful barrage of attacks. Ryu's movements slowed and his breathing became heavier. Lucian then decided to pull out his thin blade and swiped it right and then left, leaving the point aimed at Ryu.

Ryu slowed down now that his opponent had his weapon at the ready. He swiped at the blade in an attempt to knock it aside, but with incredible speed, Lucian evaded the strike and landed a blow to Ryu's knuckles. Ryu jumped back with a grimace. He looked down at his hand to see a thin stripe of red develop. The cut wasn't deep, but it stung. He re-engaged, but every strike he threw was parried by the man.

Ryu was confused as to how such a small sword could parry his with such ease. The smile never left Lucian's face and finally after wreaking havoc across Ryu's knuckles jumped out of range. He laughed loudly, "Your father no doubt taught you many things about the way of the sword, but it's clear he didn't teach you everything."

"What would you know of it, you bastard?"

"Well, my dear boy, I spent many a day with your father. I watched how he fought for many years before I ran him through that is." A malicious smile crept back into the man's face.

"You're lying."

"Oh, am I?" Lucian laughed. "Ask your fearless leader if I'm a liar. He knows me better than anyone else in your little posse.

Besides, I have no reason to lie. You will soon join Kenji in the afterlife. I will send you there myself."

Ryu stole a glance toward Abe who merely shook his head.

He needed to figure out a way to beat this guy quickly. Ryu rushed back in, he would feign one way and then go the other. Not thinking too much and just throwing wild combinations. It seemed to almost be working; the smirk vanished from Lucian's face and sweat began to bead his immaculate brows. With a deep slash of sword, the man dropped Ryu to his knees. He grasped the ground with a free hand, gathering a fistful of loose soil. Ryu exploded up and threw the dirt into the eyes of his opponent, and with a reverse grip on Sokushi, he made a hard horizontal swing.

The blade finally connected with its target, cutting a deep gash in Lucian's belly. He bellowed in pain and rage as he clutched his stomach. Lucian lunged forward and then Ryu realized the man hadn't been attacking this entire time. He was only defending, but now the onslaught was impossible to avoid. The man moved like a lightning bolt, but none of his slashes were fatal.

Tiny cuts appeared all over Ryu's body as he was unable to dodge or block any of the attacks. The adrenaline and energy had long vanished from him and his sword dropped to the ground. Lucian planted his foot into Ryu's chest and as he landed on his back he saw Abe race past him. He swung at Lucian sloppily with his hook and the man just spun around him. From behind him he lowered his position and sliced his ankles. Abe howled in pain as his ability to walk was severed.

Lucian clutched his gut as he sauntered away; he sheathed his blade and mounted his steed. "Next time," he said, "I will not be so merciful as to let you live." Jax climbed into the wagon and the two men quickly receded from view.

"You okay?" Abe asked sincerely.

Ryu was too exhausted to answer. He bled from a thousand wounds, or so it seemed, and for a long time, he just lay in the dirt refusing to move. Amelia came back, asking them if they were okay, and that's what brought him back to the reality of the situation. He realized that this was no time to be weak; his friends needed him. With all four of his limbs trembling, Ryu climbed up to his feet and sheathed his blade. Together, the two of them dragged Abe back to the nearest building where the inhabitants of M3 who were not fit to fight tended to the wounded and dying.

Hollow Man

Ryu knelt beside the tiny bed in which Storm laid; she was still alive, but was unconscious all the same. His face was contorted with rage as he looked at her motionless body. Amelia told him that as far as she could tell the only outer injuries she obtained was a broken leg and wing. There was no way to tell if she had any internal wounds, but they hoped she would recover with some time and rest.

Several days had passed since the attack on M3 and the rebel's numbers were reduced yet again. The one victory they could claim was that Lucian fled with fewer numbers as well, although, Jax was still alive and knew of their entire operation. Ryu had let one of the older people patch him up; he had shallow cuts all over his body and a few that were deep, but none that were life-threatening. The worst was the stab wound in his thigh.

Abe was directed to bed rest by one of the others which he argued about fervently. On a few occasions, Ryu overheard him being yelled at as he was trying to escape his room. His Achilles tendons were sliced open, stealing his ability to walk. Those more experienced with medical aid said that he would have to stay off his feet for quite a bit of time or else the tendons could be damaged again before fully healing.

Ryu was worried that Lucian was telling the truth about his father. Abe tried reassuring him that they wouldn't kill Kenji. He was too valuable in too many ways.

"How do you know he didn't do something bad enough that they deemed it worthy of his execution?" he asked.

"I don't know for sure. Don't lose hope, Ryu. It's all we have at this point."

Ryu walked back through the infirmary, Amelia coming in as he sat down. *She looks exhausted,* he thought to himself as she sat down beside him. As soon as she scooted her chair up she flopped her head and arms onto the table and fell asleep within seconds. Ryu just looked down at her with a smirk on his face as she snored lightly. He'd never seen her like this and it made him happy to be with her. He was proud to have her at his side.

"Poor thing," Pat—an elderly woman—said, "She's been running around here like crazy. That's a special friend you have there."

"Yes," he said. "She most certainly is."

Pat walked away as Ryu continued to watch Amelia snooze. She stayed this way for a long time and only stirred slightly when one of the others walked in and suggested she go lay down in a bed. She couldn't gather the strength to get up and walk so Ryu carried her in his arms back to an empty cot and gently laid her down. He turned back to look at her just before exiting, longing to lay beside her.

Kenji felt empty, hollow. From the moment he watched Lucian and his entourage leave the Citadel, a sinister feeling came over him. He didn't want the Resistance to be eliminated. He still hoped that Ryu would find them. This only served to cause Kenji to curse himself silently for never telling his son about the rebel group.

All he wanted was for his boy to survive. If he were to find out that Ryu had been taken from the world, his hope would be gone, and he would have no purpose in sticking around.

Kenji waited in the same spot by the gate. Waiting for Lucian's return or lack thereof. The sentries usually allowed Kenji to move about the Citadel as he pleased as long as they weren't ordered to have him in the crop fields or doing some other menial task. The guards watching him rotated every few hours. He didn't know if their nonchalance with him was out of respect or fear. The stories of how fierce of a warrior Kenji was still made the rounds among the nobles.

When they returned, Jax strode in atop the wagon and Lucian was slumped in the back of it. His horse followed closely behind. Kenji strolled over to them and said to Jax, "Hey what happened?"

The man turned his head slowly to meet Kenji's eyes. Kenji could recognize that look anywhere. The obedience serum had been applied to him at some point; he was no longer in control of his body or mind. Luckily, Kenji was never subjected to the poison, but he knew there was no cure. Jax would slowly break down and die.

Jax was still alive, but he didn't know how much more he could take before his consciousness left him altogether. That moron, Ryu, failed to kill him when he broke free of the vice this serum had on him. Jax gave him the perfect opportunity and the boy failed to complete the task. Was it his humanity, his moral compass, that prevented him from killing the man?

Lucian commanded Jax to take him to the Citadel and

straight to the medical lab as he passed out after climbing into the wagon. Jax had the Supreme Leader in his grasp, unconscious, and was unable to end the man. How unfair could life be?

Jax trembled with muscle spasms as he fought against the will to complete the command. Eventually, he just gave up. The pain was unbearable and it wasn't getting him anywhere. Jax hoped there was a cure somewhere that could rid him of this venom that now pumped through his veins.

Kenji was friendly with most of the nobles. He hoped that if he found favor with as many of them as possible, they would show kindness to him in return. Most of the people within the Citadel were slaves to the cruelty of the Order just as much as those living outside the walls. They were controlled by fear; led to be afraid of what lies beyond the safety of the Citadel. Their lives were just so much easier to handle that it seemed like paradise.

Lucian came to visit him as Kenji helped a shop owner move some heavy boxes. He had Jax in tow. "I see you still live," Kenji said.

"Of course," Lucian replied. "You think anyone in the Resistance was strong enough to defeat me? I didn't come back unscathed, however." He lifted his shirt to reveal a wound that had been recently stitched and medicated.

Kenji smirked. "Not as good with that blade as you thought, eh?"

Lucian returned the smile. "This is a compliment of your son, Kenji."

Kenji's heart jumped into his throat and he dropped the box he was holding. "My son is-"

"Alive?" Lucian interrupted. "Yes. Or was, I should say. After he gave me this nasty cut, I drove my blade through his heart."

His hope began to crumble. But then, "How do you know it was my boy?"

"Simple, really," he replied. "Jax here told me the name of everyone he knew of in the Resistance. He claimed that Ryu was your brat and then when I laid eyes on him, I knew. He looked just like you. You should have heard the way he screamed as his life faded. It was pathetic."

Kenji fell to his knees as a wicked grin spread across the Supreme Leader's face. "It was inevitable, Kenji. I am the Supreme Leader. When the Resistance finds their way to the Citadel, I will strike them all down. The rebels will fall for the rest of the nobles to see and the insolent disobedience will be a thing I won't have to deal with ever again."

Kenji was stricken, "The rebels are coming here? How do you know?" His question was met with a fit of laughter.

Silent tears streamed down Kenji's face. How could Ryu be dead? How could he lose to the swine that gloated in front of him? Kenji burst from the ground, hands reaching out toward Lucian's throat. He'd strangle the life out of him.

Before he connected with the Supreme Leader, Jax exploded between the two men. He caught Kenji in a headlock, choking him with his beefy arms. Within seconds, the world faded from the distraught father, and the last thing he saw was the devilish smile on Lucian's face.

Retracing Steps

Enough time had gone by since the attack on M3 that the Resistance had mostly recovered. Those who lost limbs in the battle would never be the same, but everyone else was recovering nicely. Ryu walked around with Kelvin, learning how they produce animals for food.

There were several rows of birthing pods in the center of the base surrounded by buildings to protect them. M3 was instrumental in feeding much of the Resistance's members. As the two men milled around the pods, Kelvin explained that there were several animals nearly ready to be brought into the world. The creatures were never close to the same age so the production would go more smoothly to avoid having long periods without animals being born.

Inside a small structure with bottles and vials of liquid all over, Kelvin said, "These are the chemicals that go into the pods. The only other thing that we add is the DNA of whichever animal we're trying to create. It doesn't always work, it's not foolproof, but our production rates are good. I imagine if the Resistance grows much larger, though, we will need to open another base with the same intent."

Ryu found it very unlikely that their group would increase much more than it was now.

Next, Kelvin showed him to the fields where they kept the livestock. He gestured to their enclosures, "Here is where the animals will live out their days until we harvest them."

"How long after being born do you wait to harvest one?" he asked.

"That depends on the animal. The chickens reach maturity fairly quickly. The pigs take a little longer and the cows can take a couple of years. There's a lot of planning that goes into this operation."

"Yeah, no kidding," Ryu chuckled. "We're pretty lucky the Order didn't attack this part of the base."

Kelvin sighed, "That would be most troublesome. Starting over at this point would be devastating to the cause."

Those who were able to move about with little hindrance left M3 to go to the Armory. The Armory was another smaller station belonging to the rebels. It was called such because they were in charge of Producing weaponry for the Resistance. It didn't take long to get there which Ryu was thankful for. Storm, now fully recovered, enjoyed getting to stretch her wings as she floated high above the caravan.

Abe shook hands with a bald man who wore the thickest mustache Ryu had ever seen. "Ryu, this is the leader of the Armory," Abe said.

The man reached out a hand and Ryu grasped it. "The name's Arms," the man said.

"Arms?" Ryu laughed.

"It's a nickname, of course," the man said defensively.

"I'm Ryu," he said. "Pleasure to meet you." Ryu didn't know if the man was called Arms because he was in charge of the Armory, or because of his massive arm muscles. His biceps bulged beneath the skin as if he had filled them with air.

Back in one of the larger buildings, Abe gathered the troops, limping around a bit due to his injuries. Storm, perched atop Ryu's shoulder. "I know recent events have made things hard for all of us; we've lost friends, family, and our home. However, the fight is not close to being over yet. If there are any of you who wish to leave because of all this, I won't hold that against you. You are free to leave, but know that you will not be allowed to rejoin us."

After some hushed whispers fluttered around the room, he continued, "Most of you probably saw Jax joined with the enemy. For that reason, I cannot allow you to return to us once you have left."

Many of the people nodded with solemn looks on their faces. Ryu thought about Jax and how he seemed to not be in control of himself. He had brought it to Abe's attention earlier, but the leader shrugged it off as if it were a figment of Ryu's imagination. He went on, "The next task that will need to be accomplished is recovering all that we can from the bunker. Now, this will be one of the most difficult things I have asked of you. Many of our people's bodies still lay there. We are weary from the battles and the journey here, however, this is important. We have technology there that may still be of use to us. If you are up for the challenge, meet me outside tomorrow morning at dawn."

Ryu found that he couldn't sit idly by and watch his allies go on this mission without him. Storm, of course, joined as well which Ryu was *extremely* grateful for. After almost losing her, he didn't want to go anywhere without the raven. She had been outfitted with some armor that fit her perfectly. How the rebels at the Armory were able to craft something like that so quickly left Ryu dumbfounded. The raven now had metallic talons and a helmet with a razor-sharp beak.

"How do you think he did it?" Storm asked, referring to Abe who now walked with ease. He wasn't moving with great speed, however, his limping had seemingly disappeared overnight.

"I've no idea," he admitted. Abe was a peculiar man. He seemed to have many secrets that he wasn't comfortable sharing, but Ryu didn't resent him for that. There were things in Ryu's life that he preferred to keep to himself as well.

They marched across the wasteland toward the bunker. The sun brought down a sweltering heat on Ryu's head. He didn't know if it was luck or strategy that put the bunker so close to the Armory, but he was thankful that the trek wasn't very long either way.

The gaping hole of the bunker came into view; Storm took flight and circled for a moment before returning to Ryu's shoulder. "I don't hear or see anything nefarious around the bunker," she told him.

The group began driving metal rods into the hard ground near the mouth of the crater and then attached the ropes for repelling into the maw. A few of the rebels stayed above while the others were lowered into the pit. Before Ryu reached the bottom, the stench of the dead wafted into his nose. The putrid smell nearly knocked him out. One of the others, Bambi, gagged and retched into the bunker from where she dangled.

The horror they found awaiting them on the floor of the bunker made Ryu's skin crawl. Signs of their dead friends littered the place. Years of work were destroyed in a single day.

"Alright, everyone," Abe announced. "Split up into groups

of two. Grab anything you think is salvageable and meet back here."

Ryu noticed Abe saunter off without a partner. There wasn't a whole lot to be found in the bunker. Ryu gathered some extra knives that he found to be in good condition. He didn't want to bog himself down with a bunch of swords or heavier weapons. Apart from that, he was able to find some rations that could be eaten.

The team met back at the opening of the bunker and started their ascension. Fresh air hit Ryu in the face as he left the stench of death behind. Ryu was glad to be out of the abyss of the bunker and back on solid ground. They began pouring over the items that had been recovered. It was odd to Ryu that Abe returned empty-handed, but he decided not to question it.

One of the recovery crew members produced some of the inner workings of a computer. Abe seemed happy about that one. Most of their finds included rations and weapons, so Ryu didn't feel too bad about not finding anything substantial.

The sun was drooping on the horizon, sending streaks of orange and pink about the sky. "Do you ever get tired of looking at it?" Ryu asked Storm.

"Looking at what?" she asked.

"The sky. When it looks like that, I can't help but be caught in its beauty."

She responded, "I agree, it is very alluring. It's one of the reasons I love flying. You could chalk it up to me being a bird, but still, flying among those colors gives me such a free feeling."

"That sounds amazing," he admitted.

The group made camp for the night. They sat around a fire,

talking and laughing their troubles away. Abe sat away from the others with his back to the flames. Ryu plopped down beside him. "Mind if I join?" he asked.

Abe chuckled, "It seems you already have."

"Fair enough," he said. "Is everything okay?" Ryu worried for the man. It wasn't like him to exclude himself.

"Many of my soldiers have now been killed," he said. "As a leader, it makes one question if they should be in the leadership position at all."

"Don't think like that," Ryu tried to reassure him. "I think you're doing great at leading us. The deaths of our friends can never be your fault, only the Order can answer to that."

Abe laughed, "I guess that's a positive way of looking at it." He paused and then said, "I have to get us to the Citadel. Soon." He looked at Ryu. "The fate of humanity depends on it." Ryu just nodded in response.

Ryu looked up, thinking he saw a slight shift of movement in the distance. At the same time, Storm began to emit a hiss. "Something is out there," he whispered to Abe.

A low growl issued from in front of where they sat. It echoed around them by the other beasts in the pack. Storm took flight, vanishing in the night. Ryu jumped to his feet, pulling Sokushi from its sheath. The rest of the group jumped up, wielding weapons as well, alerted to the danger that surrounded them. Ryu could make out the beast closest to him as it stalked forward, the flicker of flames illuminating it just enough.

Gnashing of Teeth

Ryu thought the wolves were magnificent; they were big, beautiful creatures, even if they *were* trying to eat them. He yelled out for the men to form a circle with their backs to each other. As they did so it was clear that the wolves outnumbered them. Abe quickly fastened an attachment to his nub that was like a cup with a short sword protruding from it. The Armory personnel made this for him along with Storm's new armor.

Storm swooped down at full speed and swiped at one of the smaller beasts' necks. The animal cried out in pain, but it didn't die. This attack caused them to spring into action. They rushed in, snapping their sharp teeth at the men. Two of the wolves attacked Ryu at the same time. With the sword being held in both hands, he slashed to the side and ended one life. The other wolf was able to clamp its teeth around Ryu's wrist.

The beast shook violently, tearing the flesh on Ryu's forearm. Ryu screamed out in pain. He flipped the blade over in his hand and slid the hilt in between its jaws. He then used the hilt to pry open its mouth and then kicked the wolf away. He fell back onto his butt as the wolf lunged at him again. Ryu flipped the point of the blade around and the animal landed on it, sinking the blade through its body. It yelped and struggled momentarily, but then stopped moving altogether.

Pain seared in his arm as he flopped the animal to the side and pulled his sword free. It would have to be dealt with once this was over. He looked around to see who he could help; a few of the wolves had taken their targets down, but they weren't dead. Every couple of seconds he would see a flash of black and silver as Storm swooped in and attacked the beasts with her razor-sharp talons.

The man nearest him was on his back, a metal club in between the teeth of the wolf that was attacking him. Ryu did a flip over the animal's back and sliced cleanly through its neck as he landed on his feet. The creature's head rolled onto the man and its blood soaked him. Conrad, gave a nod of thanks to him as Ryu turned to help the others. Ryu put down two more of the wolves before they had all been taken care of.

"Well," Abe said between heavy breaths, "Looks like we've got some more food to get us through the night."

Ryu heard chuckling, but couldn't focus on anything other than his throbbing arm at that moment. He'd lost a lot of blood from the bite on his arm. His head swirled and he felt woozy; he sat down hard and the others took notice of his weakened state.

Abe immediately began wrapping Ryu's damaged wrist in bandages and then had him lie down. After putting some medical ointment on, he re-wrapped the wound. Once done he helped Ryu sit up and gave him some water.

Ryu looked over to Storm who sat on a nearby rock. Blood glistened on her armor, the claws as well as the beak. "Looks like those things did you well."

"Yes, they came in handy. It was rather fun, I must say."

He chuckled, "You have a weird sense of humor."

"She's more like you than you realize," Abe interjected.

Storm began munching down on one of the wolves as the others pulled small knives from their gear and started clearing the fur from the meat. Once it was separated, the fire was replenished and they began cooking the meat. Ryu dug into a hunk of the protein; it was hard to chew but didn't taste too bad. He wasn't one to complain over food especially since it could be hard to get a lot of the time.

"Who in the world would create a pack of wolves?" Ryu couldn't help but ask.

Abe replied, "Only the Order could have, although there is no telling when it happened. The elites of old stockpiled the DNA of every animal known before destroying the planet."

"How do you know so much about our history?" Ryu asked, baffled.

Abe chuckled, "When you've lived as long as I, there isn't much you can't learn."

The men told stories and jokes, they laughed at each other and enjoyed the rest of their night. It seemed like Ryu was the only one feeling drained so he went to sleep earlier than the others. Storm joined him, taking off her armor and laying it aside. They both fell asleep shortly after closing their eyes.

Ryu was eager to get back to the Armory; he missed Amelia and wanted to see her. They were unable to spend much time together recently, thanks to being attacked and all the moving around. He enjoyed getting to sit down and just enjoy little moments with her. Ryu could tell that she felt just as strongly for him as he did her. He kept thinking about his father; Ryu couldn't wait for them to meet. Considering his father was still alive, of course.

"Why don't you slow down for a moment? You don't want to overdo it."

He turned around to see his group as small shapes in the distance behind him. "I didn't realize I was going so fast. I'm just so excited to get back to Amelia."

"I know you like her," Storm replied. "But I can sense your heartbeat. You're still worn out from the past couple of days."

"Would you just get off my back," Ryu shot at her.

"Fine," she said curtly, jumping off his shoulder and zipping up into the air.

"I didn't mean it literally," he shouted up to her. She didn't appear to be listening now though.

As if sensing that his friend had just left him, three scavengers popped up out of the dirt. They were covered in clothes that blended in with the environment in such a way that neither Storm nor Ryu were able to detect them. Storm quickly returned to his shoulder after hearing their clamoring. They all smiled greedily at the raven with her shiny armor and Ryu with his gear bag.

"Oh come on. You've got to be kidding me," Ryu said.

The big ugly one in the middle laughed, "Give me the bird and your gear and I promise to kill you quickly. Refuse, and you'll suffer."

Ryu didn't have the time or patience to deal with this. He turned his head to find his friends moving in quickly. They must have noticed the danger he was in. He decided to end it before they could even catch up. Savoring the rage that filled up. These scoundrels stood in his way. They were scum, beneath him in every way.

"How about this," Ryu said, "you get out of my way, or I kill you all slowly and then let my friend here eat what's left."

Storm clicked her beak at the men.

The three men chuckled but did not budge. Ryu took his pack off his shoulders and gingerly set it on the ground. As soon as he let go of the shoulder strap one of the men rushed him, brandishing a sword of his own. Storm sat on the top of the bag, guarding it, and watched the scene unfold.

Ryu pulled out his blade and their metal clanged, sending sparks in the air. He slid his blade down the edge of his opponent's and then flicked his wrist. The enemy's blade shot to the side and Ryu was able to use his free hand to grab the man's wrist. He flipped the blade so the edge faced the sky. With an upward motion, Ryu severed the man's wrist, the detached hand and sword clattering to the ground.

He screamed in agony and clutched his forearm as he fell to his knees. Ryu decided to come back to him later, keeping his promise to kill them slowly. The other two men rushed at the same time, the bigger of the two carried a wooden club with spikes all over it. The other wielded a dagger.

The bigger of the men reached him first and threw a hard, wild swing of his club at Ryu who easily ducked under it. As he did, he made a two-handed slash with Sokushi which cut deeply into his opponent. With his opponent now low to the ground, he spun in a fast circle, cutting through the third man's left leg as his blade came back around. All three howled in pain and writhed on the ground, blood leaking from their various injuries.

The rest of Ryu's group caught up now, sucking wind hard as they gasped for air. They looked like they were going to interfere, but Ryu just held his hand up to show that he had it under control.

The man in charge started to plead with Ryu, begging him to

spare their lives, but he was not in a forgiving mood. Ryu was a man of his word. He started with the man missing his leg. He stared at the one in charge the entire time but placed the tip of his sword on the man's forehead and plunged it through his skull. The man's movement and sounds of agony ceased. Then he moved on to the one who was missing his hand; this one tried to get up and run but was too slow.

Ryu grabbed him by the back of the collar and spun him around to face the other scavenger. He kicked the back of his knee to break his posture and as soon as his knees hit the dirt, he swung his sword and separated his head from his body. It rolled to the last man's feet as he screamed in horror, apologizing adamantly.

Never had so much rage filtered through his body as he sauntered over to the last of the bandits. The man tried to crawl away, but it was pointless. Ryu thrust the tip of his sword into the back of the man's calf. He screamed as Ryu pulled the blade free and then rolled to his back.

Ryu began slicing back and forth all over the man's body. His teeth were clenched in a fit of rage. The scavenger lay on his back, his screams fading with each strike. Eventually, they halted altogether as the man died, but Ryu continued slashing at his lifeless body. Blood spattered his hands, arms, and face. When the anger was satiated, he turned back to his friends. His chest and shoulders heaved with every breath.

They all had looks of shock on their faces. Some covered their mouths while others just drooped, slack-jawed. Abe was the only one whose expression was unreadable. Ryu breathed heavily, blood dripping from his fingers and Sokushi's tip. He looked down and finally noticed that he was covered in the scarlet liquid and as the adrenaline faded, he found himself appalled by the heinous act he'd just committed.

Sure, the men would have likely killed Ryu just as quickly if he'd allowed it. Scavengers were known to be particularly vile humans and these weren't any different. They didn't care about other people, only themselves and what they could take from others. Ryu knew there was a difference between felling someone in defense and slaughtering them as he had. The sickening part was Ryu enjoyed every second of it. He usually found himself to be indifferent when taking someone's life.

In a matter of minutes, Ryu felt like all his hard work as a youth was for naught. The Samurai spirit that he clung to had shifted—mutated—into something else. It was something evil. He felt dirty, tainted. Ultimately, he felt that by his actions, he'd brought dishonor to his father.

How will I ever atone for this?

The Cursed Warrior

Ryu could taste the iron from his opponent's blood in his mouth. He tried wiping his face, but his hands were also covered. The unrelenting strikes he made to the downed scavenger tossed droplets of blood through the air and stained his skin and clothes. He dropped down to his knees; he was usually adept at maintaining a stoic visage, especially when tensions were high. But now, in the reality that he may just be a murderous monster, dread crossed him.

He began sobbing, unable to keep the tears at bay, they flowed freely of their own volition. A small puddle formed in the dirt underneath his chin. He began punching the ground, hating himself for losing control, and loathing himself even further for breaking down in front of everyone like this. He was trained to have a resilient mind like the Samurai of old, and yet here he was, sobbing uncontrollably.

A hand gripped his shoulder, and then another on the opposite shoulder. More hands were placed all over his back which heaved with each sob. The group sat there for several minutes, and when his tear ducts had emptied, Ryu sat back on his heels and closed his eyes with his face upturned toward the sun. The other men all backed away giving him some space, except for Abe.

Abe crouched in front of Ryu and began dabbing the blood from his face with a clean rag. After his face was sufficiently clean he started to work on his hands. The clothes would have to wait to be washed, or burned, Ryu didn't care which. Abe put his hand on his head and said, "We've all made our fair share of mistakes in this life. No one passes through without losing control of themselves at least once. This anger you feel, I've felt it before too. It's a rage like the burning fires of Hell. Fan the flames and they grow. Will you give in to the anger? Only you can make that choice for yourself."

Abe pulled the young man into an embrace, or maybe he'd fallen onto the leader's chest. He wasn't sure. Either way, the way Abe held him was more fatherly than anything he'd felt in years.

Ryu nodded and stood up. He gathered his belongings and wiped his blade down then sheathed it. The group of men began their journey back to the Armory. Ryu kept his eyes on the ground as he walked. Storm perched on his shoulder and nuzzled up to his neck, offering him silent comfort that he appreciated more than he could put into words.

After the long travels, Ryu had recovered his sense of dignity after what he'd done. They entered the gates of the Armory and he walked with a sense of purpose as Arms led them back to the debriefing room. Abe shared with Arms everything that happened since they let. He told him of their findings in the bunker and about the wolf pack that attacked them.

He left out the part where Ryu went crazy on the scavengers. Ryu was grateful for the leader's discretion.

Before running into the bandits, Ryu could think of almost nothing but seeing Amelia again. It would seem that as time passed he grew more fond of the young woman. He loved her more with each passing day.

Now that the crew was back at the Armory though, Ryu didn't know how to face her. She would sense something was off with him and he'd be forced into telling her what he'd done. Wondering what she would think of him began gnawing at him as soon as he set foot in the confines of the Armory's grounds.

After the debrief, Ryu sulked to the room where he and Storm slept. He changed his clothes, putting the dirty ones in a small bag with the intention of burning them the first chance he got. He cleaned himself off with a wet rag and plopped down onto his bed. Storm jumped, startled, as the door swung open, and in walked Amelia with a worried look on her face.

Ryu didn't bother looking up at her but his heart was racing. She said, "I'm sorry I didn't knock. I figured you would have found me once you all got back."

Ryu still didn't look at her. He didn't answer. She sat down next to him on his bed. Storm said, "I'll give you two some space for a bit." Then she flew out of the room.

"What's going on? I'd be able to see that something is bothering you even if I were blind." That earned a small chuckle from Ryu.

The knot in his throat made it hard to talk. It came out as a rusty whisper, "I don't know how to tell you what I've done."

"Look at me," she demanded, placing her hand on his leg. His eyes darted to hers. "Nothing you say could make me think any less of you. Nothing you've done would cause me to stop loving you."

"So, you *do* love me then?" he asked.

She shook her head, "Of course, silly boy."

A tear slid down his cheek; he wanted to tell her but was scared. The concern in her eyes only made it worse.

"Please tell me," she pleaded.

Ryu took a deep breath and explained in great detail what happened with the scavengers. He told her how it made him feel to cut into them. The elation that ran through his body with each swing of the sword. She stayed silent, expressionless through the whole tale, and when he finished, Ryu's eyes were red from crying. His nose was running.

Much to Ryu's surprise, Amelia pulled him in tight, putting his forehead on her chest. She stroked the back of his head as he let all the sadness drain out of him.

He stood up, grabbing a rag with which he blew his nose. "How do you not hate me?" he asked. "How do you still sit there and support me after all that I've told you? I'm a monster. You should hate me."

She sighed, "Ryu, there is darkness in all of us. What kind of person would I be if I turned my back on you when you needed me most? Look at how far you've come in your life. You've traversed more of the wastelands than pretty much anyone I know. You've trained hundreds of rebels in the way of sword fighting. You would lay down your life to protect any of us. You may not think about that but I know that it's true. Look at me."

He had been fiddling with the snotty rag in his hands and staring at his feet. His eyes snapped to hers and she placed a soft hand on his cheek. "As long as I'm still breathing, you'll *always* have someone proud of you for everything you've achieved."

Ryu didn't know how to respond to something so wonderfully profound. He just pulled her into a tight hug. He didn't want to let go. Hours could have ticked by and Ryu wouldn't know or care. The depth at which he fell for this woman was so great that nothing could come between them.

Finally, he pulled away, looking into her eyes. "How do I move past what I've done?"

She seemed to ponder it for a moment, then said, "Not that I'm an expert in this area, but the next this happens, try thinking of what makes you happy. It could be your best childhood memory or something like that. Just focus on the thing that brings you the most joy."

He smiled. "I'll try that." Ryu knew that the thing that brought him the most joy was Amelia.

"I don't want you to leave without me," Ryu told Amelia, planting a kiss on her cheek.

"I won't be gone for that long," she reassured him. "Just get some rest and I'll be back before you know it."

He nodded. Amelia was tasked with leading a group to various towns. The mission was to find more recruits for the Resistance. Seeing as their numbers had dwindled significantly, they would need to beef them up a bit before moving on the Citadel.

"I want to find every last man, woman, and child that wishes to take down the Order," Abe told them.

It was important that they gather as many warriors as possible for the encroaching siege of the Citadel, but Ryu still didn't like Amelia going on a mission without him. She was capable of protecting herself but he still worried. If not for her safety, then for his sanity.

A Close Call

Amelia gathered the members designated to join her in this recruitment mission. There were 15 of them in total; 5 of them were other women like herself. Although, one of them whose name was Beatrice was the biggest girl she'd ever seen. She towered over most of the men and her arms and legs were like tree trunks.

They started their journey and before long had come across their first human contact. It was a small town, but lively. There seemed to be a lot going on; the people there were thriving pretty well. They'd figured out how to grow plants and were surviving on those plants alone. She was thoroughly impressed by the operation going on. They even had a town leader.

With Amelia being in charge of the mission, she spoke with the town leader alone. His name was Bartholomew; he was a narrow man, as were the other inhabitants of their town she noticed. He told her that he'd been in charge for several years and before that it was his father. They were particularly good at defending their possessions because of the spiked trench around their town. There was only one way in and one way out which made it easy to fight off anyone who may attack.

Bartholomew told her they hadn't received any visitors in

quite some time, and seemed excited to discuss the proposition she had for him. After telling her the reason for their visit, he became less enthusiastic. She could tell that he was a bit scared of the prospect of messing with the nobles.

"People from the citadel have visited a couple times in the past. Their numbers and weapons outdid us by a lot. I've no idea what they would be doing out here, but each time they came here, they left with some of our people. I can't imagine any one of my townsmen wanting to leave our refuge to go work for those bastards."

"So, will you help us then?" She pleaded.

"Here's what I'll do. I can call a town meeting and offer my people the opportunity to leave with you. I won't force them to fight with the Resistance, but you have my support either way. I'll provide your team with some of our food and any other supplies we can muster."

"That is more than generous of you, sir."

"Oh, please. It's the least I can do."

A couple of hours later the whole town was gathered to hear what their leader had to say. He had a small platform on which he stood and invited Amelia to join him.

She reluctantly did so; the eyes of all these strangers on her made Amelia nervous. The projection of his voice surprised Amelia when he addressed the crowd.

"My people," he called to them. "As many of you know, we have lived in harmony with the powers that be for many years. I feel that the One World Order leaves us alone because we are not a threat. Despite that, they deserve to be destroyed for the crimes they've committed. This young lady, Amelia, brings us a proposition from the Resistance."

He gestured to her, it was Amelia's turn to try winning them over.

She began explaining why she was there and how they could help.

After saying her piece, she opened the floor up for questions. There were many questions lobbed at her one at a time and she did her best to answer them.

"What if we die?"

"What's in it for us?"

"What is the plan of attack?"

Finally, a reasonable question, she thought.

"For now, we don't have a solidified plan. The goal is to amass as many people as we can so we can grow our attack force. We have many great soldiers in our ranks, but unfortunately, it's not enough yet. I know that can be disheartening, however, I just ask that you see the fight we find ourselves in is good."

"How do we know you're not lying to us? What if you actually work for the Order?"

"Listen, I know some of this is hard to believe. But I've lost many friends in this battle. Either you join me, or you don't. If you decide to come along you'll get to help humanity take back the reins from the people who have beaten us down all these years. We will be leaving your town in a few hours. If you want to join the Resistance, you know where we'll be."

She left it at that; the questions annoyed her and she quickly grew tired of the nonsense. She wasn't made for speaking to the masses, but shooting down her enemies was more her speed. She hopped down from the wooden platform and wound her way through the crowd which just followed her with their eyes.

Amelia didn't know if any of them would join, but she

presumed they most likely wouldn't. Bartholomew dismissed his people and quickly caught up with her, saying that they didn't have to leave so soon. She waved her hand and told him the sooner they moved on the better. He promised to have some rations out at the exit before they departed.

He was true to his word; when Amelia and the crew exited the town, there were a few burlap sacks of plants laying on the ground. Among the food were several men gathered around waiting for them. They introduced themselves and pledged their allegiance to the cause.

Upon further questioning, Amelia found that they were all around the same age and had trained together for many years. They hated the Order and wanted to see them fall just as much as anyone with a sane mind would. Between them, they had roughly ten or so knives that Amelia counted. Together, they hefted the rations and continued on their mission.

Several hours passed by and the sun was drooping across the horizon. The team stopped and made camp for the night. They talked fervently, sharing things about their lives up to this point. The new additions to the Resistance were excited to be a part of something bigger than them. This gave new purpose to their lives. Amelia ventured into her tent and laid down as the new members showed off their knife-handling skills to the others. The clanging metal did not stop her from falling asleep promptly.

Amelia awoke to a rustling sound, acute rays of sunshine broke through her tent. It was early morning. She didn't know if it was one of her crew rummaging through their gear or if it was something else. She thought that perhaps she was just being paranoid, but then heavy breathing and weird snarling noises told her otherwise. It would be impossible for her to silently open the flap to her tent, with the zipper being fastened closed.

She would try her best to not draw attention to herself. As slowly as she could, Amelia started unzipping her tent. The noise around her hadn't yet stopped and finally, the zipper reached the bottom. She let out a breath that she hadn't realized was being held. It came out shakily. She slipped her fingers through the flap and parted it as she poked her head out.

As soon as her eyes broke out into the open air, she noticed how horrible their situation was. A creeper crouched in front of her. He was mere inches from her face, breathing rancid breath into her nostrils. His eyes were wild and had hair growing in patches. His mouth was open and he had several teeth missing. Sores covered the skin all over his body. Drool dribbled down his chin as a near-silent moan escaped his lips.

This man's mind had been destroyed by Shade. He was too far gone to be considered as a human being. Amelia assumed there were more of them with this man; they tended to move in groups even though they couldn't communicate as far as anyone knew. Not only that, but there were several sets of footsteps she heard, plus the rustling noises still filled her ears. *How have the others not woken up yet?* she thought as her heartbeat quickened.

Her hands trembled with fear as she tried to creep back inside the tent. She was going to pretend like the two of them hadn't just made eye contact. As she grabbed the zipper though, the man sprang forward, hands outstretched. His dirt-crusted fingers entered the tent and found their way around her throat. Choke-muffled screams escaped her, and the ravings of the madman filled her ears.

She tried fighting him; her knee caught him in the crotch but had no effect on him. His saliva dripped onto her face as he attempted to bring his mouth closer, no doubt wanting to take a bite from her face. She kept her hands planted on his chest, pushing him up with all her might. Her arms shook with tremors of fatigue and he slowly descended down onto her.

Amelia was rife with fear, the shade-crazed man inching ever closer to her face. His breath smelled of rotted meat.

Suddenly, the creature was ripped out of the tent. He sounded like a wounded animal as he disappeared from her sight. She heard a couple of dull thuds and then the sounds vanished, leaving just her deep ragged breath. She wiped her face with the back of her hand and then clutched at her throbbing neck. Her pulse slammed rapidly into the palm of her hand.

Beatrice poked her head through the tent and said, "You okay, boss?"

Amelia swallowed hard, saying, "Yeah, yeah. I'll be right out."

After gathering herself, Amelia crawled out and stood hunched over with her hands on her knees. She took a few deep breaths and righted herself, looking around. Much of their gear had been strewn about, but the only casualties were those of the deranged people. This only fueled her hatred for the nobles. If not for them, Shade wouldn't exist and there wouldn't be all these mindless beasts running around trying to kill everything that breathes.

Amelia checked on everyone to make sure they were all okay. Apparently she was the only one who sustained any damage in the fight. Finger-shaped bruises appeared on her neck as they all began packing things up and moved onward. She was happy to see more structures take shape in the distance. Her hope of gaining more combatants increased as their journey continued.

In the coming weeks, Amelia would return to the Armory with so many new Resistance members that they were having to triple and double up in living quarters.

Ryu had thought about Amelia nearly every day she was away on her mission. He'd missed her greatly and made sure she knew it. He could feel her breathe into his chest as they wrapped their arms around each other. The embrace just felt right, it made time seem to slow to a standstill.

At times, Ryu would catch sight of Abe coming through the gates of their new home, which he thought was weird because there wasn't anything out there for miles. Something seemed off about him. He pondered to ask but didn't want to offend the man who had shown such care to him and Storm by accusing him of doing nefarious things.

The Armory forged as much weaponry as they could muster; daggers and knives, swords and shields, bows and arrows. They were able to create many explosives as well.

Ryu couldn't help but have a sense of foreboding whenever he thought about having to face Lucian again. The man had made him appear as if Ryu were a novice swordsman, which simply wasn't true. He voiced his concerns to Abe.

"I don't doubt that you will face Lucian again," Abe told him. "You will just have to get better by then."

It wasn't the usual upbeat positive outlook that Ryu was used to. "How do I improve if no one here can give me a real challenge?" he asked.

Abe seemed to think about it, then said, "If you can't find

quality, then find quantity. I know there are strong fighters among us, perhaps not at your level, but strong nonetheless. Just think about your father and how you wish to save him. I'm sure your heart will allow your mind to figure something out."

Ryu looked at his feet. "According to Lucian, my father is dead."

Abe sighed, "Lucian will not kill Kenji so easily. Remember, this man is evil and will do anything he can to thwart our progress. My inclination is that he lied to you. He must have seen something valuable in you that scared him. That's good, we need that. Keep your hope, your fire, and use it to drive you onto a whole new level."

Ryu smiled, a little bit of hope fluttering within, "Thanks, Abe. I think I needed that."

Abe returned the smile, "Of course. What am I here for if not to inspire?"

The Warrior

"The Samurai," Ryu told his group of trainees, "was a warrior unlike any other. Raise your hand if you've heard of them." No hands went up and he continued, "As I thought. The Samurai were revered as some of the greatest fighters known to man. They trained every day to become better in their craft. Honing their skills was of the utmost importance so that they could defend their clans, their homes."

Ryu allowed a brief moment of silence to pass. "This is what I hope to instill in each one of you in the coming days. As my father did for me."

Their training began with lifting heavy rocks overhead and running around the Armory base until their arms and legs gave out. The physical aspect of the training would increase their mental resilience as well as build muscle and dexterity. The armorers began crafting more swords in the image of Sokushi, but none could compare. It was a difficult job but the product they supplied would suffice.

Ryu worked with the rebels who had stepped forward when he gave the call to action, beckoning any who wanted to dedicate themselves to Ryu's squad of swordsmen. He trained them in the ways of sword fighting, hoping that if he made them as deadly as possible, they would in turn help to increase his abilities. It reminded him of the training he did back at the bunker, however, these were mostly new recruits who had little experience with swords.

A lot of the newcomers were more accustomed to working with knives or daggers; the sword was a foreign object. In the bunker, Ryu had focused more on teaching them techniques to cut down their enemies. Now, he was trying to prepare their minds and bodies for the hardships that came with battle. Sparring was much more frequent. It was brutal but necessary.

Weeks of training turned into months. His squad of fighters fluctuated frequently. He would lose a few members due to various reasons. Injury was the fewest of reasons that someone had to quit the rigorous training regimen. Many of them did not have the heart or soul to continue after learning how difficult it could be. The ones that remained grew more lethal as the months ticked on.

Ryu found himself surrounded by three of his fighters. They were all outfitted with wooden swords. They attacked as a singular unit. Ryu parried and counter-attacked like a madman. The sting of wood on his skin was everywhere. He simply wasn't good enough yet.

This process was repeated at least once every day until, finally, Ryu was able to hold his ground against the attackers. He was able to block every strike that came down on him and came out unscathed.

Eventually, he was able to defeat the three assailants without taking any damage from their swords.

"We're ready," Ryu told Abe. "My fighters and I are prepared to take down the Order."

"Wonderful news, my boy," Abe said with a gleam in his eye.

A smile splayed across his face. "I've grown weary of waiting for this glorious moment. We must march upon the Citadel very soon. We need to discuss battle plans immediately."

Ryu and Amelia practiced with a bow and arrow, flinging wooden missiles at a nearby target. Arms strolled up with a bright smile and said, "I've got something special for you, Ryu. It's called a kunai." He held out a small blade. It looked odd to Ryu but he took it from Arms, turning it over in his hands.

"It's best used as a thrown object," Arms told him. "I read about them once and was just thinking that it seemed like something you would enjoy."

Ryu smiled, "Thanks. It looks neat."

"Go on," Amelia told him, "give it a go."

Ryu took aim at the target, holding the blade in his hand, feeling its weight. He flung the kunai and watched as it flipped through the air. It looked promising, but then struck the edge of the target at an awkward angle, bouncing off and landing in the dirt.

Roaring laughter issued from Arms. Was this a joke? The man clapped Ryu on the back and said, "Chin up, my boy. May want to practice with that a bit before taking it into a battle, eh?"

Ryu just chuckled as the brute walked off. He retrieved the kunai and turned to Amelia. "Looks like I need some practice."

It took a while, but with time and patience, Ryu finally landed the point of his new weapon into the target.

The Inside Man

After much deliberation, it was decided that it would be easiest to split the rebels up into cohorts according to whichever base they came from. After that, the remaining members who recently joined were mixed into the groups evenly. A leader was appointed by Abe for each respective squad. Ryu, of course, would lead his group of elite fighters.

The entirety of the rebels gathered as Abe climbed up a wooden podium to deliver the orders. The march to the Citadel was nigh.

Storm hovered in the slight breeze and looked out over the troops for a while before coming to rest on Ryu's shoulder. She whispered just loud enough for him and Amelia to hear, "It appears we have more soldiers than I previously thought."

That comforted Ryu because prior to now he was worried that they wouldn't have enough to take over the Citadel. All their work and sacrifices would be for naught if they had too few members to take down the Order.

Abe climbed up a ladder onto a platform that was a few feet off the ground; he tried to calm down the rambunctious crowd to no avail. Raising his voice, he was finally able to gain their attention, "Silence!"

The chatter died down and the people took notice of the

man speaking. He continued, "I'll try to speak as loudly as possible. If you miss any of this information it will be up to those appointed as leaders, to disperse it amongst your crews."

"Who are you?" someone shouted.

"A great question. I shall answer, but please hold all other questions and comments until the end." Abe paused as if to let it sink in that he was not to be interrupted again. "Now then, my name is Abe, for those of you who have not had the pleasure of meeting me yet.

"I was part of the sentries for many years before leaving and creating the Resistance with a man named Kenji. We believe this man to be a captive of the Order. Liberating him comes only second to overthrowing our tyrants. I do have a bit of information on our enemies that I will share with you.

"Let's begin with the layout of the Citadel and outposts. The Citadel has walls in the shape of a circle that tower high above the ground. Extending away from the walls are bridges that can only be crossed by traversing the expanse of the outpost that it's attached to. The outposts are also walled cities in the shape of a circle, albeit much smaller than the Citadel. The outposts usually only have a few guards at their gates. They should be fairly easy to take over.

"It is highly likely that many of you will run across mutated humans that have been placed around the outposts and on the outskirts of the Citadel to keep anyone from entering. These mutants generally have the scent of each outpost's citizens memorized, so they will know that we are not meant to be there. The people living in the outposts are mostly slaves to the nobles so they won't put up a fight, except for the sentries that are placed there and the occasional creeper."

A loud wind began sweeping through them and Abe paused

his speech. Dust devils whipped around the area, causing Ryu to shield his eyes. It took a whole minute for the wind to cease and allow the man to speak again.

"The resources within the Citadel are unimaginable. Over time they've been able to build up the landscape; trees and lakes teeming with animals are all over. This land is more vast than what most of you are probably expecting." Whispers of a land rife with animals and freshwater arose as such a thing was unheard of. Ryu found it hard to believe as well. He didn't understand how the nobles could keep it all for themselves. *Selfish bastards.*

"The majority of their weapons will be similar to what we have, but it's best to assume they have things hidden that we've never seen. The sentries are particularly gifted at protecting themselves with full-body shields. Getting around these will prove to be difficult, but if we work as a unit, we should be able to deal with them swiftly."

Someone shouted from the crowd, "What's the plan of attack?"

Abe raised an index finger. "Ah, I was just about to get to that. Based on what I remember from having seen the Citadel and outposts, the best course of action is to start small and work our way inward. We will split our forces up and attack the outposts at the same time. The people who live there will not be harmed unless absolutely necessary.

"After taking out the sentries we will move on. Don't divulge our plans to anyone outside of the Resistance. Even though they don't live as prosperous as those within the Citadel, the citizens in the outposts are still nobles. You never know when one of them will turn on you.

"Moving onto the Citadel, we will sweep through the land,

taking out anyone standing in our way. Before we move out I will delve more precise plans to the leaders of the attack squads as we get closer to the battle. Until then, get as much training in as you can."

He then climbed down and disappeared before anyone could stop him for questions. The crowd of people began talking again, shouting over one another. Some were still confused as to what exactly they were doing, and others were too far back in the crowd to hear everything that was said.

Ryu and Amelia chased after Abe and followed him into a building. Abe flopped down into a chair and put his forehead on the table, breathing deeply.

"You okay?" Ryu asked.

He leaned back in the chair and said, "I'm getting more nervous as it gets closer to us attacking. It's always been the plan to take over the Citadel, but I never thought it would really happen."

Amelia put a hand on the man's shoulder and said, "You're a great leader. You care about your people. You want to keep them from harm's way, and that's why you're nervous. You needn't worry about that. They're all here willingly, and we have some fierce warriors in our ranks."

Ryu chimed in, "You've taken care of the Resistance for years. If anyone can lead us to victory it's you."

Abe smiled and thanked them for the kind words and then they discussed in greater detail the plans they'd contrived.

Ryu asked, "So, what kind of weapons do you think they have that are greater than ours?"

Abe replied, "I know for a fact that they have devices that expel toxins. It will fill your lungs and kill you slowly. Luckily, it can be seen by the human eye, so as long as we don't group together they will have a hard time taking out large numbers of us. Another obstacle we face is the horses which you've already seen. They will likely ride at us on horseback once they're alerted of the attack. The best thing we can do against that is to take the horses out before they can get to us."

"Do we really want to do this? I mean, are we really better than them if we slaughter all the nobles?" Ryu had thought about this early on, just after joining the Resistance. However, Amelia was the one who asked.

Abe nodded, "Not all nobles are bad. Some of them are left in the dark about what lies outside their walls. They've been lied to by Lucian, being kept inside the gates so they wouldn't find out the truth. We must uncover the truth for them, and after that, if they still oppose opening the gates to the rest of the world, then they deserve to die."

They all agreed that they would strike down those who stood in their way, and that their mission was noble. Ryu told them that he would head out to train and see if anyone needed help with sword work.

The members of the Resistance trained hard, swords clanging, arrows swooshing into nearby targets. Ryu got some good work in with one of the people he'd previously met back at the bunker, someone that he'd already trained in the way of the sword. Their blades clashed, sending sparks flying through the air.

The man called Teddy was a good fighter; he was quick and agile, but also big and strong. He put up a good fight against Ryu, but did not become the victor in this duel. Ryu thanked him for the hard sparring match and continued on his way, looking throughout the crowd of people to see if help was needed. He came upon a young boy who couldn't be more than 16 years of age; he was slashing wildly at a target with a double-edged sword.

"Hey, mind if I show you a few tricks?"

The kid regarded him with distrustful eyes and said, "Um, sure."

Ryu introduced himself and found the kid's name to be Jack. He showed Jack some basic techniques that would hopefully prove useful on the battlefield. There would be no point in having someone fighting for them if they were a poor fighter. By the end of their session, Jack had gained some ground and Ryu told him to keep practicing the things he had showed him and he'd prove to be a formidable soldier.

Ryu found a lonely training target that was shaped like a person and began working with his kunai. Normally he wasn't all that privy to working with elements that weren't his sword. He enjoyed feeling like a piece of him was extending out towards his enemies. It allowed him to be dangerous up close, but also ensured he would fight smartly. If he charged an enemy with a long-range weapon he would surely die.

He started at a short distance from the target and began tossing the blade at its chest. The first few throws clanged off the wood and the kunai fell into the dirt, but then he found his rhythm and was able to stick it into the center almost every time. After getting it down he backed up, increasing the throwing distance. He was less accurate but was still able to stick it into the target. After feeling satisfied he started aiming for the head and was less successful at hitting such a small piece of the target.

Amelia then appeared behind him with Storm on her shoulder. "Getting pretty good with that thing I see."

He smiled and said, "Oh you've been watching me, huh?"

"I mean, how could I not?" she teased.

They chuckled and embraced each other with a small peck on the lips which granted feigned disgust from Storm. They laughed at the bird's human-like humor. As they were chuckling to each other Ryu felt more happy than ever. He thought about how much he cared for Amelia and Storm, both the best friends he'd ever had but in different ways. Then he thought about his dad; being back together had always felt like a dream. Now, it was feeling more and more like a reality. He couldn't contain his excitement at the idea of introducing him to Storm and Amelia.

Feeling accomplished for the day, Ryu sauntered off, hand in hand with Amelia, and Storm on his shoulder. They wound their way through the city of tents that was spread out as there wasn't enough room for everyone to stay inside buildings here at the Armory. He felt content and didn't want this feeling to end, but deep down he knew that nothing good ever lasts and soon they'd be at war.

Without warning, Storm leapt from his shoulder and blasted into the sky. Ryu craned his head to see what was happening, but in the dimming light of the sky her black body disappeared quickly. She returned with a small bird that had a piece of torn paper tied to its ankle. Dropping it into Ryu's hands, she said, "I heard the flapping and thought to have myself a snack. But then I noticed it was carrying this paper."

While Ryu held the dead bird, Amelia loosened the string and unfurled the ripped paper. There was writing on it but none of them could decipher what it said. It was a language unknown to them. "I have no clue what this says," Amelia said.

"Me either," Ryu agreed. "It does give me a bad feeling

though. What if it was supposed to be some sort of warning to the Order?"

"That would mean we have another mole in our midst," Storm added.

"Another mole?" The voice made them jump. Turning around, Ryu saw that it was just Abe. He let out a sigh of relief.

"Look," he said, taking the paper from Amelia and handing it to him. "Storm found this bird with a note attached to its leg. What do you think it could mean?"

Abe looked at the writing with furled eyebrows, saying, "I'm not sure. It doesn't look like any language I've ever seen. Everyone in the Citadel speaks the common language as far as I know. I wouldn't worry yourselves about it, but I will take this and investigate further." He tucked the paper into a pocket and left their group with a smile on his face.

Exodus

With hundreds of rebels organized and trained, the moment they'd all yearned for had arrived. With all the extra sword practice Ryu had endured, no one could even come close to besting Ryu. Not even their second best swordsman, Rico, could compete with him. Ryu was leagues above the rest of his peers.

Abe tasked Ryu with being in charge of their elite force, the best warriors who had been hand-picked as Abe walked around to monitor the rebel's skills. For many days they deliberated as to who should be with this elite squad. Ultimately, Abe decided that no one would be better suited than Ryu. When Ryu was asked of his opinion he agreed as long as he was able to be the one to fight Lucian, then he had no problem with it. Apart from Ryu, eight more were selected from the army of rebels. They would have two people wielding the same weapon, so naturally Rico and Ryu were the swordsmen of the group.

Two of them were archers named Orian and Seraph. They were observed shooting targets with precision as they were tossed about in the air. Carrying a belt full of small daggers were Jace and Vespa. The two of them were small and fast, able to conceal themselves easily, and had agile hands. There were two brutes of the bunch; the brothers named Kraven and Thorne were born in the same pod. It was an unlikely phenomenon but not unheard of. Each of them stood well over six feet tall and their weapon of choice was a mighty war hammer. The hammers weighed roughly fifteen pounds each, but the two of them carried their hammer as if it was no heavier than a feather.

The last of the elite force was the explosives experts, Hank and Shane. Ryu thought they were crazy; he watched the two of them almost blow each other up by tossing live incindieries back and forth. They only got rid of the devices a mere second before exploding which sent them flying backward from the force of the blast, but this only made them laugh like mad men. Their skills would come in handy when penetrating the defenses of the Citadel.

Each group was divided in a similar fashion and with a second squad as their support. They broke the groups up this way so that they could be more prepared for anything that came their way. It wouldn't bode well for them to have a team full of archers if the enemy was able to get in close. The same goes for if they had a team made of all blade wielders that happened upon enemy archers.

The plan of attack was fine-tuned, the details ironed out and dispersed throughout the rebel squads. It was imperative that they stay on schedule and attack together even though they would be vastly split up. Each initial attack team were to engage the sentries at the outposts and move through as swiftly as possible. They may have to deal with outliers—the mindless Shade monsters—or any scavengers they ran into along the way.

Support teams were to stay within the line of sight of their assigned attack squad, providing supplies, medical attention, or any help they may need. Small metallic devices with pull pins were assembled by Arms and his dedicated team of weapons crafters. A pull of the pin would emit the color specified on the outside of the container. Green was to be used when all was going well. If given enough time and space between battles, green smoke would be popped to signify that a squad was moving forward. Yellow was to signify that they were running low on supplies and red was for emergencies only. If a team was being overpowered or needed dire medical attention were the acceptable uses of a red grenade.

Abe had each crew leader huddled together and hashed out the details, "As stated before, we will need to move on to each outpost first and then work our way inward through the Citadel. A lot of it belongs to homes of nobles who have no idea what goes on outside the protection of their walls, so I don't expect much resistance from them, but if it happens don't let them stop you.

"We will use these colored, explosive shells to help communicate with one another. Once your team is in position, wait for the sun to reach its apex. That is the moment our attack will be initiated."

"But sir," one man interjected, "how will we see the smoke at such incredible distances away from each other, especially after the fighting has begun?"

"A valid question, my man," Abe said. "Storm will be our eyes in the sky. She will report back to me with anything she deems necessary." Storm snapped her beak in confirmation.

"The elite force," Ryu added as he pulled out a makeshift map and placed it on the ground in front of everyone, "will be the first ones in. Hopefully, we can take on the brunt of their retaliation so that they don't send their best soldiers after the rest of you."

He pointed with his finger to one of the outposts, "Here is the outpost closest to where their most important building is, the Capitol. This is where Lucian lives along with the most corrupt nobles. We intend to make our way directly to the Capitol and strike them down before they have time to react."

Abe added the last bit of the plan, "Once the attack squads have all surrounded the city, support teams will move in and join the fight, considering they haven't already had to."

The group of leaders confirmed that they understood the plan and then scattered to delve out the information to their troops. Ryu went to find Amelia one last time, for the following day, their world would be changed. She was placed on one of the support teams; as much as he hated taking his eyes off her, he knew he'd have to be focused on the task at hand, and having her around him would just throw him off. How could he perform his best if he was worried about her safety? For this same reason, he was glad that Storm agreed to survey the battles from the safety of the sky instead of getting into the conflict.

"I can't believe we're doing this," Amelia said.

The look on her face gave Ryu concern. "It's not too late. We haven't left yet. You and I could just run away together, leave all this behind."

Her eyes snapped to his, searching for if he was being truthful. "You would do that?"

"I would leave the world behind if it made you happy."

She smiled. "I love you."

Ryu returned the smile, "And I love you."

Later that day, several of the attack and support squads left their temporary home and trudged their way toward the outpost to which they were designated. Since each outpost was a fair distance away from each other, some of the teams would have to travel further than others.

Ryu said his farewells to those he knew and bid them good luck on their fights. He begrudgingly said goodbye to Storm as well, for she was traveling with the other groups. This way she would be able to begin relaying information as each group began their attack. She told him not to worry and that they would see each other again soon which helped to ease his worry.

About half of the Resistance remained now, and they continued to prepare for the following day. They planned to move out as daylight broke. Ryu wanted to pack light for this venture because, either way, he wouldn't be returning. Either he would stand over the body of Lucian or he would cease to exist, and he was okay with that notion. He didn't think he'd be able to claim his victory over the evil man if he wasn't also willing to lay down his life for the cause.

The following morning it was time to move out. Attached to Ryu's waist was Sokushi and the kunai that had been given to him. He had a light pack on his back with his water interceptor, some bandages and herbs for the healing salve, and some rations to sustain him for a few days. The kimono felt heavy on his body, yet it was roomy enough to allow adequate mobility.

He knew the trek across the wasteland would take some time and he was prepared for it, but didn't want to wear himself down with unnecessary items.

Their exodus began and soon the groups dispersed across

the land, each one heading in the direction of their assigned outpost. Abe and the rest of his support team traveled with the elite squad so that he'd be able to communicate with everyone more efficiently. Before the elite squad moved out, Ryu noticed that Abe looked less weary, more excited.

He told the crew, "Today is a glorious day, gents. For today we find out what the Order and their nobles are *really* made of. We shall see if they can withstand what we've prepared. Either way, my enemies will fall." The speech left Ryu silent as the others cheered. Abe seemed… off.

Along the way Ryu witnessed a few birds circling over a dead corpse and it made him miss Storm. He wondered what she was up to and if she was okay. *Stop thinking like that,* he chastised himself, *it will do you no good to wonder if she's alive or not.*

Ryu couldn't help but be nervous at the prospect of facing Lucian again. His confidence had been built over the past few months, only to falter now that they were heading into battle. He asked Abe, "Is there anything else you can remember about Lucian? Anything that may help me beat him?"

The rebel leader thought about it, then said, "He is very arrogant. I'd imagine that since he has already defeated you once, the next time he will underestimate your ability. Use that to your advantage and you can win."

"Right," Ryu agreed. "If I can get him to drop his guard, I can get the better of him."

"Honestly, I wouldn't worry too much. I've watched you over the last few weeks. You've grown into a fine swordsman. You need to take into account the physical state you were in on the day he beat you. You'd just fought an enraged Jax and countless others. Your body was exhausted already and then you had to face him. Plus, this time, you'll have me at your side."

"And us." The two giant twins said in unison causing the rest of the group to chuckle.

Ryu hoped they were right. He took a dive into his memories, nostalgia taking over him as he thought back to his earliest remembrances. He could see it clear as day as his father gave him his first sword lesson. The first time he showed him how to kill a wild animal. The day he ventured out on his own and then ran across Storm.

He reminisced on the first time Storm saved him from a scavenger and the first one he ever had to remove from this world. His first kill was the hardest, but it had gotten easier ever sense. He knew that it was necessary to survive, although now he wondered if it only got easier due to the blood lust curse that was thrust upon him. He thought it best not to dwell on something like that right now, but he would keep it in the back of his mind so that he doesn't forget how to overcome it in the heat of the moment.

A Raven's Recollection

Storm floated high above the group of traveling rebels. She agreed to be the communicator for this battle, reluctant to leave Ryu's side. The raven knew it was important that they had a solid way to attack as closely to each other as possible, but she still didn't want to leave him.

She had grown rather fond of the boy over the years. She needed him as much as he needed her. Storm felt the wind rifling through her feathers as she remembered her life before she met Ryu. She hadn't told him everything from her past, declining to talk about certain things for fear that he would pity her, and she did not want to be pitied.

Storm remembered being pulled from the animal birthing pod at the Citadel. Her creator, Marvin, nurtured her until she was a young bird. He added a mutation to the formula, not knowing what it would do, but with time discovered she could speak the language of humans. At first, he thought this was all she could do, but being able to talk as a human also cursed her with having human emotions.

It was very difficult on the bird for a while; she lived for a long time with only the inclinations of a normal raven. Then when the humanity began to spread through her DNA, processing it left her often feeling confused. It took some time for her to learn words and the human emotions she felt went unexpressed.

The aviary and human inside of her constantly battled for reign in her head. Having human emotions tormented her more than anyone could ever know. After seeing that she could speak, Marvin would parade her around, making her out to be a party trick for his friends. He wasn't a powerful man, living on the outskirts of the Citadel, but he thought having a pet like her would make him more popular among the nobles.

Marvin traveled with Storm in a wooden box all the way to the Capitol. She never saw it, but when he presented her to their leader, he reviled the two of them. He called Storm an abomination. Her creator was so distraught that when he made it back to his abode, he tried to end her life. With tears blurring his vision he pulled out a knife and tried to sever her head, but she fought back. The blade merely put a gash across the skin around her eye, leaving a deep scar.

She fled his grasp, the fear, anger, and resentment flooding her mind as the wind lifted her into the sky. She remembered flying for a long time and didn't come down until exhaustion and hunger riddled her body. That day she learned that humans could not be trusted.

Storm was by herself for a long time after that. She found that surviving on her own was more difficult than she originally perceived. Food was often hard to find and water was even more so. Hunting the prey that she came across often left her feeling exhausted, the return of energy from her food was hardly worth the trouble. The bird would often pilfer through human's belongings to find any sort of sustenance. Then she found a companion in that which she distrusted so much.

She approached what looked like a dead person lying on the ground. The thought of eating it made her want to vomit, but to her excitement, he had a bag near him. She hoped that he would have something worth eating in there and as she began rifling through it, the body stirred. *How could I be so dumb?* She thought to herself.

Storm had thought the person would surely kill her and eat her, but as she peered at him she noticed how young he looked. There was something about him, something in the way that he looked at her that made her believe he could be trusted. He had held his hand out to her.

"Come here," his sweet voice beckoned. "I won't hurt you."

In any other situation, she wouldn't have believed the human. Storm recalled hopping into his hand. He stroked the top of her head. He didn't know she could speak, and yet, he introduced himself as Ryu. When she replied, "You can call me Storm," he nearly lost it. She laughed as he fell into the dirt with wide eyes. In the end, he too laughed about it.

Since then the two of them traveled the earth together looking for his father. They'd saved each other many times over and would both probably be dead had she not found him. Storm had gotten so lost in thought that she didn't notice she was being hunted. It wasn't until she heard shouting from below that she broke from her entranced thoughts.

"Look out!" someone yelled, and as she looked around a dark shape entered her vision just above her.

She twisted and pulled her wings in close to her body, diving down and then spreading her wings out again. As her body rolled in the air she noticed there was a slightly larger bird intent on making her a meal. It seemed to be a hawk of some sort. She flew upward, trying to gain altitude on the bird so that she could drop down and attack the top of it.

The hawk was too quick and blocked her path. She tried to double back and go for a different route, but again the bird foiled her plan. It dropped on her again, this time just barely getting its talons caught on her wing. She screeched and flailed, feathers ripping free as the bird lost its grip on her. As the talons cut through her wing she noticed that it wore the same metal talons as herself.

As Storm fell with her back to the ground the hawk quickly tried to grab her again, but this time she was prepared. Had she not also been wearing her armor, the hawk would have most likely gotten the better of her. As the hawk got within range she grabbed its talon with hers and flipped backward, flinging the bird toward the ground. The hawk spiraled out of control and she dove on it.

The raven drove her metallic claws deep into the back of the predator bird and rode it all the way to the ground. They landed a few feet in front of the group of rebels where she hastily tore at the thing's throat with her steel beak. The hawk resisted and squawked in pain for a few seconds before finally becoming silent.

Once the kill was complete she asked the leader to look her over and he obliged, telling her that she had some minor scratches. She did a quick circle and noticed her wing was a bit sore, but not enough to keep her from performing her duties despite a few missing feathers. She resolved to ride on the shoulder of the group leader, allowing her wing to get rest. The bird was aware she needed to perform at her very best when the battle ensued.

Breach

The elite squad was in position and waiting for the sun to reach its peak. Ryu enjoyed the breeze that was blowing through his hair. His father's red headband was tied around his head. With luck, he would be able to give it back to him soon. He had also wrapped strips of white cloth around his hands and wrists for some extra support and stability.

Ryu could see the rocky steps that led up to the front gate which was guarded by a few sentries. He couldn't tell what they were armed with at this distance.

The sun was high in the sky. Ryu looked back to Abe. A thumbs up.

"Move in!" Ryu ordered his elite crew.

They darted away from the support team with Ryu in the middle of their formation. The two hammer-wielding twins were in the back of the formation, being slower than the others it only made sense to put them in the back. As they got closer, Ryu could see the sentries begin to stir. He saw one of them brandish a weapon he didn't recognize. The female sentry put one end of the wooden weapon on her shoulder, holding it with two hands. He heard a sharp snapping noise and a second later an arrow whizzed passed his head. A couple of inches to the left and he would have already been dead. It was a bow of some sort.

"What was that?" he asked.

None of the crew could come up with an answer, however, they continued moving in. Ryu saw the sentry reload the weapon and take aim.

"Scatter!" Ryu shouted so that everyone could hear.

The attack squad began zig-zagging to avoid being struck by the darts being launched at them. The archer fired more arrows, but Ryu noticed that it took longer for her to fire them than it would with a regular bow. Once they were in range, he ordered his archers to fire at will, and as they did so the other two sentries deployed tall shields. Their bodies were completely covered, making the bow and arrows ineffective.

Ryu then ordered the archers to move in and fire if they saw an opening. They pushed on, dodging the arrows that came their way, and finally got close enough for close-range fighting. The shield-bearing sentries stalked down the steps onto level ground and Ryu motioned for the twins to attack.

Kraven and Thorne lumbered past, already breathing laboriously. Despite being tired, they chuckled as they began swinging. Just as their hammers dropped in unison, the sentries tossed their shields at the men and rolled to the side, narrowly escaping a deadly blow. They got to their feet and yanked their swords from their waistband, grasping them with two hands.

Kraven was quicker to the punch; he thrust his hammer into his opponent's face, dropping him with a sickening crunch. The other sentry swung at Thorne who side-stepped, dodging the strike. He swung his hammer low, sweeping the man off his feet and then Kraven jumped in the air with his hammer overhead. He brought it down with all his might, connecting with the sentry's chest as his back touched the ground. He didn't stir.

Before anyone else could move, Ryu heard the twang of the bow-like weapon. An arrow ripped through Thorne's calf muscle. He dropped down to one knee with a howl of pain. Ryu saw his opportunity to react. As the archer was reloading her crossbow he rushed forward. He kicked off of Thorne's massive back, launching himself in the air. He pulled his kunai from its holding place on his belt and flung it at the sentry. It landed dead center in her chest. She clutched at the blade, pulling it free. Blood spurted and she wore a pained expression as she collapsed.

Thorne grimaced as Ryu bent down to check out the damage. It was a flesh wound.

"Can you go on?" he asked the brute.

"It's just a scratch," he said, with a chuckle.

Ryu quickly wrapped bandages around his leg and then Kraven helped heave him upright. Ryu tossed down a green grenade as the support team caught up. He wiped off his kunai and pointed at the foreign weapon, "What is that thing?" he asked Abe.

The leader picked it up and smiled, saying, "This is a crossbow. It fires bolts similar to arrows, as you've noticed, but at a much slower rate. However, the speed of the projectile is much quicker. Never mind that though, move forward!"

Upon reaching the gate, they found that it could only be opened from the inside. Ryu called Shane and Hank to do what they do best. The two were happy to oblige and suggested the others take a few steps back. Once it was clear, they placed some charges that Ryu didn't even want to try to understand. They joined their squadmates and pressed a button on a small switch. Immediately a blast shook the ground.

The gate fell along with the walls around it. They climbed their way through the rubble and started walking through the small town that was the outpost. Ryu didn't think it looked too decrepit. People stared at them, fear displayed in their wide eyes. Men shifted in front of women as the group of armed rebels passed by.

Abe reassured anyone close enough to hear, "Don't worry. We're just passing through to the Citadel. Everything will change soon."

No one had yet attacked them and Ryu figured they were roughly halfway through the outpost when they came into contact with a group of creepers. Their eyes bulged from their sockets. Veins protruded all over their bodies and white drool dribbled from their mouths. The elites were outnumbered but Ryu wasn't worried about the odds and found himself looking forward to the fight as the creatures began screeching.

Storm flew around the battlefield as fast as possible, taking note of each color of smoke she came across. So far she saw no red plumes, however, she did see a couple of yellows. She swooped down to each one to determine what was happening. It was only minor injuries that needed medical attention and by the time the raven had landed each one was being tended to by their support team.

She made her rounds and changed course back to Abe. She was already becoming tired and would soon need to take a break and eat something to replenish her energy. In order to cut down on time, she flew directly over the Citadel. So far she couldn't tell that anyone knew what was happening outside their walls.

Storm had made it across the distance and located Ryu and the rest of the elites walking through the outpost. Abe with the support team trailed not far behind them. She landed swiftly on Abe's shoulder and between staggering breaths said, "The others.. are in.. position."

"Good, good. You're not tired are you?"

Her breathing slowed, "I'd be lying if I said no."

Abe rummaged in his pack to try to find her some food, but she noticed and told him not to worry, she'd just spotted a live snack not far off.

She flew away, more slowly this time, and found the rat she spotted scurrying along the ground a short distance away. The raven dived down and pierced the creature's body, killing it instantly. The rat was devoured heartily.

The group of beasts charged and a flurry of blades met them. The two swordsmen and the small dagger-wielding assassins stabbed and slashed in every combination imaginable. The group of Shade-destroyed humans painted the rocks with their blood and as the elites walked on, more citizens popped up. Some even gave their thanks for ridding their town of the monster's presence and then warned that more exist in the outpost. It took the rest of the day to get through the city and when the sun dipped behind its walls they began looking for shelter.

They found a small building that was seemingly abandoned and waited for the support team to arrive. As they were waiting wails echoed off the buildings and Ryu thought it was incredibly eerie. Luckily, the support squad showed up quickly and they were able to take refuge inside the ramshackle structure.

Abe announced to them, "Let's get some sleep. We'll take turns keeping watch. Tomorrow, we breach the Citadel."

Siege

Just before sunrise the elite squad ventured out with their support not far behind them. They made it the rest of the way through the city without anyone or anything getting in their way and then came to another gate that was, once again, guarded by sentries. It was just two this time and they were fast asleep.

Ryu wouldn't allow his group to attack them in their sleep so he cleared his throat right next to them. They shuffled awake, startled at the sight of these weapon-clad rebels. They grabbed their swords and jumped to their feet. They both swung their swords at Ryu who was standing in between them. He rolled forward at the last possible moment. Their blades narrowly missed him and then sliced each other. Ryu pointed at Rico, signaling for him to finish the sentries off. With a quick swipe of his blade to the left and then to the right, Rico struck the two men down where they died swiftly.

With the two sentries disposed of, they were able to unlock and open the gate. Once it was raised they locked it in place so that it would stay open. On the other side, Ryu could see the blazing sun creeping over the tall walls of the Citadel. Directly in front of them was a tall, stone pathway. On either side was nothing but wasteland.

He peered over the edge and said, "A fall from this height would kill any one of us. Be mindful of where you step."

There were large piles of rock and other debris scattered about the path and it became a hassle to move as a solid unit the further they made it. Ryu glanced behind them and saw the support team had made it through the gate and up onto the bridge.

Ryu made the mistake of allowing a couple of his comrades to get too far ahead of him. They became stagnant in their vigilance and no one saw it coming.

A massive beast of a man sat up from behind a pile of rocks. Once he stood he was easily seven feet tall. His mouth looked like it had been sewn shut and his eyes appeared to be black pits of darkness. A mutant.

His hands had been removed and long serrated blades were attached where the hands should have been. There was a large OWO carved into his fat belly. He moved quicker than a beast of his size should have been able to.

Seraph just so happened to be closest to him and was unable to move. She was frozen in fear as the creature swung his bladed arm at her. It connected with her, sending pink mist into the air. Ryu's breath caught in his throat as she fell to her knees and slumped face down on the path.

He threw down a grenade that burst into a red plume of smoke as he felt the flames of rage ignite his soul and got tunnel vision that focused on the foe ahead. His legs pumped with energy, and adrenaline coursed through him as he sprinted along the stones. He barely noticed that his teammates were retreating, thrown off by the sudden fight. All but Orian who was frozen at the sight of his fellow archer lying in the pool of her blood. He couldn't take his eyes off her and was unaware of the blade headed for his neck.

Ryu came flying through the air; his foot planted on Orian's back, pushing him out of the blade's path. In the last second, he sprang his Sokushi from its sheath and blocked the monster's. The giant kept swinging with a ferocity Ryu had not yet dealt with in an opponent. Each time he blocked a blow it knocked him back. He was inches from dropping over the ledge when Rico came to his aid. He slid behind the monster and sliced the backs of his knees.

The thing groaned and dropped down, giving Ryu time to recover and launch an attack. Now that he was at eye level, Ryu could reach his neck. He swung his sword upward and connected with the man's flesh. For the first time ever, his blade didn't sever a person's head from its shoulders. The beast's neck was too thick for the sword to glide through completely. He yanked it back out and swung again. Three more blows from Sokushi and the mutant's head finally rolled.

Ryu kept slashing at the lifeless body of the beast. The blood lust mingled with the anger of having one of his elites fall victim to this *thing.* It wasn't until he heard Rico yelling his name that he remembered what he needed to do. The blade shook in his hand as he closed his eyes and pictured nothing but Amelia's face. He blotted out all other thoughts and focused on her. After a minute his blood lust had passed and he opened his eyes and took in the carnage around him.

Orian knelt with his hands digging into Seraph's shirt. He rocked back and forth, wailing into the sky. Abe knelt next to him, his hand on the younger man's shoulder. Ryu flicked the blood from Sokushi and put it back in its casing. He walked over to their fallen comrade and knelt beside Orian.

"We have to move on," Abe said, "she would want that."

"Don't claim to know what she'd want!" Orian vociferated.

Abe told him, "Now is not the time for mourning. Do not let her death be in vain. We have to continue. The others can't wait for us. We can mourn our losses when this is all over. Be strong, my friend."

Orian nodded and reluctantly let go of his companion then stood to his feet with wobbly knees. He wiped his face and walked away without so much as a glance back. Ryu heard him say, "I'll make them all pay for this."

Abe ordered Draven—one of the older men in the support team—to take Seraph's place. He was very good with a bow and arrow as well, but not quite as good as she was. The rest of the support squad wrapped her body up in a tan cloth as the elite force moved forward.

The front gate of the Citadel was in view now. Sentries lined the front and were preparing to defend it. Ryu could feel his heartbeat quicken as he thought about how close they were to the real battle. Above the tall iron gates, in large bold letters was the title, ONE WORLD ORDER. The sight caused a shiver to run down Ryu's spine.

The Citadel

To Ryu's surprise, there were no archers that he could see. He spotted six sentries gather up their full-body shields and begin marching toward his squad. There were a few more behind them preparing something that he couldn't see. His group took cover behind a couple of large chunks of rock, trying to come up with a plan to dispose of their enemies quickly.

After some deliberation, Hank interjected with a, "Leave this to me." He hopped up and pulled the tab on one of his many incendiary devices and tossed it toward the shielded sentries. It rolled to a stop close to their feet and they turned in an attempt to flee. They were too slow. A loud pop was heard and a couple of the sentries screamed in pain.

The men who were further away had simply lost parts of their legs. The closer ones were killed on impact. The elite squad ran forward, jumping over the bodies. As they were about 30 feet away from the other sentries, one of them stopped rifling through a bag and tossed a small, glass cylinder. It burst on impact and yellow dust spread through the air in front of them.

As the substance began to make contact with Ryu, he was grabbed by the back of his shirt and yanked away from the airborne powder. "That looks like the toxins we were warned about," Thorne—the one who pulled him to safety—said.

They all backed away slowly. Because of the yellow particles, they were unable to clearly see the sentries, but Ryu could tell that they were shuffling around. He wondered what sort of weapons they were preparing now. When the dust finally settled, the sentries were nowhere to be found.

"Oh no," Ryu said, "they're going to warn the others. We have to stop them!"

With urgency, he held his breath and dashed forward just in case toxins still remained in the air. The others followed and they came upon the tall iron gate. It cost them more explosives this time, but with a little work, they got through it. They clamored over the rubble and what waited for them left Ryu shocked.

Storm continued flying in the circle above the Citadel, checking on each team as she went. She never saw red smoke except for with the elite squad. Diving down to Abe, she learned that they'd lost one of their archers. She decided not to dwell too much on the yellow plumes for the time being. Each squad was progressing as they needed to and as she flew back in the direction of Abe she noticed a few people down below running toward the tallest building. She lowered her altitude and saw sentries coming from the direction of Ryu and his group.

She picked up her speed and finally, the front gate came into view. She passed overhead as explosions shook the metal and rock apart. Abe and the others appeared and she dropped down, not far behind the elites.

Landing on the ground in front of him she said, "Everything is going according to plan thus far. Although, I just spotted some sentries running away from Ryu. I'd bet they're going to alert the nobles."

"Thank you for the report. Your skills are invaluable, Storm."

She clicked her beak and once again took to the skies. As she passed back over the elite squad, she saw a group on the inside of the Citadel wall waiting for them. There was a gaggle of sentries with massive beasts just on the other side of the gate.

They were incredibly ugly; patchy fur covered their bodies and their lower jaws protruded passed the upper. Jagged teeth poked out and drool dribbled from their mouths. The creatures stood on four stubby legs with flat paws. Each of the three beasts stood about six feet tall.

Ryu gawked at them in confused horror, not believing what he was seeing, and also not knowing what he was looking at. A sentry stood behind each one with a confident smile. The man in the middle had scars on his face and lines from a tattoo on his neck. His clothing was different from the other sentries he'd seen and he wore a golden badge on his breast.

He turned to Abe who didn't look as surprised, "What the heck are those?" he asked.

"It's a special breed of animal developed by Lucian's most insane lab technicians. They're born as small blobs of cells and can be put into a machine called a shifter. The creatures can be shifted into all sorts of beasts, but it has never been anything normal. Shifting them into a dog would be too easy, right?"

"Can they be killed?"

"Generally, severing the head is a good way to go. I'm sure that will hold true for these as well. As for the man in the middle, he's the current commander of the sentries, hence the badge on his chest."

"Duly noted." Ryu would make sure to take him out as soon as the beasts were dealt with.

They needed a diversion. Ryu ordered his archers to spread out and begin firing at the sentries while Rico and himself dealt with the mutated animals. The others were to provide backup in case other foes showed up or they became overwhelmed.

The sentries pedaled backward, creating more distance, as the archers began firing away, their arrows zipping by. Ryu and his fellow swordsman launched themselves into an attack on the mutated animals. He was surprised to find they were much slower than he thought they'd be. They disposed of the creatures quickly and with minimal effort. Ryu was almost disappointed at how easy it was, but then he saw something else that piqued his attention.

Coming toward them was a group of sentries atop horses; some carried variations of blades and others had spears. Dust was billowing up behind them as they got closer. Ryu looked over his shoulder and yelled, "Let's get these three now!"

Jace and Vespa ran past them and began fighting one of the sentries together. He struck at them with his sword but they dodged each blow and easily overwhelmed him. Kraven charged at the other sentry who ran screaming at the sight of the giant which left just one. He made eye contact with Ryu and sneered, pulling out a spiked mace.

The man came forward and raised his mace over his head, but before he could swing, Ryu had drawn his blade and cut through the man's wrist. He clutched it, wailing just before his head was also removed from his body.

Ryu was momentarily concerned that Kraven was going to allow his foe to escape. The sentry was much faster, but before he got too far, the hulking rebel hefted his hammer overhead. He flung it with a loud grunt. The hammer flipped end-over-end until it smacked the coward in the back. Kraven was able to catch up and finish the man off.

With the beasts and sentries easily culled, the elite squad began preparing for the horsemen. They'd be upon them within seconds. Ryu glanced around quickly, just now realizing there was a small grouping of dense trees nearby. Ryu would have to admire its surprising lushness later. He ordered his crew to follow and they ran for the forest. Ryu believed this would help to mitigate the advantage of having horses.

When they reached the trees, Ryu began climbing and the others followed suit, picking up on what he was thinking. The horsemen charged in blindly and even though they saw them climb up it didn't matter. As soon as the opportunity presented itself, the squad dropped from their perch, each one taking out an enemy. There were few opponents left who were stabbing at them with spears.

Without the room to move as freely as they would in an open area the horsemen were defeated and the elite squad tried to take their horses. However, they found that riding them wasn't as easy as just sitting there and letting the animal do all the work. Reluctantly, they elected to not use them and trudged on toward the Capitol after popping green smoke.

Ryu looked around him; the lush green and sparkling water of a nearby pond gave him a new motivation to win this war.

Amelia and the rest of the support team she was assigned to moved quickly through the Citadel. The gates they breached led to a large fielded area with crops growing everywhere. Amelia found herself wondering how they were able to grow things from the ground so easily. The attack team ahead of them moved through their gates with relative ease, only one person being injured and another needing a replenishment of arrows.

Small houses were scattered throughout the land which ranged far and wide. The Citadel was much bigger than she anticipated. The ground didn't seem to be ruined as it was in the rest of the world. Plants grew freely and she could see very tall buildings in the distance.

They'd moved pretty far into the walls of the city and hadn't seen any people since entering the gate and defeating the sentries. An eerie feeling came over Amelia, as if their group was being watched. She looked around, scanning the surroundings, but didn't see anything. She looked over her shoulder and that's when she saw it. It was brief, but she could have sworn she saw someone dart behind a tree as she turned.

Amelia turned to one of her squad mates, Archy—who was the oldest person on their team—and said, "Don't look, but someone is following us. What should we do?"

She waited for his wisdom and finally he said, "One of us should swing wide and arc back around, get behind them, and then the others slow down. We'll force them into our hands."

"Good idea," she said and began veering off to the side.

She ducked down in a cluster of bushes, staying as low as possible to the ground. Her squad got further away and she just hoped the follower hadn't seen where she went. A few minutes later a small man appeared. His footsteps were silent on the rocks which unnerved her slightly. He darted in and out from behind cover as he crept along the path.

Amelia followed suit after he got far enough away that she was sure he couldn't hear her. As the time passed she could see the distance between the man and the support squad diminishing. He seemed to notice this and tried to backtrack, but that was when she decided to act.

She popped out from behind a large stone and nocked an arrow, aiming it at his chest. "Who are you and why are you following us?"

He looked shocked to be caught and said, "Please don't shoot me."

His voice threw her off; it was higher than she thought it would be.

"Answer the question."

Her squad had turned and jogged all the way back to them as he said, "Okay, okay. My name is Jekkel. I live in Sector 5. I saw you guys following the other intruders and just wanted to see what was going on. My mom always said I was too curious for my own good."

"Wait, you have a mom?"

He looked at her as if she asked him something silly. "Don't *you* have a mom?"

Amelia lowered her bow and Archy answered for her. "None of us have parents, young man. That's what it means to live outside these walls."

"Oh. That sounds sad."

Archy nodded, "Indeed it is."

"So, are you gunna kill me?"

"No," Amelia said, "but we can't just allow you to run off. You might warn someone about us and we can't have that. You'll just have to come along." She put on her warmest smile.

The boy didn't argue and they all began heading toward the buildings once again. He talked a lot which annoyed some of the other support team members so they put a little distance between themselves and him, but Amelia didn't mind. She learned that he always looked older even though he was only 14 years old.

"The city is split up into different sectors," Jekkel told her. "Sector 5—where I live—is mostly a farming sector. We don't get a whole lot of respect from the other nobles, but I don't mind it too much. Mom says we're nobles but sometimes it doesn't feel like it. I think we may be the least powerful of all the nobles."

"The nobles rank themselves like that?" she asked.

He nodded, "Yep. Where would you all fall on the nobility scale?"

She replied grimly, "We wouldn't." That seemed to shut him up for a bit.

Amelia shared part of their plan with him, feeling that she could trust him, but still not dishing out all the important details. Apparently, he had no idea that there were *actually* people living outside their walls. None of the nobles were allowed to venture outside of them and he recalled hearing stories when he was a small kid of the monsters that crept around in the wastelands.

"Well, there are definitely monsters out there, but people too," she told him.

The buildings became larger as they got closer and it appeared that the attack team was fighting once again. Amelia dialed in her focus on the battle and then saw the red smoke. She looked at the boy and told him what was about to happen and decided to free him. She found that he was fairly open-minded to all the things she told him.

"You can go now. We have to help our friends."

Without checking to see if he left or not she followed the rest of the support team into the battle. She pulled her bow and one arrow off her back as she ran. A couple of the attack squad already lay on the ground with the life gone from them. Amelia didn't have time to stop and check on her fallen comrades. She began firing arrow after arrow.

For the first time since they'd entered the Citadel, Ryu was able to look around at their surroundings and take it all in. It was breathtaking. Grass and trees covered the landscape, things he'd rarely seen. Plants did not grow so liberally in the wastelands of the world outside. They walked with the Capitol building in their sights now.

The Capitol was a tall pristine building, the likes of which Ryu had never seen before. It was made from gray stone-looking material and had many glass windows. He checked behind their crew and could see the support team trailing in the distance.

Ryu couldn't see anyone milling about as he assumed he would. *Where is everyone?*

It was odd that they weren't being met with an onslaught of sentries.

He turned to his crew, "Where do you think everyone is?" Shrugs were the only response he was met with.

They crept closer and Ryu had an eerie feeling come over him. Something wasn't right.

Ryu held up his fist, signaling for the crew to stop movement. He looked around; plumes of smoke rose in the distance. *Maybe all their forces went after a different squad.* That had to be it. There was no other logical explanation he could conjure. The elite squad stalked further into enemy territory. Ryu made sure his head was on a swivel.

He halted their progress again as they were now becoming surrounded by some of the Citadel buildings. He looked around. The support squad was nowhere in sight. That wasn't part of the plan. They were always supposed to be within each others' line of sight. *This can't be happening.*

His intuition kicked in. He ordered his team, "Run. It's a trap!"

Break Free

Kenji was being held on one of the higher floors of the Capitol; Lucian thought it would be humorous to have him watch as the Resistance was ambushed. Two sentries stood watch over him, the tips of their spears gently poking his back. It wasn't enough pressure to bring pain or draw blood, but it was a stern reminder that they could end him with one false move. For an extra measure of security, his hands were tied behind his back. His nose was nearly pressed against the large glass window as he saw a small group approaching the city streets.

Is this it? Has the Resistance been reduced to such meek numbers that this is all they could muster? He looked around and saw plumes of red smoke in the distance. It would seem that they were craftier than he gave them credit for.

His eyes weren't as keen as they once were, but a father would recognize his son anywhere. A gasp cracked his dry lips apart as the face of his boy, Ryu, led the small group of rebels.

No. He's playing right into Lucian's hands. The Supreme Leader knew they were coming. He knew their battle strategy. I must do something!

Kenji stole a peek over his shoulder. The sentries' foreheads were already beaded with sweat. The point of one of the spear tips pressed harder. "You know the rules," the sentry said.

"Gotta watch the whole thing. Supreme Leader says so."

He had to think of a way out of here. "Do you even know what's going to happen once the Resistance is destroyed?"

"Eh? What's that?"

"Lucian is going to dispel the sentry program," Kenji lied. "He told me so. He said he's going to feed you all to the mutants that lay outside the walls."

The other sentry shifted nervously, saying, "Why would he go and do a thing like that?"

Kenji smiled. "Well, it's simple. He won't have any use for you after that. The sentries were created to protect the nobles against the rebels. After Lucian destroys the rebels, he'll have no use for you."

There it is. The slight release of pressure on his back. It was subtle but it was enough. Kenji spun away from the spears and closed the distance between himself and one of the guards. The man launched himself toward the closest. A resounding crunch created by Kenji's head connecting with the man's nose. The guard fell with a scream, clutching his face.

The other sentry thrust his spear at Kenji but he was ready. The man kicked the shaft of the spear with one foot and then planted the other in the sentry's chest. He flew backward. Kenji fell onto a spear and slid the rope binding his hands along the sharp tip until it gave way. He was free.

He finished the two men off quickly. They stood no chance against him now that he knew Ryu was so close. With a glance outside, he saw the group of rebels turn and attempt to flee as a plethora of sentries began pouring out of the buildings, surrounding them swiftly. They had nowhere to run. Kenji flew out of the room and bounded down the stairs.

Snake In The Grass

Storm flew around the Citadel which was now more of a battle arena, taking note of all the yellow and red smoke being popped. She made sure that support teams were responding to the red plumes and continued on. She was making her way back to Abe when she realized something was terribly wrong. Amelia and her group were struggling to gain the upper hand against their adversaries.

The raven dived down as fast as her body would allow; she swooped in on an unsuspecting enemy archer and sliced through her carotid artery with her metallic talons. Storm careened sideways and swooped back up as another man swung at her with a sword. She circled back around, rocketing back at the foes and helping to take them out. Once all the archers were incapacitated she flew back off, trusting that they could handle the rest.

All of the teams were closing in on the Capitol. It was at that moment she realized something was going awry. Ryu and his elite squad were being surrounded. She darted in the direction of where Abe and the support team should be. She had to report this back to him. She hadn't made it far when she found him covered in blood. He was the only one of his support squad left.

Ryu looked around frantically as sentries began flooding the streets. His elite squad went back-to-back in a defensive position. Ryu knew it wouldn't matter. They would be overwhelmed instantly when the enemy decided to attack. He searched the crowd for Lucian's face but didn't see it yet.

"Put your weapons away," he ordered.

Orian retorted, "Are you insane? They'll kill us!"

"Just do it," he said. "We'll die either way. Let's just try to talk our way out of this first."

The squad did as they were told and the atmosphere seemed to relax a little. Ryu looked around at their faces. He got the feeling that most of them didn't want to be doing this either. They all probably had someone they cared about. Dying there would be needless.

A slow calm emitted from somewhere in the crowd. The sea of people began to part and out waltzed Lucian and his entourage. He smiled from ear to ear.

Ryu hadn't yet laid eyes on the nobles who made up the Order. Long blonde hair and blue eyes. Each member of the Order looked eerily similar save for Lucian. They were like the twins in his party but there were ten instead of two. It was impossible to tell if they were male or female. Each of them wore silky white robes and was barefooted. A dagger was brandished in each of their hands. They looked both human and not at the same time.

"Well done, Ryu," Lucian patronized. "Well done, indeed. You've managed to break into my Citadel and make it all the way here. Too bad it was all for nothing. We've been expecting your arrival."

"How did you know?" Ryu demanded.

"Be more specific, dear"

Ryu sighed, annoyed. "How did you know we'd be attacking today? Jax didn't know, he wouldn't have been able to clue you in."

Lucian threw his head back and laughed. The soft swoosh of something flying through the air cut through the Supreme Leader's laughter. A spear soared over the crowd and then landed right between Lucian's feet. Gasps and murmurs scattered throughout the crowd as they began to part again.

Ryu dropped to his knees with tears in his eyes. The man standing before him was the one he never thought he was going to see again. He looked mostly as Ryu remembered, if not slightly thinner. "Father?"

"Hello, son," Kenji replied. He had a sword of his own strapped to his waist. He walked over and pulled Ryu to his feet. They hugged each other tightly as tears silently slid down Ryu's cheeks.

He couldn't believe it. Was it a dream? Was this some sort of trickery put on by the nobles? His father was alive and standing there with his arms wrapped around him. Not only alive, but healthy.

When they broke apart, the nobles adorned in white had surrounded them and were closing in with daggers poised to kill in synchronized movements. "Together again only to die so soon," Lucian jeered.

Ryu smirked and looked at his father. Kenji smiled and said, "I've been waiting to end these fools for a lifetime."

The nobles and everyone who bore witness found that they were not all that fierce in battle. The slaughter was quick. They stood no chance against his elites. Ryu was happy to find the cocky smirk wiped from Lucian's face. With a snap of the leader's fingers, sentries began dragging the fallen Order members away from the crowd. The smirk returned to the wicked man's visage.

"Well done, Ryu," a familiar voice from behind him called out. He turned.

"Abe?" Ryu asked. The man looked insane. He was covered from head to toe in blood. The scarlet liquid dribbled down his face and dripped from his fingertips. The most disturbing image of all was the smile displayed on his face.

"Abe, what has happened?" Kenji asked with great concern in his voice, but Abe didn't answer. He walked past them over to Lucian's side.

"You?" Ryu asked. "How could you do this?" The hurt in his voice was unmistakable.

Abe was the mole in their ranks. Their leader had betrayed them all. He didn't see any of the others from the support team around. The thing Ryu couldn't figure out though was why he'd do such a thing. Why would he lead the Resistance for so long, only to betray them in the end?

Lucian seemed unable to contain his laughter. When Abe made it over to the group Lucian ordered for him to be cleaned and clothed. Immediately, two elder women burst from the crowd and began washing the blood off of him. They removed the dagger attachment from his arm and stripped him naked. The women put fresh clothes on him which included an ensemble of gray pants and shirt. They placed a pair of shiny black boots on his feet. His appearance had shifted so quickly and he now looked immaculate.

He turned back to the group of rebels, "I know you all have a lot of questions." He let that simmer for a moment before continuing, "I will give you all answers in due time, but first lay down your weapons."

"Not a chance," Kenji had stepped forward, his hand trembling on the hilt of his sword. Ryu followed suit. "How could you betray your people like this?"

Abe snapped, rage and venom spewed from his words, "Me, betray you? No! You betrayed me! Or do you not remember?" He walked back and forth in front of them, pacing with fury. "Let me refresh your memory then. I was one of the first to help build everything around us. I am the one who kept humanity from going extinct for so long. And then, I went undercover to see how our sentries were coming along. I played at this for years—long before you came around—allowing you to be appointed Commander of the sentries. Time is but a fickle thing for someone like me. I saw your traitorous virtues early on. I was supposed to be your friend, and yet you couldn't even tell me about your relationship with Sari. I had to find out from someone else. Even when I told you of my feelings for her, you pretended like nothing was happening between you two."

"That's why you're doing this?" Kenji asked. "Because of a woman?"

"Of course not, you fool! Shortly after I found out how chummy the two of you were, you came to me with this plan to start the Resistance. I was able to keep my identity hidden for a thousand years, and then you came along with this endeavor to ruin everything I'd worked for! I told my baby brother here about everything. I wanted to let you amass a large following and then eradicate the lot of you."

Lucian chuckled, "Oh, my brother and his theatrics. I thought it was a bit much, but now that you are all here, I must admit, this is delightful."

Ryu stepped forward, he could feel his body shaking with

blood lust. Through gritted teeth, he asked, "What would be the point of that? It doesn't make any sense. Why even let the Resistance be formed when you could have stopped its progression from the beginning?"

Abe's eyes narrowed on Ryu. "All to send a message, really."

"A message?"

"A message that would prevent anyone from trying something so foolish ever again. We nobles are the commanders of humanity. There is no room for disobedience. Now that you've killed the rest of our Order, my brother and I will usher in a new age. We will write history to show the world that we will not be trifled with." He looked to Kenji. "And then you had to go and disappear. All to raise this brat of yours," he said, pointing at Ryu.

"Watch your mouth about my son."

"I could have just killed you while Lucian had you in captivity, but no, we knew you had a pod to yourself and did the math. We had to wait to get you both, to put an end to you and your filthy bloodline. And now, we have you. Once the two of you are dead we'll sweep the rest of the Citadel and put down your sniveling comrades like the dogs they are. Word will spread throughout the world of how you built a mighty army and were still unable to defeat the Order."

As if on command, the remaining forces of the Resistance sprang forth from around the buildings. They were still outnumbered, but with the sentries having enemies on both sides, they would find it far more difficult to claim victory.

Ryu smiled and yelled for all to hear, "Sentries of the Citadel, if you wish to live past this day, lay down your weapons and flee!" Few of them complied. A wicked grin was on Abe's face.

He held his injured wrist out to his brother, saying, "It's

funny how we only allow people to see what they want." Lucian pulled a large needle out from behind his back and jammed it into the man's skin. A thick black liquid was pumped into his body. He grunted and within a few seconds, a new hand had appeared out of the nub as if nothing had ever happened to him. Abe laughed.

"All this time," Kenji began, "you could have healed yourself. Why wait?"

He shrugged, "It endeared everyone to me. I couldn't *possibly* be considered a traitor or a threat if I was stunted in such a way. It made the acting much easier."

"You're sick," Ryu said. Then he addressed the sentries again, "How can you all follow these men? Can't you see how wicked they are?"

Lucian retorted, "Of course they see how wicked we are, however, they know who is going to win this war. They choose the winning side!"

"I'm done with this," Ryu said. He'd had enough. The betrayal was almost too much to take. The battle needed to end now.

Bloodshed

"Attack!" Ryu yelled as he launched himself at the leaders of the Order. Ending Lucian had been his goal the entire time, but now he wanted Abe. He didn't even want to picture what the bastard did to the rest of his support team.

I hope Amelia is okay.

Through all the trials they suffered to get here like gathering forces in the bunker just to have half of them squashed like insects. Every step of the way was part of some master plan created by Abe. The traitor allowed them to grow just big enough that they'd be confident in the plan to raze the Citadel. He wanted to lead them to slaughter in front of all the nobles. A parade of death.

Ryu refused to go down easily. As he charged toward Abe, the man disappeared into a sea of bodies. It was all Ryu could do to protect himself. Sokushi was becoming more and more soaked in blood. The young man claimed every life presented to him.

Ryu found his father and stood back-to-back with him. "You okay?" he shouted over the clang of weapons and cries of pain. The rebels on the outside were steadily working their way through the crowd. Those in the middle just needed to survive long enough.

"I'm good! You?" Kenji replied.

"We have to get out of this circle!" They fought together as father and son. They were moving in a dance of their blades, striking down the sentries that worked to end their lives.

Ryu glanced around and saw the giant twins swinging their hammers. Screams and the scent of blood filled the air with each blow they dealt. Orian and Seraph were both dead already. In his glance around, Ryu didn't see Amelia's face anywhere. A knot was growing in the pit of his stomach.

After losing a third of their men, the sentries began laying down their weapons. They were falling to their knees in surrender. Everyone was breathing heavily. Ryu searched the faces, panic rising as he couldn't find her. Then he did. Even covered in sweat and dirt, Amelia looked beautiful. He smiled at her.

A roar and a crunch of bones alerted Ryu to Craven smashing a sentry's head in. He rushed over and placed a hand on his shoulder. "Stand down!" he ordered.

Craven spun on him, his eyes were large and crazed. "Calm yourself," Ryu said. "They've laid down their weapons. If we continue to slay them, then we are no better than they are." With a few deep breaths, the giant appeared to relax a bit.

Kenji grabbed him by the shoulder, "We must find the brothers! This will not end until they are dead."

"Agreed," Ryu replied.

The doors to the Capitol opened and the two brothers walked out with another in tow. The man looked starved and emaciated. Abe had a golden spear in his hand and Lucian was armed with the same thin sword as before. The third man had nothing.

"We'd like you to witness firsthand the power of the Order,"

Abe said. Then he plunged a needle into the man's neck. "Jax, kill."

Kenji shook his head solemnly. Ryu asked, "What did they just do?"

"They've turned your old friend into something less than human. The merciful thing to do is to end him."

"Poor Jax," Ryu said as he took a defensive stance.

Jax's body began to seize and shake aggressively. He bent over as his bones began to break and contort. His limbs stretched to impossible lengths and his jaws elongated. His teeth became like that of a wolf and he charged at Ryu on all fours. In a flash, Kenji had darted around Ryu and met the beast halfway. Ryu was awestruck watching his father use the sword. It erupted from the sheath and passed cleanly through the neck of the creature.

"What a waste," he heard Lucian mumble.

"Feel like surrendering yet?" Ryu asked them. The remaining rebels began closing in around them. "See, you've underestimated us. We all have been fighting to survive our entire lives. Your sentries are still green in the art of killing. I would have thought Abe would know that, now that I know he's a traitor."

Abe held up a hand. He seethed, "Be that as it may, I have a challenge for you."

"Go on," Ryu said.

Kenji shook his head. "Whatever it is, don't listen to him."

"A duel between you and I. The winner takes control over the Citadel and, effectively, mankind as we know it. I planned to have cleared you all out by now, but it would seem my sentries have gotten soft in my extended absence." He leered at Lucian who seemed to cower from his gaze.

"I'll do you one better," Ryu replied. "I'll take on the both of you. Neither of you deserves to live after everything you've done."

Kenji grabbed him by his arms, "Ryu, no. You can't do this. It's suicide."

Ryu smiled at his father. The last time he smiled at him, he had to crane his neck upward to meet his gaze. "Don't worry about me. I've got this."

"You're sure?"

He nodded, "I'm sure."

Kenji stepped aside. Abe and Lucian said together with sly grins, "We accept."

Fallen Hero

Ryu slipped the pack from his shoulders as the sentries and rebels cleared out. They formed a wide circle around the three of them. "I'll be right over there," Kenji reassured the young man. Ryu gave a nod of thanks.

Storm flew down and landed on his shoulder and nipped at his ear. "Father, this is Storm."

"Hello, there," Kenji said.

"I've heard a lot about you," Storm replied. Kenji jumped back in shock, eliciting a chuckle from Ryu and the raven.

Kenji smiled, recovering his wits. "I wish to hear what he's told you when all this is over," Kenji told the bird.

"I look forward to that," she replied. Then to Ryu, "This is foolish. You know that, right?"

"Just go with my father. I can do this." The raven hopped over to Kenji's shoulder and they retreated into the crowd.

Ryu closed his eyes and took a few calming breaths. He could hear his heart slamming against his ribs. He gripped Sokushi tightly and approached the brothers who were waiting on him with maniacal looks in their eyes. They began to circle him.

"Did you bid them farewell?" Abe asked snidely. Ryu let the taunt roll past him.

Good. Let them think they have the upper hand here.

Attacking simultaneously, Abe lunged with the tip of his spear heading toward Ryu's chest. Lucian slashed with his blade. Ryu expected such an attack and was able to anticipate it. With his sword, he blocked the strike from Lucian and with his other hand, he caught the golden shaft of the spear before the tip could penetrate his skin.

He yanked on it but Abe did not budge. Ryu never considered him to be a physically strong man, but he was being proved wrong now. Abe pulled on the spear himself, knocking Ryu off balance. He fell to the ground.

Lucian jumped into the air and brought the tip of his sword down. It was poised to pierce Ryu's eye but he moved his head just enough. The tip of the blade made a shallow gash in his cheek. Lucian made the mistake of getting too close. Ryu entangled the man's legs with his own and was able to trip him. Ryu scrambled to his feet as another attack from Abe ensued.

With Lucian on the ground, Ryu knocked the spear aside with his sword, and with a quick slash, severed the tip from the shaft. A back kick to Lucian's nose kept him from getting to his feet as he tried to recover. Ryu could hear his comrades cheering for him now. It was a distraction.

The broken wood of the spear was rammed into Ryu's gut. He didn't know for sure, but the searing pain was enough to make Ryu believe it broke through his skin. With a grunt, he knocked it aside. Abe let it fall, lunged at him, and tackled him to the ground. Lucian was back on his feet. This was not a good position to be in. Abe fought to get his hands around Ryu's neck.

Ryu bucked his hips as hard as he could and pushed against Abe's chest with all his strength. The man tumbled off of him.

Lucian attacked with a ferocious flurry of slashes from his sword, leaving lacerations all across Ryu's arms as he tried to block. Sokushi lay a few feet away.

"You know you can't win," Abe goaded. "Tell you what. Give up now. Get on your knees, beg for mercy, and we'll make it quick."

"How about a counteroffer," Ryu replied. "You shove it."

The two men growled and charged Ryu. He dove for his sword. Abe was now unarmed and jumped back, leaving just Lucian. The two of them engaged in a clash of metal. Neither of them had the upper hand until Lucian made the mistake of allowing Ryu to get too close to him. Ryu grabbed the man's weapon side wrist with one hand. An arm snaked under the young man's chin. Abe was on his back choking him but Ryu had to take the chance.

With maximum effort, Ryu sliced upward, taking off Lucian's sword hand. The man screamed in agony. Ryu dropped Sokushi and clawed at the arm that was choking him. Shadows were creeping into his vision. Abe had his legs wrapped around him now. A mistake. That was the secret to defeating a strong opponent. Wait for the mistakes and capitalize.

Ryu grabbed Abe's thighs and flung himself backward with all his might. Black spots dotted his vision as they slammed into the ground. He felt the air blast out of Abe's lungs. Ryu rolled off of him and shook the dizziness from his head as he retrieved his sword. Lucian was dragging himself through the dirt with his good hand.

I don't think so.

Ryu retrieved the needle-like blade belonging to Lucian and plunged it through his calf, nailing him to the ground. The wailing that ensued was a welcome sound. He left him there and went to deal with Abe. His lungs burned and his limbs were like stone.

"I do not know how you became so evil," he told Abe as the man heaved deep breaths. He was getting his feet back under him. "But you no longer deserve to live." Wasting no more time, he plunged his sword into Abe's chest and didn't stop until he rested against the hilt. "The world is better without you in it."

Ryu stared into his old leader's eyes and watched the light fade. His body slumped to the ground. Ryu let out a sigh of relief. It wasn't completely over yet but he'd won. He only needed to deal with Lucian. The cheers from his comrades had disappeared and everyone looked on in awe of what they'd just witnessed.

As Ryu turned to finish the other leader of the Order, the sound of a bolt being fired from a crossbow filled his ears. He saw a flash of black to his right as something soared by his head. He caught sight of Amelia dashing toward the sentry who took a shot at him as he waited for the impact that didn't come. He didn't want to believe it, but only one thing could have saved him. He turned his head to find Storm lying in the dirt with a bolt protruding from her minuscule body.

No, no, no.

Ryu let loose the most desperate, blood-curdling scream as he dove for the raven.

Storm knew what her actions would incur. She didn't know it before now, but death no longer scared her. There were more important things to life than just surviving. The feeling of not having a purpose in life plagued her for a long time, thanks to her curse of gaining the full scope of human emotions.

The raven's purpose was clear now; she was destined to be more than just another bird on this war-torn Earth. More than just a madman's science experiment gone awry. Her fate was to be Ryu's protector. She thought it funny to consider herself as a guardian of a human when she was such a small creature.

The pain was immediate and excruciating. The raven could hardly breathe after the bolt penetrated her body. She knew it would be temporary; soon, her troubles and burdens would be no more. Storm had joined Ryu all those years ago to aid him in finding his father. They succeeded. It was time to move on.

He didn't know what was happening around him. His ears seemed to be ringing as he dove to Storm's side. She lay in the street with an arrow sticking through her. He gently put his hands on her and could feel that she was still breathing and conscious. His lips and hands trembled. The bird's chest was rising and falling rapidly, but slowing down.

"No, you don't die on me now. Not after all this!"

"You.. did well.. little one." she sputtered between gasps.

"I won't let this happen. I have to save you!"

"Let me.. go. It's finally.. my time. Thank you.. for giving me.. a purpose."

Her breathing slowed to a full stop and Ryu screamed into the sky. Tears rolled down his face with a force he had never experienced. He felt as if his heart had been ripped from his chest. He broke the bolt's point off and removed the shaft from his companion's lifeless body, soaking his fingers with her blood as he pulled her body in tight.

There was a hole in his chest now that he wasn't sure would ever be mended. His bond with the raven was unlike any he'd ever formed and had he known it would be ripped away from him so soon, perhaps he would have made some different choices. Hatred filled his soul for the people of the Citadel.

The sound of a body stirring in the dirt and a clicking noise startled Ryu from his emotional torment. What now? He looked at Lucian; the man had blood trickling down his chin as he sat up, pointing a wicked-looking device at him. The sword now removed from his leg. Smiling with reddened teeth, he chastised, "Crying so abundantly over a *bird*? Now I've seen it all. If I am to die today, then I'll just have to take you with me."

Ryu couldn't form a response, only breathing heavily with the lifeless raven in his arms. Kenji crept around to get behind the man. He continued, "The firearm. One of man's most devastating inventions. I never got to use it. I figure I may as well see how well it kills before I leave this God-forsaken world." Lucian coughed again.

A memory flashed in Ryu's mind at the term 'firearm'. He remembered his father's journal saying something about it being a particularly deadly weapon. Ryu laid Storm down gently and rose to his feet. He growled as he stalked forward without his sword. He didn't care about anything else. Didn't care about knowing what a firearm was or what it could do. All his mind was focused on was ripping the man before him apart with his bare hands. The tip of the weapon followed Ryu as he moved. Kenji's sword rippled through the air toward Lucian's neck. A loud bang emitted from it as a small flash of yellow light appeared and vanished within the same breath.

Pain struck Ryu in his ribs, halting his movement. Lucian smiled as his head was separated from his body. Ryu looked down, pressed his fingers to the spot that ached, and pulled them away to find they were slick with blood. He wasn't sure if it was the pain that dragged him into unconsciousness or if he was dying. He hoped for the latter. He and Storm would be reunited in the afterlife if there was one and that was comforting to him. As he faded, Amelia and his father's faces were the last things he saw before black encompassed him.

Near Death

It all happened so fast. The relief that flooded Amelia's body as Ryu began winning the skirmish was immediately replaced with dread. She had noticed the crossbow being aimed at Ryu too late. Her feet didn't allow her to reach the assailant in time and she was able to get a shot off. Storm came out of nowhere, saving Ryu from certain death.

She reached the female just after the arrow was loosed and dropped her with a punch. Her head whipped around and she spun as she fell.

Amelia turned slowly, panic filling her as she heard Ryu scream. Her feelings contradicted themselves. The arrow was intended for Ryu, but instead, he was holding Storm in his hands. She was relieved that it wasn't him, but felt guilty for that almost immediately.

Her body froze as Lucian slowly sat up, seemingly rising from the dead. No one had checked for a pulse. There was no time. It was a careless mistake. She watched as the firearm exploded, causing her ears to ring and then Ryu fell to the dirt. Ryu's father beheaded the man. She flocked to Ryu's side as he slipped away.

His eyes were rolling into his head as she dove into the dirt next to him. Kenji was there too. They tried to shake him awake but it was futile. She grabbed his wrist, his pulse was beating faintly. "What do we do?" she yelled to Kenji. He didn't answer. His eyes were wide in fear, or shock, maybe both.

A woman stood next to them. "Let's get him to the infirmary!" she ordered.

Kenji pulled Ryu's limp body from the dirt and followed the woman. Amelia retrieved Storm from where she lay. "Everyone stay put!" the woman yelled to the others around. It was obvious she held some sort of respected position among the nobility. Amelia was worried that they would all start brawling again if left alone for too long without a leader.

They ran to a small building down the street and into its doors. There were white beds all around and the woman began frantically cleaning her hands before putting on a pair of elastic gloves.

"Lay him here," she pointed at a table. Kenji did as she said and the woman began strapping wires to him, injecting him with needles. Amelia felt helpless. All she could do was hold the raven and cry. She sobbed and Kenji put his arm around her shoulders. She could see where Ryu got his kindness from.

"Is there anything we can do to help?" he asked.

"Not unless you are trained to remove shrapnel from someone's body," she answered as she rolled Ryu over to expose his back. "See? No exit wound. Which means it's still in his body."

"What is?" Amelia asked between sobs.

"Whatever came out of that weapon."

There were shallow scrapes on his stomach from the broken spear shaft that Lucian had tried to impale into him.

She pulled out a series of medical instruments. An incision

was made across the hole in Ryu's ribs. The woman spread it open slightly, peering into it with a light. She inserted a metal instrument with grooves meant for gripping wet objects and pulled free a small mass of metal. Blood seeped out liberally.

She eyed it curiously in the light. "Appears to be fully intact, that's good. That means there shouldn't be any small chunks floating around in there. Looks like it broke a rib, but that seems to be the extent of the damage. He will most likely be sore for a few weeks; he'll need to take it easy, but he'll be fine."

Kenji and Amelia both sighed loudly. "I'll stay with him," Amelia told him. "You should go make sure no one else is killing each other. We're all going to need a leader."

He smiled sadly and said, "I don't know that I'm the man for that job."

"Kenji," the woman interrupted, "you're the perfect fit for a leadership position and we both know it. Your boy will be okay; get out there." He nodded and left the room.

The woman was closing the wound in Ryu's ribs with some form of threading. Amelia watched with intense curiosity. She'd never seen such practices before, but the lady looked like she knew what she was doing. "What's your name?"

She didn't look away from Ryu as she answered, "Mae. Yours?"

"Amelia," she responded.

"That's pretty. Quite the predicament we all got ourselves in here, huh?"

Amelia chuckled, "To say the least. I'm not sure where we go from here."

"Well, that's the good thing about not being in a responsible party for people," she said. Amelia looked at her questioningly. "You don't have to make the difficult decisions. Just keep your head down and do as they say. That's how I've survived anyway."

Amelia's face was a welcome relief when Ryu's eyelids fluttered open. She was smiling at him but he could see the sadness that filled her eyes. He didn't feel like returning a smile of his own at the moment. He tried sitting up but a pair of hands held him down. Another woman told him, "Take it easy. You've narrowly dodged death today." He sat up as slowly as he could, wincing from the pain. It hurt to breathe.

"You have a broken rib and some minor tissue damage," the woman said. "It's going to bruise and will be sore for a while. Take things slowly. No sword fighting for a bit, okay?"

He nodded. "Who are you?" he rasped.

"My name is Mae. I'm a scientist of sorts. A pleasure to officially make your acquaintance." Ryu shook her outstretched hand before heading outside with Amelia.

Ryu took his dead friend from Amelia's arms and allowed her to hug him tightly despite the pain it caused. He was thankful for the embrace. Tears threatened to spill over his bottom eyelid.

A loud ruckus was breaking out among the people gathered around the courtyard where the two previous leaders of society lay dead. Sentries were becoming restless, their loyalty to the nobles of the Citadel proving true. It was a virtue that did not die easily. Ryu heard his father trying to shout them down. Weapons were being brandished. Ryu could do nothing but watch. Even if his body would allow him to move enough to get into a fight right then, the ache in his heart would not motivate him to get involved.

Eventually, Kenji was able to calm everyone down, sending

the remainder of the Resistance away to cool off. "These next few months will be hard," his father shouted. "But if we can agree to get along, I promise, in the end, it will be worth it."

"You have no authority over us, slave" someone shouted. Many in the crowd of sentries echoed in agreement.

"Have we all not been slaves under the rule of these criminals?" he shouted. None answered and he continued, "I understand this is hard, but please bear with me. I used to be the commander of the sentry program. I do not intend to take over and rule over all of you as your previous leaders did. I see a vision of a more prosperous society with free men and women. I implore you to go back to your homes for now." The group dispersed with fewer complaints than Ryu would have thought.

Kenji walked over and hugged Ryu gently. He pulled away and just looked at him.

He put his hand on Ryu's shoulder. "I'm truly sorry for the loss of your friend, son. From the brief introduction she gave me, Storm seemed to be an amazing creature. I look forward to hearing all about your adventures together when you're ready. I'm proud of you, I want you to know that. You are the embodiment of the Samurai I told you about all those years ago. I couldn't be happier with the man you've become."

A knot choked Ryu as his father's words moved his emotions. "Thank you," was all he could croak out. An awkward silence filled the air as Ryu, Kenji, and Amelia all looked from one to the other.

Finally, Amelia broke the silence, "My name is Amelia."

"Kenji." They shook hands.

Ryu shook his head slightly, and said, "Sorry. I guess I'm still a bit out of it."

"You have nothing to apologize for," Amelia reassured him. "You fought bravely today. You've been through a lot and now it's time for some rest."

"But we still have so much more work to do," Ryu argued.

"She's right, son. Let me take things from here. You've done well."

Ryu nodded and hugged his father again. Kenji said, "Well, we better gather the troops. This is going to be a long road to recovery for mankind."

Humanity's Redemption

A few weeks had passed since the fall of the leaders of the One World Order. All who remained within the walls and anyone else surrounding the Citadel who wanted to join had been gathered. They crowded together in the courtyard directly in front of the Capitol building. Kenji climbed atop a shorter building so that everyone could see him more easily as he addressed them. He could have ruled over everyone if he wanted to, but what would the point of all this be if he were to do that? He declared that he would not be replacing the fallen tyrants, but instead would put together a group of people to make decisions on behalf of humanity.

Along with himself, Kenji gathered Ryu, Amelia, and a few others who were happy to represent the nobles. Ryu suggested Mae be added to this group of authority and she was willing to step in. She was very helpful in showing the rebels how things had been for a long time. The rebels had their minds blown more than once by the advancements in technology they had in the Citadel.

Mae told them that she remembered when Abe was around as a leader. He was more in the background of the operations whereas Lucian was the mouthier of the two brothers. The elderly woman claimed to have no idea where Abe had gone off to or the ruse he was planning. She gave them a tour of the Capitol building, showing how the two managed to stay alive for so long.

"And in this room over here," she said, "is where the brothers would strip unborn children from their pods before it was time. Using a special extraction tool, they'd suck out the fetus's spinal fluid and mix it with a chemical called Xenoflex. Then they would inject it into their own spines. This is why they seemed to never age. It's also incredible for healing injuries, however, they had strict rules that no one was to utilize it besides them."

"Destroy it," Ryu told her definitively.

"I'm sorry, what?" Mae responded.

"I want it all gone. No one should have the power to be immortal. Are there any objections?" Ryu looked around at his cohorts but they all just shook their heads. Those who were previously known as nobles were more reluctant to agree. From the moment the group was formed, everyone would be known as citizens. They didn't want anyone to feel they were more or less important based on previous titles.

In the end, they agreed that it would be best to destroy it all and find another purpose for that room. After that, Mae showed them the Shade lab and once again they agreed to destroy it. Mae and the others didn't argue with that proposal, agreeing that the drug was the biggest flaw in their society at this point.

"I never understood why they wanted to pedal this out to people," Barlow—a particularly burly, bearded man—said. "Of course, telling them that would get you a one-way trip to an eternal dirt nap."

They had a surplus of solar panels to keep everything going.

There was plenty of energy to go around and they had people who specialized in building and repairing the panels. With the combination of nearly endless sun and the panels, they had all the energy they needed to keep everything running.

Mae showed great delight to find that the gates would remain open for anyone who happened to travel upon the great walls. Already more homes were being constructed to support the influx of people from the outside.

"I often considered leaving the Citadel," Mae told them, "but the safety of being behind these walls kept me here. I wouldn't have fared well in the wasteland."

Some of the people previously known as nobles were not supportive of all the new changes and didn't want to leave the gates open. They were fearful of what could come in and attack them just as the Resistance had done. Kenji told them that the new leaders of society would not force anyone to stay within the walls. They would also make sure that guards remained at each gate, but in order to be fair, everyone would have to pitch in. This wouldn't be the humanity that thought others were beneath them, but rather a humanity that sought kindness and fairness for all.

Kenji's experience as commander of the sentry program gave him a little more trust from the group. They were apprehensive at first, but soon enough, even the most hardened sentries eased up. The sentries were led to believe that those they protected, the nobles, were far superior to those lying outside the walls.

The sentries who came from beyond the walls were treated poorly even by their sentry comrades. They were convinced that those humans were nothing more than monsters to be struck down on sight. That way of thinking was unacceptable for this new age of humanity.

"I know it will take some time," he told the group, "but this is the way things need to be. Everyone pitches in if they are able. No single person is more important than the next. I truly believe this will bring us to a more peaceful and prosperous society, but if any of you has a better idea, I will gladly hear it." None did.

Some of the people who were loyal to the old government abandoned the Citadel, but most of them remained. Ryu thought how large of a mistake they were making. Those people didn't know the nightmares that lay outside these walls, and after living in the Citadel for their whole lives he knew they wouldn't last long. They'd either return within a week or perish in the wastelands.

The rest of the Resistance had made it to the Citadel and were getting settled into their new homes.

The sentry organization was dispelled; the need for them was no more with Kenji's new plans to have all of the citizens man the gates on a fair rotation. He believed it was the people's civic duty to protect their homes. However, the group of leaders agreed to put a few people in charge of making the schedule so that things didn't get too confusing.

With every statute that was put into place, the group of leaders took a vote on the issue. Majority rule took place so that there wasn't one person making all the decisions for everyone. Kenji had a lot of changes he wanted to make and many of them were brought to fruition, but not all.

The leaders agreed to have anything reminiscent of the One World Order removed, as long as it didn't degrade whatever structure was in question. The gates were to be rebuilt, but remain open, just in case there was a bigger threat looming outside the walls that no one yet knew of.

Everyone that was old enough and fit to work was given a job. There was a lot to do around the Citadel, whether it was working the human pods, tending to the fields of crops, or managing the growth of livestock. It was a large machine with many moving gears, but with teamwork and a strong work ethic, they would once again flourish.

In order to give Storm the proper death ritual, Ryu held a small procession for her where her life was celebrated. It was an intimate affair; he figured the nobles wouldn't have understood his connection to the raven. They would have thought her just a bird. Of course, he and those close to them knew she was more than that. Kenji was so busy with implementing the changes that Ryu had not been able to sit down and chat with him much.

Storm was an ally, not just to Ryu but to the Resistance, in their war against the tyrannical government. She was an intelligent creature with a greater mind than most humans. She was a listening ear to anyone who needed it, and most importantly, she was Ryu's greatest friend in this life. Nothing could ever change that.

Silent tears slipped down his face as he said, "Storm paid the ultimate price for me so that I may live. She sacrificed herself and I will never forget that. Because of her, this new age of humanity was born. We all owe a debt to her."

He placed her in a small wooden box among a bed made of the shredded clothes that he wore in his last battle. Those in attendance offered up some words of gratitude for her as she was laid in her final resting place. At the conclusion of the ceremony, Ryu lit the box on fire, incinerating Storm's body to ashes. He buried them beneath the Earth, putting a large stone with the inscription carved into it reading "Here lies Storm, the Raven." The metal claws and armor she wore were placed atop the gravestone.

Ryu knew that Storm wouldn't want him to dwell on her death, and so he moved on from it. However, he would never let it slip from his memory. She would have wanted him to find a way to be happy despite how difficult it would be. He wanted to be productive here and also wanted to keep his mind busy for a while.

After discussing with Amelia, they decided to live together. He began building a home for them with other's help and soon a small wooden house was erected. They built it in an empty field that lay a couple of miles from the Capitol, surrounded by wilderness. There were many trees and flowers around their new home. It was a beautiful sight to behold.

The two of them spent their days as members of the committee that made decisions for mankind and their nights at their house together. Ryu found himself without want; all he needed was right there, except for his late friend. It took a while, but eventually, he found a way to be okay with Storm not being there. It had to end this way, didn't it? One of them would have had to leave the other behind in this cruel world at one point or another. He had only hoped that it would have been much further down the road.

New Beginnings

"We finally have some time to talk about everything," Kenji said.

Ryu smiled and said, "I still feel like this is a dream. I honestly never thought I would find you, but I always clung to the hope that we would be reunited one day."

"And here we are," Kenji returned the smile. "I'm just fortunate that they wanted me to suffer more than they wanted me dead."

The father and son sat in a chow hall discussing everything that led up to that point. Ryu pulled out Kenji's journal. "This was all I've had of you this entire time. If not for this, I may not have had any hope of finding you in the beginning."

The man took the journal and smiled as he leafed through the pages, saying, "I can't believe you have this. So, you were telling me about Storm."

"Right," Ryu said. "She found me not long after I left to search for you. Shortly after that, she spoke to me; kind of freaked me out at first, but I thought she was so cool. I'd never heard of a talking animal before. I told her about you and your disappearance, how I was looking for you, and then she decided to join me. She saved my life more than once."

"I'm glad the two of you found each other. I hope you don't

ever regret taking her on as a companion."

"No," Ryu said, "I could never. I'll cherish her friendship forever."

Ryu followed his father around the city one day as the man disappeared from one of their leadership meetings. He didn't tell anyone where he was going, which Ryu thought to be suspicious. He was sure to stay far enough away to not be spotted, ducking around corners to stay hidden when Kenji turned around to check his surroundings.

Finally, the man led him to a small building near the edge of Sector 3. He followed him inside, being as quiet as possible, and caught his father in the act. He was kissing a woman! Ryu saw that they had entered the records building.

He looked around and saw that there were tomes and books lining every inch of wall space in the building. His love for reading had clearly been passed from Kenji to him, but for now, he just wanted to know why his father was keeping this a secret. Brazenly, he marched out from behind a shelf of books and said, "Well, what do we have here?"

The two of them jumped, startled by the outburst.

"What are you doing here?" Kenji asked.

"I was going to ask you the same thing." Ryu crossed his arms and raised an eyebrow.

"Listen, it's not as if I were sneaking around." Ryu scoffed at that remark because that's exactly what he'd been doing. "Okay, maybe I was, but that's just because I'm a private man and don't want everyone in my affairs."

"Fair enough," Ryu said, "but you still could have introduced us before I found you out like this."

Kenji sighed, "You're right. I'm sorry, son."

"Oh, so you're the Ryu I've heard so much about. I'm Sari," the woman said.

They extended their hands as he said, "It's nice to meet you."

She nodded her head and said, "Kenji has always spoken very highly of you. How proud he is of the man you've become."

"Sari kept me from going insane," Kenji told him. "She was the only support I had as a prisoner all these years."

"I would have helped him escape a long time ago," she admitted, "but the fear of what would happen to us if we were caught was enough to keep us from trying anything."

"I understand," Ryu said.

Ryu bid them farewell, telling them that their secret was safe with him, and then left to peruse the plethora of books.

His eyes landed on one that looked tattered and bland. Unsure of what drew his eyes to it, he grabbed its ratty spine and pulled it from the shelf. Its title read *The Journal of Victor Yorkshire.*

He opened it and noticed that the book was poorly bound. The stitching was coming loose and the pages were aged and frail. He was very careful as he flipped through its tan pages. He sat down on the floor with his back against a wall and stayed there for hours, his eyes glued to the words.

The way the letters were poorly scrawled across the pages made it clear that this was the original handwriting of Victor Yorkshire. There were anecdotes that talked about how he created the birthing pods that saved humanity. After tinkering with the formulas, they were finally perfected. He states that he created a son from his own DNA and would call him Abe and then later on created another called Lucian. They were the first two successful human births from the pods.

Ryu broke his eyes away at that point, his face rife with

shock. A small laugh escaped him. He sat there, pondering that information, and then returned to reading. Several pages and many experiments later he found excerpts about trials to create a solution to death. He found how Xenoflex was created and how the cure for dying was made. It was a lot of trial and error but the man finally figured it out. Based on the scientist's words, he seemed to want nothing but the best for humanity. He didn't know how vile his children would become.

The more he read, the more eccentric his ideas became. At some point in his life, Victor began to become increasingly paranoid that his sons were going to murder him. The boys were becoming more aggressive the longer they lived. He often found them torturing small animals for fun, or dissecting them while still alive. He contemplated killing them.

With no idea how much time had passed, Ryu finally made it to the final page where the scientist noted this would be his last journal entry. He mentioned a plan to end the lives of his boys and then that of himself. It was clear that they were on to the old man and probably killed him themselves after all. Ryu assumed that Abe and Lucian stole all of Victor's work to keep themselves alive forever. He had no idea why they would keep this book, or if they even knew it was here. No one on Earth needed the power to live forever. The information would die with him.

Amelia was relaxing atop one of the walls of the Citadel as the sun dipped in the sky. Kenji had stairs placed here and there around the inside of the walls. Ryu found her up there with her legs dangling from the edge. He plopped down beside her, putting his arm around her. It was a beautiful sight to behold.

She let out a sigh and laid her head on his shoulder. They watched the sunset on the horizon, casting orange and pink streaks across the sky.

"How was your day?" she asked him.

"It was… interesting."

"How so?"

Ryu chuckled, "Well, I found my dad kissing that woman, Sari, who keeps the records building going."

She laughed, "That's funny. Is that all?"

"No, I also found a journal of the man who created the birthing pods. There was a lot of crazy stuff in it, but I got rid of it."

"Oh, well I guess you'll just have to tell me about it sometime." She sighed again and then said, "For the first time, I'm finally happy."

"I am too," he agreed, kissing her atop the head.

"I used to be so angry at everything, and then I met you. I haven't been the same since then. I love you."

Ryu put his fingers under her chin and lifted her head to kiss her. They smiled at each other, content. They gathered themselves and walked down the stairs where Ryu picked some purple flowers to give her. They went back to their home and lay down as it became darker outside.

* * *

A full year had gone by since the One World Order was overthrown once and for all. Ryu and Amelia vowed to spend the rest of their lives together, as had Kenji and Sari. There was peace within the world as they knew it. The Citadel had become slightly crowded and many people relocated to living in the outposts.

They'd already spread the chemicals that would change the soil outside the walls into fertile dirt that would grow anything that was planted. When the previous Resistance members found out about it, they were infuriated. They couldn't believe it had been there all this time. Ryu and his father still trained with their swords every day. A school of sorts was started so that people could practice their fighting skills.

Very few fights had been fought since the takeover and all of them were mutual due to the nature of a law that was passed. The statute stated that fighting amongst one another was unacceptable unless it was mutual. Terms were to be stated prior to the fight as to what parameters would be set and at least two witnesses were to be there. If anyone broke this rule, then they would be banished from the Citadel.

Ryu found that he missed fighting with his sword. Anytime he heard of a duel being planned out, he'd be sure to be there to watch. He may not quarrel with anyone else, but he was happy to watch other people take out their frustrations on one another. Most of the time they would agree to fight to the death or yielding. Ryu thought it was a lot of male posturing; their egos would get in the way of thinking clearly. Death had yet to be the cause of stopping a tussle; it was usually a bloody nose or something similar. It was fun to watch. They'd walk off like best friends after releasing the tension.

With every new law set into place, they would present it before all the people. The leaders didn't want to take a chance on someone claiming they didn't hear about the new rule after breaking it. A list of names was kept and people were made to sign a piece of paper stating they'd been briefed.

Mutated humans and creepers still existed beyond the

Citadel and would occasionally wander into an outpost. Because of this, cohorts of people were sent out periodically to eradicate the creatures from existence. Ryu hoped that, in time, all the evil concocted by the Order would dwindle out.

As far as Ryu could tell, all was well within the Citadel. The anger and rage that once plagued Ryu's mind was now gone. The blood lust never reared its ugly head at him. He couldn't remember a happier time in his life than now. He looked forward to living the remainder of his days in the Citadel. Ryu's one wish was that Storm could have seen the harmony in which they lived before her passing.

Epilogue

Sebastian ran up to Kenji and began wrestling with him as they always did. It was like an unspoken agreement that this was how they would greet each other. Kenji often let the little boy win for he had become a softy over the past few years. Sebastian dragged his grandfather down to a knee and jumped on his back. The kid had a love for fighting that proved he shared the man's DNA.

He held Kenji in a chokehold and jovially yelled, "Mommy! Daddy! Look at me!"

Ryu and Amelia laughed as Kenji flipped their son over his shoulder and put him in a shoulder lock.

"Ha!" Kenji said, "You thought you had me."

The two of them giggled abundantly. Sebastian jumped to his feet and hugged Kenji. It was the boy's eighth birthday. Eight years since he emerged from his pod and they were determined to make it a special day. Sebastian had Amelia's eyes and hair. Everything else was reminiscent of Ryu.

They cooked him his favorite food and invited his friends to come along as they went to swim in the new lake. Kenji did some research about creating lakes, and then with some help from the engineers, they constructed a massive lake for recreation. Most of the other bodies of water were filled with life and they didn't wish to disturb it.

He spent several months digging and filling the hole with

water. They spent Sebastian's birthday at the large lake and it never occurred to him that none of them knew how to swim. There's no time like the present and, after a while, most of them had gotten the hang of it and began teaching the kids who were there.

In the past few years, the population had grown quite a bit, and they were beginning to build cities further away from the outposts and Citadel. The soil was becoming richer and greenery was finally spreading outside the walls. They had a method for drilling for water that the people of the Citadel had used for years prior.

Ryu often thought to himself that maybe the planet would one day return to its former glory. It's funny that all it took was for mankind to stop being selfish and share their resources with the Earth to help it once again begin to sustain itself. Animals still weren't able to reproduce but the plant life had found a way to overcome this inconvenience and now spread its seed all on its own.

At the end of the day, Sebastian asked to play swords with Ryu who of course obliged him. Each time he sparred with his boy, that old fire would ignite in his soul and remind him of all the fun he'd had training with his father and then with Storm. Memories of the troops he prepared for battle would flood his mind. He brought out two wooden swords; one for himself and the other one small enough to fit in his son's petite hands.

They began clanging them together. Ryu was unlike his father in that he refused to take it easy on Sebastian. He never took it so far as to hurt him, but wouldn't let the boy win any time they dueled. He believed it would make him stronger and a better fighter. As much as Ryu didn't wish for Sebastian to ever have to defend himself, he couldn't rule out the possibility and wanted him to be prepared. One day he may even thank him for the tough love.

Sebastian never complained about losing to his father, even at a young age he understood the value of what he was being taught. "I want to be a great swordsman just like you, Daddy!"

"Keep it up and I bet you'll be even *better* than me!"

"You think so?" Sebastian asked excitedly.

Ryu nodded, saying, "Of course. But I won't make it easy on you."

The love that Ryu felt for his boy was insurmountable. He and Amelia did everything in their power to make sure their son was happy. Every night they would take him outside to peer up at the stars. They would tell him stories, often ones that had actually occurred. Ryu told him of Storm and how she had saved his life countless times. Part of it was to carry on her legacy, and part was to make sure that Ryu never forgot her.

On one particular night, they bundled up to stay warm in the chilly air and went out to their normal spot. It was a patch of grass where they would lay out a large blanket and pile up on each other to see the twinkling stars.

Something was different this time. As they all lay down on the blanket, Ryu realized that the stars weren't visible. They seemed to all notice it at the same time. Dark clouds covered the sky, blocking the stars from their vision. A loud boom echoed around them, rumbling their chests, and purple streaks flashed around the clouds. Sebastian gripped his father's neck, startled, but Ryu assured him that they were safe. Something about it was calming to him.

He thought to himself that this was more beautiful than the stars had ever been. As they fawned over the light show above them, Ryu felt tiny droplets land on his face. They all laughed heartily as the rain intensified slightly, the drops growing and the frequency increasing. Perhaps the world would make a full recovery one day after all, Ryu was just glad that he could be a part of its restoration.

Acknowledgments

First and foremost, I'd like to thank God, my Lord and Savior for giving me the ability to put my thoughts on paper. Without Him none of this would possible.

I have much gratitude for those that take the time to read this book, without you I would have no reason to write. If you enjoyed "Blade of The Raven" please leave a review! Reviews are what make it possible for us indie authors to continue working!

Thank you so much to my family for supporting me through all of this, my many hours of being behind my keyboard. I appreciate you guys more than I could ever put into words.

About the Author

DC Sumner goes by many titles. Some of them include Christian, husband, father, and now, writer. Mr. Sumner serves as a Unit Training Manager in the US Air Force and hopes to be a best-selling author one day.

Besides reading and writing, some of his hobbies are hanging out with his family, watching The Office on repeat, and practicing Brazilian Jiu-Jitsu. DC loves to make new friends and meet new people. One of his biggest hopes for this writing journey is to inspire others to follow their dreams.

You can connect with me on:

🌐 https://dcsumner.com

❎ https://is.gd/qkC1u1

Also by DC Sumner

Shadows Rising

Book one of the Chronicles of Ash series follows the story of Ash, a 13-year-old boy who was abandoned as a baby. He learns he can control lightning when he has an outburst with his adoptive father. After fleeing, Ash meets other people like him. Together, he and his new friends face a dark enemy that aims to destroy the magic that keeps their island alive, and they must work as a team to stop him.

Merchant of Darkness

Merchant of Darkness is book 2 in the Chronicles of Ash series. The adventure continues as Ash, Kane, and Quinn go on an epic journey to a lost city. Their goal is to find the cure for that which is destroying their source of magic. Aros, King of Demons, grows stronger. Ash faces tragedy and tosses himself into the prison of his mind.